25x 5/16 ✓ 2/21

The Scenic Route

ALSO BY BINNIE KIRSHENBAUM

An Almost Perfect Moment
Hester Among the Ruins
Pure Poetry
A Disturbance in One Place
History on a Personal Note
On Mermaid Avenue

AN **ecco** BOOK

HARPER ⬤ PERENNIAL

NEW YORK • LONDON • TORONTO • SYDNEY • NEW DELHI • AUCKLAND

Binnie Kirshenbaum

The Scenic Route

A NOVEL

HARPER PERENNIAL

P.S.™ is a trademark of HarperCollins Publishers.

THE SCENIC ROUTE. Copyright © 2009 by Binnie Kirshenbaum. All rights reserved. Printed in the United States of America. No part of this book may be used or reproduced in any manner whatsoever without written permission except in the case of brief quotations embodied in critical articles and reviews. For information address HarperCollins Publishers, 10 East 53rd Street, New York, NY 10022.

HarperCollins books may be purchased for educational, business, or sales promotional use. For information please write: Special Markets Department, HarperCollins Publishers, 10 East 53rd Street, New York, NY 10022.

FIRST EDITION

Designed by Sunil Manchikanti

Library of Congress Cataloging-in-Publication Data is available upon request.

ISBN 978-0-06-078474-4

09 10 11 12 13   OV/RRD   10 9 8 7 6 5 4 3 2 1

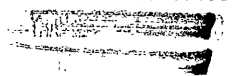

Tony and Susan, my bookends

Acknowledgments

My friends are my good fortune. For their wisdom, support, suggestions, thoughts, advice, patience, and for being my dear ones, I thank (in alphabetical order): Elisa Albert, David Alexander, Lucie Brock-Broido, Lauren Grodstein, Maureen Howard, Richard Howard, Tree Swenson, B.W., and William Wadsworth.

To my dear friend *and* savior agent, Ira Silverberg, I am forever and profoundly grateful.

Thank you, thank you to the brilliant and indefatigable Kimberly Burns.

I am indebted to Dr. Matthew Avitable for miraculously and generously recovering my lost pages.

My colleagues and my students at Columbia University are a wellspring of inspiration, and to all of them I wish to express my admiration, affection, and appreciation for the alchemic admixture of artistic and intellectual integrity and warmth of community.

I am grateful to the New York State Writers Institute at Skidmore College for the opportunity to read work-in-progress. (BLU, too.)

To be published by the Ecco Press is a joy and an honor. Many, many thanks to Virginia Smith, Rachel Bressler, Michael McKenzie, Carrie Kania, Amy Baker, Allison Saltzman, and Juliette Shapland.

Dan Halpern, I can't thank you enough; it's infinite.

O irrevocable
river
of things:
no one can say
that I loved
only
fish,
or the plants of the jungle and the field,
that I loved
only
those things that leap and climb, desire, and survive.
It's not true:
many things conspired
to tell me the whole story.

—Pablo Neruda, *from* "Ode to Things"

The Scenic Route

Here is the story of Henry and me. I wish it had a different end.

It had a good beginning.

That's what I would say. If Ruby would hear me out, I would say, "This is the story of Henry and me," and no matter that it's of the recent past, past is past, and to tell Ruby this story now would be to call on memory, to travel back, and, as it was, to be with Henry was never quite of our time but of another time better than all that. A time before my time. Like how it was in New York during the last days of the Automats, when there was still the Biltmore

Hotel and that pink place for ice cream, the name of which escapes me, and Henry, he was not quite of our time either. "I wish it had a different end," I would say to Ruby. "It had a good beginning."

Also, I would apologize to her.

I would say, "Ruby, I am so sorry."

Ruby is living some six-hundred-plus miles away at her mother's house, which is never a good thing, a middle-aged woman living with her mother. That Ruby lives with her mother, it's my fault. In a roundabout way, but still my fault.

Rumpelmayer's. The pink place for ice cream was called Rumpelmayer's. I would apologize to her not for what I did because I *did* nothing. I did nothing and I said nothing, and for sins of omission, such as mine was, there is no good excuse, and I'd say that, too, and again I'd say, "I am so sorry."

And Ruby, she'd say, "You're sorry? You're damn right you're sorry," and then she'd hang up on me and I'd be standing there holding the phone with no one at the other end.

Or, who knows? Maybe she would say, "It's okay, Sylvia. It's over. Forget about it now." Not likely but possible because all things are possible, and it could happen that she'd say it's okay.

'It's okay, Sylvia. Really. It's okay. It's all behind us now.'

And I then could tell her, as I could tell Ruby and only Ruby how it is that, precisely that, that it's all behind us now, that is what I am most afraid of, that everything good is over, and where do I go from here?

To which Ruby might say, "You give up. Or you begin."

'You begin.'

.   .   .

To begin. Florence, to begin. Florence, the one in Italy. I had not been to Europe or to anyplace else much either in how long? Eight years? Maybe six. Before I quit travel as a thing to do, I'd done my fair share of it, but then it happened that I stopped because effort expended is not always worth the price of getting there, and it's not as if New York doesn't offer a surfeit of art and music and theater to feed on, much the way a goose is force-fed to make foie gras, which, for the record, is something I consider to be immoral, the way geese are force-fed to make pâté. Ducks, too. In New York, we've got culture coming out our ears, plus the Empire State Building, the Statue of Liberty, Grant's Tomb, and the cuisine of all nations, so who needed to pack a suitcase or fret over the decline of the dollar or worry about how, just like that—*poof*—a plane can vanish from the sky? Travel became something I thought of as fixed in my past, something done and over, a youthful avidity, perhaps, until I got to thinking about how I had never been to Italy, and how that fact seemed to · alarm people. Coincidental to thinking about how I had never been to Italy, that is to say, right around the same time, I got a letter in the mail. A registered letter. A letter that you have to sign for, you know it's not going to be a greeting card or a love letter either. Walking from the living room to the kitchen, I read it, the letter, the letter that exuded the same milk of human kindness as a letter that begins with "Dear Occupant." I read the letter regretfully informing me that as a result of company downsizing, I was to be let go.

The Scenic Route

Let go.

Let go: dropped carelessly, the way an empty soda can is let go from a car window. Let go, and so what that "this decision bears no reflection on your job performance," blah, blah, blah. The words boiled down to their essence, which was a pink slip. A pink slip that matched the pink of my face as it went hot, pink and hot from shame, which is a category of embarrassment but embarrassment entirely unlike embarrassments such as a trail of toilet paper stuck to your shoe or your dress tucked into the back of your panty hose or getting caught in a lie or in a compromising position. Those embarrassments we get over, those become funny stories we later tell, but shame is a pyric ember of humiliation, and it lodges within the core of us. The burns are searing; shame leaves scars.

My function, the letter said, was to be absorbed.

Absorbed: a spill mopped up with a sponge. Absorbed. My services were no longer needed, although if I were to be perfectly honest, it's something that it took them, what, fourteen years to figure that one out. My services were never needed. Often I wondered, What exactly is it that I *do* here and why?

Oh, there would be a great display of sympathy, solidarity even, from my colleagues, and I would be sorely missed for two or three days. Then no more. Then my office would be turned into a conference room or be used for storage.

I folded the letter and put it back in the envelope and left it on the kitchen counter as if it hadn't yet been read.

There I stood: five feet, six inches tall, forty-two years old, divorced, no children, without—for all practical purposes—any family, and now, let go. Unemployed, and think about this: how everyone always said, repeatedly said, "Sylvia does not live up to her potential." Broken-record said how I am, how I have always been, the paradigmatic underachiever, which means I was let go from a job that was beneath me, a fact that was not a source of comfort.

Such a life was not inclined to elicit envy, although I did receive a severance package, enough money to tide me over until I could figure out what comes next. A severance package, which was not entirely an ungenerous one, although it wasn't as if I was especially grateful for it, either.

But I took the money and I went to Florence, and on my fifth day there I got on a bus, a dark green rickety bus that went seven kilometers north, fifteen to twenty minutes up, up, uphill to the ancient Etruscan town of Fiesole, now famous, if *famous* isn't pushing it, for a handful of Roman ruins. A light breeze billowed the air, but it was hot. Midday in June, in Italy, that kind of hot, and because the ruins weren't going anywhere, rather than rush off to see the sights, I went directly to a café. Umbrellas advertising Cinzano shaded tables set with matching Cinzano ashtrays of the sort that tourists are inclined to pocket, as if a free ashtray comes with your *limonata*. There I had a view of the amphitheater that could knock your socks off. I ordered an espresso. The thing about a view, even one that could knock your socks off, is this: once you've seen it, you've seen it, and it's not likely to offer up anything new while you are sitting there. Changes in the landscape are slow in coming, and my attention drifted.

The Scenic Route

5

To observe people is ornithologic in design, and throughout Europe, in cafés where tourists flock, you are likely to spot an American sparrow: ordinary, without brilliant plumage or anything much distinctive, these are solitary creatures but not by choice. In the cafés they read guidebooks, read intently about where they are, as if all experience belonged to someone else. That, or they will be writing in their journals or on the backs of postcards. "Dear Diary," or "Dear Aunt Louise," whichever, the words will not address the loneliness, the loneliness this trip was supposed to assuage but instead served only to exacerbate. The one desire articulated is predictable and flimsy: "I am seriously considering moving here." That desire, to pack up the house in Portland or Amherst or Indianapolis and move to Florence or Prague or Barcelona, is a desire that, once they are home, fades the way all dreams do in the light of morning, but the man seated at the table next to mine, although unmistakably American and alone, he wasn't reading a guidebook or writing in a diary or addressing the back of a postcard of the Ponte Vecchio. He was reading the *Wall Street Journal*. Without my glasses, I could not make out the date or even the headlines, but it was the *Wall Street Journal* that, along with the kelly-green *kelly-green!* Brooks Brothers polo shirt he wore, led me to peg him as a person to whom I'd have little to say and nothing to share, and that was a damn shame because he was someone rather lovely to look at, and I am not entirely beyond superficiality.

And back to the view it was. Looking out over the hills to the ruins, I brought the demitasse cup to my lips, and accidents will happen: espresso dribbled down the front of my dress. A white dress, too, so there was no pretending otherwise. He, that man at the next table, held out a handkerchief for me to take, to blot the coffee stain. A handkerchief. For real.

'A handkerchief? He had a handkerchief? There's an item we don't see much of anymore.'

Yes, a handkerchief, and I'd have bet there was a seersucker suit hanging in his closet, too. He was something of an anachronism, how, in his dress and in his ways, he was nearer to that era between the wars, the world wars, when young men from America, young men of means, went off to live in Paris just as, so I came to learn, he, as a young man, went off to live in Paris. He lives there still. Someone should've told him: it was over; the others had long since packed up, gone home. All that remained of the movable feast were the bones on the plate, and you never want to be the last one to leave the party because that's about as sorry as it gets. An American in Paris is a cliché, and a cliché is something no one should aspire to be, although really I'm not in a position to talk about ambitions, given that I never had any.

'There's that movie, An American in Paris. *It starred Gene Kelly and Leslie Caron, with music by George Gershwin.'*

Henry was that: an American in Paris, as American as Gene Kelly, although sometimes I kidded around and called him Henri. Kidded around because despite nearly two decades of an address on rue de Grenelle in the sixth arrondissement, and some years before that on rue Monge in the fifth, he wasn't any kind of an Henri.

He was from North Carolina.

'Oh, he's one of my people.'

The South. Ruby, too, was from the South, and as if everyone born south of Maryland and north of Florida, excluding the District of Columbia and surrounding suburbs, was in some way related to her by blood or by marriage, she referred to them all as "my people," which, she believed, gave her license to make broad and unflattering remarks about them. Which is often the case, that people feel free to criticize their own.

'One of my people. You know, we can try to change who we are, but trying, that's about as far as we get.'

It was true that Henry could have lived on rue de la Moon from now until forever and still, right off the bat, you'd have recognized him as a son of the Confederacy, an alumnus of William and Mary.

Tall and lanky and he had light brown hair that was going gray, light brown hair going gray that fell forward in boyish exuberance. He wore steel-rimmed eyeglasses with clip-on shades, and he favored blue jeans and those polo shirts, ordered from Brooks Brothers and shipped to him in Paris. Brooks Brothers polo shirts that sported—rather than the European-preferred Lacoste alligator—a sheep *Poor little lambs who have gone astray* for a logo.

I did not take the handkerchief he proffered because it was too late for that now. "Thanks anyway," I said.

"You're American," he noted, and I said yes, and he introduced himself. With more than a trace of his North Carolina accent coming into play, he said, "I am Henry Stafford, and I am pleased to make your acquaintance."

'You know how we do that. Pile the accent on thick when talking to Yankees. We think you all are taken in by it.'

For Ruby, the Mason-Dixon Line was as concrete a divide as before and after, or an iron gate.

Henry Stafford introduced himself to me, and I introduced myself to him, and as if to commit my name to memory, he repeated it twice. "Sylvia Landsman. Sylvia Landsman." Landsman, he said, as if it was a spondee, both syllables stressed equally. "Sylvia Landsman, I am pleased to make your acquaintance," to which I, suddenly in possession of the social grace of a twelve-year-old girl, said, "Yeah," but as it happens when two Americans find themselves to be two Americans in a café somewhere else, we started chatting. About what? I can't recall precisely. Even at the time, there seemed to be no sharp definition to the talk, as if our words were made hazy by the heat of the summer afternoon, as if the present moment was happening years ago, but it didn't take long for him to move from his table to my table, and I noted that his newspaper was ten days old. At some point in the conversation it came up that, distinct from the other Americans there and for that matter unlike the French and the Japanese visiting Fiesole that afternoon, he was not on a day trip, although maybe he was going to leave tomorrow. Or on Saturday.

"Why?" Not why was he leaving Fiesole. I wanted to know why was he there in the first place.

"Oh," he said. "I am nursing a broken heart."

"A clean break?" I asked. Because I did not believe him, I made light of what was not. "Or did it shatter into countless pieces?"

He paused, as if this question deserved thought. "Since you put it that way," he said, "I'd have to reconsider. Perhaps it's not really broken at all. Perhaps it's just bruised. Or embarrassed."

"So it will heal," I said.

And he said, "I believe it just this minute has."

'There's a line.'

Oh, he talked pretty, he did, in hyperbolic bloom, yet there was truth to what he said. His heart was not broken, but something else, some other part of him, was. Broken or missing, I knew because *birds of a feather* we recognize our own, and we are drawn to what is familiar to us.

Together he and I walked all of Fiesole, coming full circle *In my end is my beginning* to where we began on the Palazzo Communale, and there, the way an excuse is pulled out of thin air, not quite seamlessly, he took a Cinzano ashtray from his pocket. "For you," he said. "A souvenir. To remember the day."

Souvenir. From the French: remembrance, memory, something that serves as a reminder.

Back when I was a child and not exceptionally literate, I was sure, as sure as sure can be, that the word was *silverneer.* The etymology of it found in the "silver" part, the permanence of the metal being key. If you don't lose it, you'll have it always. As opposed to perishables. Perishables turn to rot and attract bugs; and the experience, the moment, the moment that you wish to remember, well, that doesn't last at all. A photograph fixes the occasion so that you can't remember it any other way except that which is in the picture, and memory is an unreliable narrator, selective, open to embellishment, eager to be shaded, or flat-out wrong. Silverneers were the tangible expression of a time at the Bronx Zoo, the Museum of Natural History, Rye Playland, the educational excursions to Washington, D.C., to Lancaster, Pennsylvania, to Stockbridge, Massachusetts, the vacations to Martha's Vineyard and the Bahamas, and there was no point to going anywhere unless I got a silverneer, a thing *people, places, things,* a thing to rely upon to retain memory within itself, within its matter.

The silverneer was the evidence to be had, the evidence needed, the proof that it happened, that I didn't dream about Amish people, I really saw them, and I know this because I got a hand puppet dressed like an Amish man, and it had a rubber head and black felt hat.

Before memory became like the morning mist—the mist that Henry called *nebbia*, which is the Italian word for "fog," only he pronounced it "nebyah" —to remember the day, he gave me an ashtray, white plastic and shaped like a tricornered hat, advertising Cinzano in red and black Art Deco letters.

To remember the days there is an amber ring from Krakow, a bit of the Berlin Wall encased in Lucite, a small gilded notebook from Ljubljana, garnet earrings from Karlovy Vary, Wolford stockings from Vienna, a necklace made of glass beads from Prague, a snow globe from an Alpine rest stop, perfume— Eau de Juliette—from Verona, a Cinzano ashtray to remember Fiesole, to which I said, "I won't forget."

I won't forget, but it could happen that I might not remember either; the distinction being the distortion of memory, but I do remember the feel of Henry's mouth on my mouth, when there, on the Palazzo Communale, he kissed me, and it was a kiss *would I yes to say yes* that told us all that we needed to know ` for now, and we never did get to dinner that night.

A shimmer of moon came through the part in the curtains, heavy brocade curtains in Umbria red and gold, and I said to him, "Well, that wasn't half bad."

"You're none to shabby yourself, Buttercup," he said. *Buttercup, Poppy, Forget-Me-Not—These three bloomed in a garden spot.* Peach Blossom. Tulip. Snap Pea. Appellations of affection are often flowers or parts of fruit and the occasional vegetable, and while I never thought that I was the first girl he'd called Buttercup, I came to believe I might well be the last of them.

Henry slept with one arm draped over my waist, his hand cupping my breast, and in the morning, he kissed the nape of my neck to wake me from a dreamy slumber. A while later, we got up from the bed and the sunlight was white, and we took breakfast—black coffee and bread with preserves made from figs, *figs!*—at a marble-topped table in the courtyard of his hotel, which was once a villa.

We finished all the bread and the sun was moving higher in the sky, and we had one more cup of coffee before he drove me back to Florence, to my hotel, where I assured the desk clerk, who feared I was displeased with the accommodations, that no, there was *no problema*, I was leaving sooner than planned, that was all. Pulling my suitcases behind me as if they were a pair of *So much depends on* red wagons—how did we manage before the advent of suitcases on wheels, such a small but significant advancement for the coming and going of mankind—I stepped out from the hotel to find Henry sitting on the hood of his car. A forest green Peugeot, which was parked on the sidewalk because the streets of Florence are that kind of narrow. A gentleman of the old school, chivalrous, Henry rushed to relieve me of the suitcases and, at the open trunk of the car, with one hand he lifted the first of them a few inches from the ground before having to put it down again.

I don't prioritize well, and when packing my suitcases, I found myself incapable of sorting out what I was likely to need—underwear, tampons, sun block SPF 55, a few books to read—from what I was less likely to need—dishwashing detergent, an Ace bandage, the *Chicago Manual of Style*—so I took it all.

"I might have overpacked," I said to Henry, and he did not contradict me. "Yes," he said. "It appears that you did."

I did overpack but not so much that I would be legendary for it. Compared to the likes of Imelda Marcos with her shoes or Hannibal with his elephants or Alma Schindler with her treasures, compared that way, I traveled with nothing more than a toothbrush.

All things being relative.

Having now braced himself, prepared for the heft, Henry hoisted one suitcase into the trunk, followed by the other, and then he flexed his left hand as if working out a kink.

I fiddled to buckle my seat belt, and Henry reached across to the glove compartment and got out a map, which he handed to me. The car was in idle but raring to go, and he said, "Where to?" With the road map of Europe, open and spread over my lap and beyond *This much!*, my finger went like a pointer on a Ouija board moving in fits and starts to Madrid to Prague to Munich, to places with names requiring lingual dexterity—Mrakov, Bolesławiec, Perchtoldsdorf—and then my finger came to rest and I said, "How about here?" to which Henry said, "Seems as good a place as any."

Folding the map like a newspaper, I could follow the route, the red and yellow lines that were the roads from Florence to Trieste, and once we got beyond the city limits, Henry switched gears and turned on the music. The three oboes of the first Brandenburg Concerto filled the air, sweetly suggesting the pleasures of pastoral diversion, and we were off.

This is how it began.

I had nowhere I had to be, and he had nowhere he had to be. We had money in our pockets and time on our hands.

It was that easy.

Except.

'Except nothing is ever that easy.'

2

The landscape went by—the rolling Tus-
can hills, golden fields and olive groves and
blue flowers like an Impressionist painting—and in that same kind of vague, soft-
around-the-edges way, Henry asked, "And
is there a Mr. Landsman?" Which was a
question that, we could say, came a little
late in the game.

"I'm divorced," I told him.

"Recently divorced? If you don't mind
my asking, that is."

"I don't mind. Recently divorced on paper but separated for quite some time before that."

"And married then for what number of years? Assuming it was years and not months or a matter of days, although I do confess to a certain admiration for those whose marriages don't make it through the first week."

'He'd admire the hell out of me, then. Wouldn't he?'

"Four years," I told him. "I was married for four years."

"Happily married?" Henry asked.

"Very," I said.

Married. Separated. Divorced. What Vincent and I hopped-skipped-and-jumped over was the part where you get engaged, the lag time before the wedding. There was never occasion for me to refer to Vincent as my fiancé, when I could have said, "This is my fiancé," which was not something I would have said regardless.

Fiancé. Now, there's a word kept aloft by the warm air of an empty head.

When my brother, Joel, and Laura got engaged, which they did soon after Vincent and I got married, Laura used the word *fiancé.* A lot. *Ad nauseam* a lot.

Only a woman such as Laura would consider my brother to have been a catch. Joel is, I'm sorry to say, a miserable person. He was born miserable; he was a baby born with an acorn wedged up his ass. An acorn that did as acorns do and grew into a mighty oak. There is another side to him, of course. Because there is more than one side to everyone, more than what they show us, more than what we allow ourselves to know, and so there *is* more to Joel, something that makes him afraid, afraid to cut loose, as if to cut loose would be to free-fall, free-fall out of control, but I'll be damned if I know what it is that scares him, and the fact remains: instead of orgasms like the rest of us have, Joel's load of joy shoots out tightly wrapped, like a pellet or a kidney stone.

Laura, she was a darling—could she be any more perfect?— whereas I was, to my parents' way of thinking, *Well, Sylvia is Sylvia,* which is to say they considered me to be, at the very least, a fuckup. Oh, they had reasons. They did, which was why they were deeply relieved when I married Vincent, because he was a respectable husband and not a manager of a motel or a shady character dealing in auto parts. That Vincent and I got married at City Hall by a civil servant who wore a comb-over hairstyle and a brown jacket or maybe it was marine blue, but whichever the color, it was the same fabric as foam rubber, there came the blow. A glum little ceremony was one thing but to refuse to have a party was, as my mother put it, "Why are you doing this to us, Sylvia?" What I was doing to them was this: I was denying them the pleasure of making me a wedding. To be sure, denying my parents pleasure was not my intent, although the concept of pleasure in this context did give me pause, because since when does pleasure mandate a to-do list? Invitations, music, menu, flowers, *something borrowed, something blue* and then you are fitted, pinned like a butterfly mounted for display, into a bouffant gown, and don't forget more flowers, the bouquet of roses and baby's breath, and each detail like a marble to lose one by one, *kerplunk,* and when all your marbles are gone, what is left for you to do but crawl into the laundry hamper, pull the soiled sheets over your head, and stay there until it is all over.

Know thyself.

Laura and her fiancé, my brother, Joel, they would have the wedding with all the frills and pom-poms, and also they had an engagement party.

"I had a big wedding," Henry said. "But I don't remember any of it." As if the brain were an accordion envelope and memories were stored in the folds like receipts saved for accounting at tax time, sometimes they get misfiled or they get wet, rendering them illegible. "The day I got married," he told me, "I was that kind of drunk. As a skunk in a trunk."

"You were married, too?" I said, and he corrected me. "Am. I am married." *Am? Is?* Then he wanted to know, "Does that concern you any?"

I wasn't sure if he meant "concern me any," as in: Does it worry me? Or if by "concern me any," did he mean: Is it any of my business? I mulled that over, too, and I came to the conclusion: no.

No, because we were alone, the two of us, in his car, driving through Tuscany; alone, the two of us, in a world of our own design, a world not unlike the desktop biosphere you can buy at Sharper Image. Or a snow dome. Other people? Who were they to us? Other people, they were the stuff of stories to tell; they were the characters who populated our stories, the stories we told to each other, to entertain ourselves, to explain ourselves, to be. And how happy we were, Henry and I, telling stories, as if stories offered possibilities where there had been none.

Like Scheherazade, we all tell stories as a means of staying alive. We can exist in the context of the tale, but only the storyteller dwells beyond the tales that are told. "Happily married?" I asked Henry.

"No," he said.

Husbands, wives, mothers, Cinderella, Humbert Humbert, former lovers, Cain and Abel, friends and family, Emma Bovary, characters all, and his wife was no more real to me than was Jordan Baker, who was also a minor character in a story, a peripheral character and one not viewed altogether with favor, either.

You could say that an engagement party is a way to collect double the number of gifts, and you wouldn't be wrong. Joel and Laura had their engagement party in a banquet room at a country club where Laura was doing that fish-on-land thing with her hand, making sure we all got a load of the *Diamond As Big As the Ritz* ring. I am not one to be bowled over by a diamond, a lack of appreciation I let be known whenever the subject came up and for reasons I can't determine, the subject came up often enough, and then it came back around to bite me, but for now, that—to gush over the rock—was what she was after, and why deny her the compliment she sought? "Oh," I gasped. Gasped. "Laura, the ring is beautiful."

As if she were the queen or the pope, she held out her hand as if I were expected to kiss the ring and curtsy. "It was your mother's," she said. "Your mother's engagement ring. She gave it to me."

And that was a slap in the face. I admit it, a slap in the face that stung all through the night, and when Vincent and

I got home, I said to him, "I know my mother has every right to give her engagement ring to whomever she pleases, but I'm hurt." Vincent said that my being hurt was not unreasonable under these circumstances, and I trusted his judgment because he would've been the first one to tell me if I'd been making a big deal out of nothing. Vincent and I, we had that, that way of telling each other what was what and neither of us taking offense because offense was never meant, which is the nutshell definition of a good friend. That's how it was with Ruby, too. Ruby, she was like a sister to me but better than a sister, because we had separate mothers.

"*Was?*" Henry asked. "She *was* like a sister to you?"

"Was," I said, although there is no way to accurately parse the verb tense of such loss.

"What happened?" Henry asked, and I told him, "It's a long story. For another day." Which was not entirely true. It wasn't so much that it was a long story as that it was an uneasy story.

The morning following Joel and Laura's engagement party, I called my mother on the phone and I told her that I was hurt about the ring, that she gave it to Laura, who was practically a stranger off the street.

"I gave the ring to Laura," my mother explained, "because Joel's practice is just getting off the ground, and right now he isn't in a position to buy her a nice ring like that." My brother is a podiatrist—a foot man—who specializes in sports injuries to the ankle and related tendons, and how many children do you know who have that dream, the dream of growing up to someday be a podiatrist?

"Vincent will *never* be in a position to get me a ring like that," I said. I was not casting aspersion on Vincent. It's that Vincent is an astronomer, which is not a profession you go into for the money.

What Vincent does exactly is called mapping the universe, which, even though it sounds like something else entirely, is mostly physics and has far more to do with mathematical calcu- · lation than it does with the romance of travel and the sorrowful beauty *Up above the world so high* of stargazing.

"You don't even like diamonds," my mother said. "You always make a point of it. How you don't like diamonds. Moreover," she added, "it's an engagement ring. You didn't get engaged," and that was true, too, and what's done was done, and there wasn't anything left to say, and that conversation was over.

Vincent and I had a good marriage. As if we'd been brought together by a matchmaker, there was that kind of compatibility, as easy as two rocks in a stream. Symbiotic even, like flowers and bees. Respect and affection were mutual and genuine between us. I loved Vincent and he loved me in the abiding way most couples in good marriages love each other, that way in which every once in a while there is a longing for someone you haven't yet met. A longing that comes upon you while you are loading the dishwasher or weeding the garden or sitting in front of the television or turning out the light to go to sleep, and you don't even know what it is, this longing, and you think maybe you're in need of a vacation or maybe you are dying because the ache of it hurts so fucking much.

In other words, Vincent and I had a good marriage, but we weren't in love. Again, the same could probably be said for most couples in good marriages; the difference being we put an end to ours, which we did because we liked each other a lot.

That ache, it went away when I met Henry; it went away as if it had been a headache instead of located nowhere precisely.

It's not that I *wanted* to fall in love with Henry, but I did just the same because you can't keep from falling in love any more than you can keep snow from falling from the sky in winter.

'Gravity is gravity.'

When Vincent wanted to get married again—not to me but to someone else—that's when we got divorced officially, on the books, and if ever there was a no-fault divorce, it was ours, but even if I had been at fault, Vincent was never one to hold a grudge. Further illustration of Vincent's overall excellence as a person, beyond the general amicability of our separation, was demonstrated in the division of property. "Why don't you keep the apartment," Vincent said, "and I'll take the stock portfolio. That's about right, don't you think?" No. That was hardly even-steven, because our apartment, never you mind itty-bitty, is primo property—location, location—whereas our stock portfolio was a grand way of calculating peanuts, but as I've always said, you'd be hard-pressed to find a man as fine and decent as Vincent.

It is small, our apartment. What is now my apartment. A turn-of-the-century shoe box, but a great fuss is made over the tin ceiling and the claw-foot tub, which was centered like a coffee table in the middle of the living room until the building went co-op and market-value inspired renovations. Slum *de siècle* is what it is, but cozy and charming are the preferred descriptives, and it would be as adorable as a dollhouse if it were furnished with dollhouse miniatures, if I could sleep in a bed as big as a matchbox or eat from a plate with the circumference of a pill, and if my possessions were few.

There are, in this world as we know it, plenty of mathematical constants—pi, zero, the square root of three—and in physics, too, there are constants, but not in human nature. Stories retold word for word are not to be trusted. People oscillate like floor fans. From the day we are born, we are a surprise party.

For example: there's no rhyme or reason for my attachments to things and people past, or lack thereof. My best pal from kindergarten? I haven't spoken to her since first grade. You won't find an old boyfriend's smelly sweatshirt stuffed in the back of my closet. No crapped-up one-eyed teddy bear sits on a pillow on my bed, which is a reason I can get up in the morning. Because a woman who keeps a teddy bear on her bed, it can't be easy for her to face the day. My high school yearbook got lost, I think in a garbage pail, just days after graduation, and if I had been consistent in this regard, in this deficit of wistful sensibility, I'd have a white couch, a Danish modern coffee table, a futon instead of a bed, and not a damn thing else.

Instead, I've got reams of stuff. Souvenirs from other times and foreign lands and gifts given and keepsakes and things *Oh irrevocable / river / of things* passed down from generations before me: vases, photographs, jewelry, figurines, plus my grandmother's china, which is Wedgwood, cream-colored porcelain garlanded with ivy; it was once service for twenty-four, which was a lot of dishes.

"Why am I not surprised by that?" Henry asked, no doubt alluding to the heft of my suitcases, to which I said, "All things being relative."

The Most Beautiful Woman in All of Austria: Alma Schindler was married to Gustav Mahler, but only for a few years because he died, thus making her the widow Mahler, and something of a merry widow, too. Mistress and muse to Gustav Klimt, Alexander Zemlinsky, and Osckar Kokoschka, to name a few with whom she carried on before, after, and during the time when she was married to her second husband, Walter Gropius. He was the famous Bauhaus architect. Alma favored accomplished men. Her third husband was Franz Werfel, the author of *The Forty Days of Musa Dagh* and *The Song of Bernadette*. To say that Franz Werfel was not a handsome man is something of an understatement. He looked a lot like a potato. Lumpy, like that.

At the time of the Anschluss, the Werfels, Franz and Alma, fled from their home in Vienna to the south of France, where they lived in exile, but to be in the jurisdiction of the

Vichy government was not a safe haven for them, either. It was a lucky thing for the Werfels and for some thousand or so others that a largely unsung hero by the name of Varian Fry—a name you'd think Graham Greene had come up with if it hadn't been for real—made it his mission to get artists and writers and big thinkers—those of them in peril—out of France and into Spain, to Barcelona, where they set sail for America. You might, and you could, question why only artists and geniuses were aided in escape and not tailors and fishmongers and housewives, and you could get all sanctimonious about the elitism and you might even have a good point, but at least Varian Fry did something, something brave and grand, rather than closing his eyes and picking his nose like pretty much everyone else did.

Arrangements for these escapes were elaborate and involved forged documents, black-marketed money, and danger. The routes taken were carefully mapped out, and the refugees went in small groups because a parade over the Pyrenees would not have gone unnoticed. There were five to the Werfels' group: Franz and Alma, Heinrich Mann and his wife, and their nephew Golo (there's a name for you), who was Thomas Mann's son.

Despite Heinrich Mann's advanced years and Franz Werfel being as fat and soft as a goose-down pillow, the plan was to cross the border, at night, on foot, over the mountain pass. Final instructions were given: when and where to meet; which documents to keep and which to leave behind; do not, under any circumstance, forget to bring the cigarettes that were the currency with which to bribe the border patrol. Varian Fry told them, "Pack only what is absolutely necessary." The scout would come to collect them, and on the night that they were to make their way in the dark over the Pyrenees and into safety, Mrs. Werfel waited alongside her pudgy husband and the nine steamer trunks filled with her necessities.

Mr. Fry tried to explain to her that not only couldn't she take nine steamer trunks, *Was she out of her mind?*, she could not take so much as one steamer trunk, but Alma was not about to leave behind the scores of music composed by the great Gustav Mahler, and she would not leave behind Kokoschka's paintings, and she wasn't very happy about leaving behind her beautiful dresses or her diaries either.

Plans were changed. Lives were risked, but in 1964 Alma Schindler Mahler Gropius Werfel died a natural death in her apartment in New York City. The paintings, the music, and her diaries survived. They made for juicy reading, those diaries of hers. Detailed among her other flings is the story of her affair with Kokoschka, which began before World War I, just after Mahler's death. From 1912 to 1914, Oskar Kokoschka was either painting Alma Mahler or fucking her. Either way he was obsessed with her, and she, in turn, in 1915, perhaps tiring of him, urged him to enlist in the army. She sent him packing, off to the Russian front, where he was seriously, although not mortally, wounded by a bayonet.

Kokoschka returned to Vienna, where he made himself a life-size doll, one that bore a startling likeness to Alma. Anatomically correct, the doll was perhaps the first of what would become a small industry: blow-up dolls with pocket mouths and cunts.

One night in 1919, during a wild party in his studio in Dresden, Kokoschka went out of his mind with hatred, that kind of non-ideological hate, hate of such ferocious intensity, hate that only love could spawn. In a mad frenzy, Kokoschka tore apart the Alma doll, ripping off her head.

One way or another, we all carry excess baggage.

.

The money Henry had in his pocket belonged to his wife. That's what Henry did for a living. He was Elinor's husband. Elinor was rich, and she was from England, where she grew up in one of those *Brideshead*-y, Masterpiece Theatre–type houses: thirty-eight rooms and all of them damp.

But wanting for nothing, as far as they could say, Elinor and Henry lived what is commonly, albeit sometimes mistakenly, referred to as the good life, and Henry, he was what I thought of, with a wink, as a Communist of the French school: *liberté, egalité, fraternité,* and *douceur de vivre*; the little extras, such as *les pullovers cashmere* and good wine, good food and fine china, and sterling flatware and the occasional piece of art, and hotels with at least four but preferably five *étoiles*.

'Those little things, they sure do have a way of adding up on a person.'

There's a question: Why did my grandmother have service for twenty-four when pretty much no one came to dinner and dinner was pretty much limited to scrambled eggs and toast because she didn't know how to cook and she was too delicate to learn. My mother could cook, but there was no appealing presentation to the meals she set out, and whatever the food, it all tasted like Hubbard squash, which is a squash about nothing but texture. Despite periodic rhapsodizing over the pot roast, the noodle pudding, the mushroom and barley soup of his child-hood, my father never complained about the slop my mother served up, although he often laughed at it, as if laughter were a way of giving thanks for this food we were about to eat.

Love does that, spins flax into gold.

For me, cooking falls apart in the planning stage. I'll go to the store to buy food for dinner and come back with fresh pasta, an Idaho potato, and a jar of orange marmalade.

Because my grandmother's china was not to my mother's taste, she kept it packed away in the attic, but I liked it, insofar as I was ever going to lose my head over dishes, and because such is the way things are passed along from one generation to the next, like blue eyes or a bump on a nose, I assumed that someday my grandmother's china would be my china. So it was surprise, surprise, when one night my mother called me to say hello, and then, all matter of fact, she said, "A nun came by the house today." Like nuns were always stopping by our house. "She was collecting things for the church rummage sale. Finally I had an excuse to get rid of Grandma's china."

It is possible that I never did articulate the assumption that my grandmother's china was to be my china, but it never oc-curred to me that my mother would give away Wedgwood from Tiffany's, service for twenty-four, as if the nun collecting for the church rummage sale were Christ Himself and you had to go overboard with the generosity. Plus, it was *her mother's* china. Isn't that supposed to mean something in terms of great sentimental value? Although I suppose great sentimental value isn't the gold standard. Over time it is likely to be devalued, ultimately as worthless as Confederate dollars or reichsmarks, all of it currency of the vanquished, and my mother was the sort of woman who would weep and sniffle at the treacle expressed in a Mother's Day card from Hallmark, get herself all choked up over it and then, wiping away the tears, there-you-go, she'd toss the card into the garbage can along with the eggshells, the morning's coffee grounds, and a banana peel.

"You have to get it back," I said, as if some serious connection had been severed, like an artery, and I were watching myself bleed out, the calm of it detached and disembodied yet dire. "You have to go to that church. Tell that nun you made a mistake."

"Okay, okay," my mother said. "I'll get it back." And she did. In part. Service for twenty-four got more or less halved, some rummage sale volunteer having helped herself to twelve dinner plates, which was okay because it wasn't like I was ever going to have twenty-four people to dinner, either. All of the coffee cups *Good to the last drop* were gone, although none of the saucers were missing. The pristine soup tureen was not to be found, and one of the gravy boats got cracked in transit, but all in all there was plenty left for me to retain the reference to my grandmother, which was all I really wanted from the china. A tangible means by which to remember her, to touch what she

Almost no one marries for the sake of
love alone. Ask people. Ask them, Did you
marry the love of your life? Eight times out
of ten, they'll pause, and if they are honest
people, they will say no. They will own up
to a high school sweetheart left behind or
an ill-fated, star-crossed love affair or having bowed to family pressure, the way my
mother's aunt Semille did. Semille wasn't
really my mother's aunt; _aunt_ was a catchall
word for "related somehow." She died many
years before I was born, and I am named for
her, in her memory.

"Where is your wife now?" I asked
Henry.

3

That we do not marry our one true love is not to say that we don't love the people we do marry. It just means there were other factors in the mix.

"Elinor is in India," Henry said.

"And you didn't want to go to India?"

"She is in India," he told me, "studying with her goo-roo," which was how Henry pronounced guru: goo-*roo*. Elinor would be in India studying with her guru through the summer and into the first half of September. "Three months of meditation or levitation or some such flapdoodle," he said.

"Three months is a long time to spend in the lotus position. She must be devoted."

"This season she is devoted to the guru. Last summer she was sculpting the human form from clay to be cast in bronze. The year before that, it was archaeology, and off she went to Egypt wearing khaki short pants and a sun hat. Oil painting. Rock climbing. She has her interests. Interests about which she is passionate, interests that come and go, never to be heard from again."

"Not that it's any of my business," I said, "but," and then I hesitated.

"But what?"

"I was just wondering if she suffers from some kind of manic-depressive psychosis. Because spells of mania will induce new enthusiasms like that. It's a symptom."

"She doesn't suffer from anything," Henry said. "She's bored, is all it is."

"Were you one of them, then? One of her passionate interests?"

"Me?" Henry laughed. "Hardly. No, I was never one of her passions, although she does hold a small interest in me." A small interest in me, Henry made it sound as if he were some stock she owned, a piddling-size investment in a dot.com likely to go belly-up.

I never came flat out and asked, and Henry, he never came flat out and said, but there it was: motive. Henry married Elinor to have this life of his, to keep hold of his idea of himself as a carefree young man of means living in Paris. Although he was no longer young in years, he was without responsibility, which can pass for carefree and engender a kind of youthfulness. His was a very comfortable life, and an idle one, too, and I was never sure which mattered to him more: having money or not having to work.

'Not having to work. I know my people, Sylvia, and there's no one more trifling than a Southern man. Each and every one of them, lazy as an August afternoon.'

"Why don't I ever have the good sense to marry well?" Ruby used to ask me, but that's not a question you answer. More than once, she said, "Next time, I'm going to marry for money," but always she married for other reasons. Some of her mistakes were more extreme than others, although none of her marriages was a good plan from a sound mind.

Love and money. Ruby claimed that was all she ever wanted: love and money.

"That's it?" I asked. "Love and money?"

And Ruby said, "What else is there?"

Love and money. I was never sure which of the two Ruby wanted more, or if she really wanted either one at all, if *love* and *money* weren't stand-in words for something else, labels when she didn't know what to call it, or maybe that was me, because all I ever wanted was nothing much that I could name other than a vague sense of something else.

There are things to be said in defense of ignorance.

The middle of September was far off in the distance.

Keeping to the back roads, the mountain trails, the scenic by-ways, Henry did not take the path the crow would fly, yet we got to Trieste in a matter of minutes, which is an exaggeration on my part but not by much. For someone who had no place where he had to be, he sure liked to get there fast, and so when he told me that his parents had passed, together, in a crash—passed, he said, as if he were talking about an exam they took, the bar exam or the test to get certified as a lifeguard, and they passed—I assumed they had died in a car accident.

"No," Henry said. "Their plane went down."

"Is there more to that story?" I wanted to know.

"Probably," Henry said.

It could be said that "probably," without the definitive quality, the certainty of a yes or a no, implies a lack of commitment, but I don't read it as wishy-washy. Rather, I read it as nearer to a promise; a word that takes more of a risk than does its corollary: possibly.

Having arrived in the city center of Trieste, we followed the sign posted for the hotel with five stars. There, Henry parked the car, and waving off my offer to help, he got our suitcases from the trunk, and when we got to our room, it was as if we didn't have all the time in the world. As if we'd been through a drought, want for each other became need. My skirt went up and Henry's jeans came down, and that's why, after, when we were ready to go out, getting dressed took us all of ten seconds, if that.

At the water's edge, benches, like park benches, were set along the coastal wall, and sitting on one of them was a young woman, seventeen or eighteen years old, and she was crying; maybe because she'd had an argument with her parents or maybe she'd been dumped by the local Romeo. We sat two benches away from where she sat, her head in her hands, palms covering her eyes as if that would stop the flow of tears, and I asked Henry, "You don't think she's going to try and drown herself or anything like that, do you?"

"No," Henry said. "I think not," as if he knew this for a fact, but you can't know that for a fact.

The sun was an orange semicircle on the horizon, and golden rays fanned out on the water like a full skirt on a girl sitting under a tree. After a few minutes, the crying girl walked past us, and then we went for dinner.

There *was* more to the story, the story about Henry's parents and how they had died. Just as there is more to every story, the way we close a book but still we wonder what happened to these people after that last page, how did they go on from there. In the telling, where and when we end a story is artifice. Stories come to their ends when and where we choose to end them, and in that way, stories are unlike how things really are.

Henry's father had a pilot's license, and he flew not to get from one place to another but for the fun of it, much the way, I noted, Henry drove. Or maybe fun had nothing to do it; maybe it was the illusion that going somewhere meant getting away from where he was. Whichever, that's what his parents were doing, zipping around the sky in a two-seater Piper Cub, flying high over a peach orchard in Georgia, when his father radioed air traffic control and said, "Everything is spinning. I'm dizzy." The plane took a nosedive and, upon impact, which was not a smooth landing, it broke apart. And just like that, his parents passed.

The air traffic control report coupled with the autopsies, and also evidence from what was left of the plane, determined, as best as these things can be determined, that his father was struck with a severe attack of vertigo. "I'm dizzy," he'd said, and he slumped over the control panel, which was nothing more than the bad luck of being in the wrong place at the wrong time.

'Vertigo. That is a title of a movie, too. One directed by Alfred Hitchcock, starring James Stewart and Kim Novak and Barbara Bel Geddes.'

Had he been at his desk or, say, on the golf course when this happened, he would have passed out on the soft green grass by the ninth hole, and after a few hours of observation at the hospital, they would have sent Henry's father home with instructions to take it easy for a couple of days, and that would've been that.

Henry's mother, in the seat behind her husband, did nothing but wait out the time it took for the plane to hit the ground. "Mind you," Henry said, "she was heavily sedated."

"Because she was afraid of flying?"

"No. Afraid of living is more like it."

It was not the last time that Ruby and I spoke to each other, on the phone, but it was near to the last time, when I asked her, "What's with you and the movies?" because Ruby was never much of a moviegoer.

"It's pretty much what we do here," she said. "After dinner, we open up a big bag of popcorn and we sit on the couch and we watch a movie. Sometimes two movies. My mother favors the old ones. From her day. Uplifting movies. The kind that are supposed to make you feel good about being alive."

"Does it work?" I asked. "Those movies, do they make you feel good about being alive?"

"No. But sometimes my mother picks a movie of suspense, and that'll get me to the next day. The best I can say for myself now," Ruby said, "is that I'm not my cousin Kimmy. She came to visit yesterday. You remember my cousin Kimmy?"

Ruby's cousin Kimmy had a lantern jaw that kept her from being pretty, and she had a job at the Tyson factory. Each of her four children had a different father, but what was interesting about that was how all four of the fathers were named Tommy, and she met them at Alcoholics Anonymous meetings, which was where Kimmy went trolling for men. She'd get them on that first day or two of sobriety when they were vulnerable and confused.

"You could never be like your cousin Kimmy," I said.

"Yeah, you're right about that. Not with my mother bound and determined that I rise above my raisins. Better I do nothing all day than pluck chickens for Tyson."

I considered how Southerners have the oddest way of putting things into words. Raisins. Odd but nice.

"Not *raisins*," Ruby clarified. "Not a sun-dried grape or the stuff of Raisinets. *Raisings*, i-n-g-s, as in how I was raised. To rise above my raisings is to come up in the world."

"You came north, to New York. North is up, geographically speaking."

"Above my raisins does not mean *away* from my raisins."

During the time when Ruby lived in New York, she went back home often and easily, as if the south side of Virginia were as handy as the South Street Seaport, but her attachment to what she quaintly referred to as "the home place" afforded only some relationship to affection. It was stronger, more urgent, than affection, but it wasn't much like love. "We go back," she told me, "every chance we get. We always go back, if for no reason other than we get to be all braggity about how we don't live there anymore."

Not Henry. When Henry left home, it was for keeps. "Other than to go to England for Christmas, I do not leave the continent," he said. "Home was a place where I lived for a time, and then that time was over." Henry said he needed something vast and deep like the ocean as demarcation between then and now.

"Was it all that terrible?" I asked him.

"No." Henry said. *"Au contraire."* That was how he said "on the contrary." In French. *Au contraire,* but it sounded like regional English. Like Ruby's *raisings.* "My life was a charmed one," he said, "and what can you do with a charmed life but leave it behind? Leave it behind, and don't look back. Looking back," Henry said, "brings nothing but remorse."

The plane crash left Henry with ties to no one except for a grandfather who had long since been in the advanced stages of Alzheimer's. "He was more like a turnip than a person," Henry said. No family, no close friends, but Henry was left with a more than modest inheritance, which inspired him to quit William and Mary in the middle of his senior year. "I was a lackluster student," Henry said, "although I did well at the parties." From there he *Pass Go and Collect $200* hightailed it to Paris, where he did some serious squandering of his days and his money, and then he met Elinor, who was in need of a husband, and so they both got some of what they were after.

"In *need* of a husband?" I asked.

"Oh, yes," Henry said. "Need. Because of the way her trust was set up. Her grandfather, not being an enlightened man, stipulated that she had to be married before any money was rightly hers to spend, and I am the perfect husband."

Because you could argue the fact that someone else's perfect husband wouldn't have been tootling around with me, I said,

"Don't get me wrong here, but the perfect husband? I'm not see-ing it."

"Oh, I am exactly the man she was looking to marry. A pre-sentable escort, and we understand each other to the letter. Elinor does not like to be refused, and I am in no position not to be agreeable," he said, as if this were a cheerful thing.

A cheerful thing when it was not that at all, like the way boys go off to war singing and goofing around, as if they were going on a school trip.

"Is she very beautiful?" I asked.

And Henry said, "Elinor is a somewhat handsome English-woman," which led me to picture her as one of those good-size British gals with legs like tree trunks. Women who played a solid game of tennis in their day, and as they age, their bodies don't grow fat so much as they grow thick like Doric columns.

'You think that might explain their fondness for those corgi dogs? A similarity in shape?'

Being Elinor's husband did have significant benefits, but with assets come liabilities, and it's true: things, they do have a way of adding up on a person.

On one of her visits back home, with nothing much else to do, Ruby said, "Oh, why the hell not?" and off she went with Kevin Wiley to his place, which was a broken-down school bus. Cinder blocks set behind the wheels kept it from rolling away from his parents' backyard. "It was like a guest cottage, except it was a yellow bus. He got it fixed up," Ruby told me. "Took out most of the seats to make some space. Put a bed and a table in there and rigged up a generator for electricity and a pump for water. You wouldn't know it to see him," Ruby said, "but he was the handsomest boy in town. No lie, but if you took his picture from back in the day and put it alongside a picture of him now, you'd know that the time between didn't offer much in the way of accomplishments. And the saddest part is how he could play baseball. Good enough that he got recruited for a farm team. But that would've meant going to live in Ohio, and oh no, he wasn't going to leave Mecklenburg County, no way, no how. So now he's missing a front tooth and his liver is shot from the drink. But his mama is happy because her boy, he might be living in a school bus, but he stayed right close to home." Then Ruby said, "Tennessee Williams, he had it right, you know. What every Southern mother really wants is a drunk for a son and a cripple for a daughter."

After moving back home with her mother, Ruby got fat. Or so she said. I can't picture Ruby as fat. Ruby was willowy despite a diet of Snickers bars for breakfast, and once we were out for lunch and she asked me, "Can I have your pickle? I haven't had a vegetable all week." She had that kind of metabolism, revved up, and she could eat and eat and still, always she was willowy. Then there were the times when she had no appetite. No appetite at all and she would grow too thin.

"You? Fat? Impossible," I said.

"It's true. I'm fat. And," she added, "my hair is falling out." Her hair—some months blond, other days black, and one time, years ago, she dyed it pink—was never its natural color, but

The Scenic Route

mostly it was long, except when she'd go to the other extreme and have at it with a Weedwacker. Long or short, and whatever the color, it was always thick, healthy hair. "It's the lithium," she said. "And the Depakote. Significant weight gain and hair loss are common side effects."

Some side effects—dry mouth, constipation, do not operate heavy machinery, even frequent urination—we shrug off easily enough, but there are other side effects—sexual dysfunction, · significant memory loss, death—that give us pause, and I asked her, "How fat is fat?"

"Fat," she said. "I've considered going off the medication. I might rather be a crazy person than a fat and bald one."

Although her rationale was not without merit, I did not say anything to encourage her to go off the medication, and although my mother's cousin Danny sprang to mind, I didn't mention him either because that was the sort of story Ruby might obsess on. Ruby was prone to obsessing, and drugs, they are good for only so much.

I suppose if you didn't know otherwise, you could easily have assumed that Ruby never lived elsewhere other than home, that ever since graduating from—I don't know—Longwood College in Farmville or perhaps the University of Virginia, Ruby had been doing mostly nothing but sitting on her mother's rose-print couch, leaving the house only on those days when she was called in to be a substitute teacher at the local high school. You could have thought that was the whole story.

"Oh, yeah," Ruby said. "I took the scenic route back, but I got here just the same, didn't I?"

My Mother's Cousin Danny: According to my mother, Danny was the way he was because of his mother Alice, who was one of my grandmother's sisters and also Alice was a Froot-Loop. My grandmother, Beatrice, had three sisters. Hannah, Alice, and Thea, and one brother. Five children born into privilege, but things went wrong with them, as they suffered from problems in living. Suffered collectively, although each of them in their own way, from neurasthenia, hysteria, melancholia, and Alice, Danny's mother, she was mean. The other three sisters turned in on themselves, but the way Alice was twisted, all the ugliness was directed outward. "It's her sickness, the way she is cruel and vicious," my mother had said. Alice was the opposite of my grandmother, who was good and kind and sensitive. That's what was wrong with my grandmother: sensitivity.

That's what everyone said she had. Sensitivity. "She is sensitive. And delicate."

What is delicate can shatter, and the sensitive are easily bruised

What my mother meant, about Danny being the way he was, was this: Danny, Alice's only child, was circus-freak obese. Also, he was bald, which maybe, like the obesity, was stress-related if only because our families are predisposed to the lean side and we have good hair, too, but the way Danny was pathetic was not part and parcel of his obesity. It was a whole other order of business, the way he engendered nothing but pity, the way no other response to him was to be had.

One time I came home from I don't know where to find Danny sitting on our couch, his girth pretty much filling it up, and tears, fat tears, were streaming down his blubbery, woesome moon face, and I was sure that this was the saddest thing I would ever see, that even though I was only five or six years old with my whole life before me, I was sure that Danny was the saddest person I would ever know.

Yet soon after that, he found someone to marry. A very fat woman named Leora, and I was the flower girl at their wedding.

Danny and Leora had two children, which means they did have sex, about which I will own up to a mild curiosity, the physical logistics of it, the same way I had a curiosity about the woman with the wooden leg.

"I forget her name," I told Henry. "The woman with the wooden leg. We worked together for a few months. Every morning, at the coffee station, she would waylay me, to tell me about the night before. Specifically about the sex she'd had the night before. With whom, and where, and for how long, and who was on top, and she didn't scrimp on any of the details, either, but it was never very interesting."

"It wasn't? I would have thought, you know, the novelty of it, would have rendered the details" —Henry paused, groping for the right word, but there wasn't one and he settled on— "colorful." Colorful, and he blushed, too.

"This was before I learned about the wooden leg," I said. All I knew then was that some woman I barely knew was cornering me at the coffee machine to tell me about the pubic hair stuck in her throat or her very responsive nipples, and so I wasn't sorry when I heard that she was moving to Los Angeles. On the morning of her last day at work, we, yet again, met up at the coffee machine. Attempting to sidestep the daily clitoral report, I said something about Los Angeles and sun and surf, and she said, "Oh, I don't go to the beach because of my leg."

"What about your leg?" I asked, and she patted her left thigh and said, "That it's wooden. This is a wooden leg. Didn't you know?"

I suppose she did walk with a limp, but I never thought anything of it, and I didn't see that she had a wooden leg because she always wore pants and boots, but this, a wooden leg, now I wanted to hear all about who was on top, and I had other questions for her, too: Do you mention it before you undress, or do you just kind of spring it on him? Do you leave it on, like socks? Is taking it off foreplay? But I never saw her again, and my questions went unanswered.

"To spread one leg," Henry said, "could be one of those deep thoughts for ridiculous people. One hand clapping kind of fool-headed nonsense, don't you think?"

"That's rude," I said.

"What's rude? To suggest that contemplation of one hand clapping is nothing but a whole lot of hooey?"

"No. The spreading-one-leg thing. That's rude."

"It's *your* story," Henry said.

'He got himself a point there.'

.   .   .

It happened that my mother's cousin Danny wound up with only one leg, too; the other one got amputated because of his diabetes. Which is what he died from, diabetes. Leora died from one of the especially grotesque types of cancer. Maybe it was cancer of the rectum.

Those two children of theirs, the boy was *Jack Sprat could eat no fat* as thin as a blade of grass and the girl *His wife could eat no lean* was a butterball, and they were six or eight years younger than me. After Leora died, the thin boy and his fat sister went to live with Leora's brother and his wife. I never saw them again, the same as if they, too, had died, together, maybe in a car wreck.

Two days Henry and I spent in Trieste, eating and drinking and walking aimlessly through the town and walking aimlessly along the water's edge and exploring each other with purpose, and then we'd had our fill of the town and its coast, and we checked out of the hotel and got in the car. I opened the map and my finger went to Vienna, and Henry said, "Seems as good a place as any." We were back on the road, and that, toward Vienna, was the general direction we took until Henry said something about how Vienna and Venice sounded as if they could be the same city in two different languages. "Yet they are entirely dissimilar in topography and temperament. Still, I wonder if anyone ever mixes them up."

"I would think not, but what do I know? I've never been to either of them."

To which Henry said, "You've never been to Venice? That just won't sit. I have got to take you to the Lido." He turned the car around. "It's right handy to here."

"What's so special about the Lido?" I asked, and Henry told me, "The Hotel Des Bains. Last summer I spent near a month there. At the Hotel Des Bains."

"Doing what?"

"Nothing."

'The Hotel Des Bains. From Death in Venice. *They filmed some of* The English Patient *there, too.'*

"Right handy" was, give or take, three hundred kilometers to the southwest, but it wasn't as if we were going out of our way to get there and, sure enough, in no time flat we were crossing the Ponte della Libertà. Henry parked the car at the privately owned Garage San Marco. From there, we took a water taxi instead of a vaporetto. "Because," Henry said, "the vaporetto is like a bus."

"And you'd rather not travel with the riffraff?"

"No, that's not it. It's that they won't take kindly to the suitcases." Then Henry gave a truer explanation. "The water taxi doesn't make stops along the way. It's faster."

"And we don't want to be late," I said.

The water taxi left the vaporetto behind in a spray of water, and it was luxurious, too. The seats were upholstered in blue leather, more like a limousine than a taxi.

The Lido is narrow, barely a mile wide, so that even as we came in close, the optical illusion of it made it look like land far off in the distance; as if one of us should have called Land Ho!, as if we had discovered a new world.

4

Our room overlooked the sea, and all of the Hotel Des Bains—Palladian style and Art Nouveau—was imposing and gorgeously gloomy. Dark Oriental rugs covered dark wood floors. High ceilings and salons and there was a billiard room *a billiard room!* and throughout the place there was a whiff of shabbiness to the opulence, a slight fraying at the edges, and it seemed as if no one walked, but rather they wafted, as if every single person in the hotel, guests and staff alike, were dead. Dead, as if this were some kind of purgatorial afterlife for the well-heeled and slightly wicked, where the food was abundant, the drink was plentiful, the sex was kinky, and yet no one quite wanted to be there. The sound track would be faintly heard organ music, lugubrious and mournful.

The next day we took another water taxi to the Piazza San Marco, where we didn't climb the Bell Tower or visit the Basilica or Palazzo Ducale or step foot in the *museo* either. We did, however, cross the Bridge of Sighs, and then we walked through alleyways until it was time for lunch.

We sat at a table by the window, which I was glad of because Henry was eating squid that was stewed in its own black ink, and I didn't much want to look at that. "It's raining," I noted.

Henry turned to the window. "Maybe we'll get the *aqua alta*. That's when the lagoon overflows," he explained "and the streets flood," and the lagoon did overflow, and the Piazza San Marco and the surrounding streets got flooded. The floodwater wasn't more than ankle deep, but Henry said there was no easy way out, so he ordered another bottle of wine.

My grandmother, the sensitive one, Beatrice, and two of her three sisters, Alice and Thea, were as lovely as the beauties of the silent movies. Clara Bow types, with big eyes and eyelashes like palm fronds. Their mouths were full and rosy-round, and they had bosoms to match. To see a photograph of the four sisters together is to conclude that my great-grandmother was raped by a Talmudic scholar because Hannah, she could have been the second coming of Alice B. Toklas. Skinny and flat-chested, and she had a nose that could chisel stone. You might not notice that her eyes were set too close together because she wore

Men seldom make passes glasses with lenses an inch thick. Her hair was the opposite of soft, and unlike the peaches-and-cream complexions of her sisters, Hannah's skin was sallow. Although not at all beautiful, Hannah was somewhat brainy, and she got a Ph.D. in logic and rhetoric, which didn't entirely compensate for a lack of comeliness, but it was something.

In her day, a day that fell during the Depression, which was, for so many, a time of desperation, Hannah had no choice but to compromise in terms of her career. A schoolteacher was as good of a job as there was to be had for a woman back then. Which doesn't mean it wasn't something of a letdown of a job, too. For a person who aspired to be a university professor, teaching fifth-graders where to put their commas and when to begin a new paragraph and, "Yes, *there, they're,* and *their* all do sound alike, but no, they don't mean the same thing," well, who bothers to get a Ph.D. for that?

When it came to getting a husband, Hannah relinquished all standards relating to quality. Nathan Lasky was a pattern cutter in the garment district and also he was a drunk and a child molester, so the best thing to be said about Hannah's marriage to Nathan was that they did not have children.

Even though her sisters were sorry for Hannah because she wasn't beautiful and she had a loser for a husband, they envied her, too, because, unlike them, Hannah was strong, a rock, of sound mind.

Except she wasn't.

She was as crazy as her sisters—the difference being only that for many years Hannah's insanity was under wraps. Like a predatory animal hiding in tall grass, crouched and waiting, ready to spring, and no one saw it coming. I never met my grandmother's brother because he killed himself when he was still a young man, which led me to assume there were more than a few bats flapping around in his belfry, too.

As is the way with all things touch-and-go, whatever it was that was off with my grandmother and her sisters, it would go off, like an alarm clock telling them, "It's time," but they weren't uninterruptedly crazy. There were months, years even, when they were mostly all there in the head. By and large, day to day, they functioned, except for Alice, who was never right. It would seem that the way a lamp is either off or on, Alice was either tra-la-la delightful or schoolyard-bully cruel, but it was all one and the same. Delightful was the trap she set for the unsuspecting.

Alice lived with her husband—I'm sure there was a husband, although I don't remember him—on the Upper East Side of New York, and my mother and I were once invited there for tea and strawberry shortcake. After her second piece of cake and probably sugar-buzzed, Alice stood up and took me by the hand into her bedroom. On her nightstand was a small box. Deep green leather, and the inside was lined with ivory-colored silk, and like a crown set upon a tufted pillow, there was a ruby ring. A child's ruby ring, for a girl of nine or ten, which I was. Ten. A small ruby on what was called a Tiffany setting, the prongs raised like arms reaching up to the stars, so that the stone rose above the band. "This was mine when I was your age," Aunt Alice said to me. "I want you to have it."

I dutifully kissed Aunt Alice on the cheek, tasting her powder, which didn't taste terrible, but when I showed my mother the ring, she said, "No. That's very nice of you, Aunt Alice, but she's too young for good jewelry."

"You are ridiculous," Alice said. "My father gave me this ring when I was her age. It's a precious family heirloom, and I want to pass it down to Sylvia."

My mother relented, but I could tell she wasn't happy about it.

The following day, in a pique of generosity or not caring enough either way, I gave the ruby ring to Carolyn, who was not my best friend, but I wanted her to be my best friend. Perhaps I thought the ruby ring might effect devotion.

"And did it?" Henry asked me. "Did the girl become your true-blue friend?"

"No."

Carolyn slipped the ring on her finger, and she admired the red of the ruby in contrast to her creamy skin. Then she went home.

That night, after dinner, my mother found me in my room, doing homework. "The ring," she said. "Alice's ring. Where is it?" My mother was clearly angry, but I knew she wasn't angry at me, and so for no good reason, I lied.

"I lost it," I said.

All too familiar with, and nearly resigned to, my incorrigible carelessness, my habit of losing things—my eyeglasses, my wristwatch, *You'd lose your head if it wasn't attached* library books, my winter coat—such a declaration—I lost it—had come to elicit not much more than a sigh, an exhalation of exasperation, but not this time. "Where? Where did you lose it? We have to find it." My mother got down on her knees and was feeling around under my bed as if on the hunt for an errant shoe. From there, with the single-mindedness of a pig rooting for truffles, she went through the drawer where I kept my socks. "I should have known better." My mother slammed that drawer shut and pulled open the next one. "I should have known she'd pull a stunt like this."

Having rummaged through my sweaters, my mother folded them and put them back neatly, which was *not* the way she'd found them because I was not a tidy child, either. "We need to find the ring," my mother said. "Alice is raising the roof about how you stole her ruby ring."

"I didn't steal it," I said. "She gave it to me."

"I know she gave it to you. But she does crazy things like this. All the time. For no reason. Except that she is a vicious woman, and she is going to make me miserable until I get that damn ring back to her. I knew I shouldn't have let you take it."

"I didn't lose it," I said. "I gave it to Carolyn."

To compensate Carolyn for her loss, for having to give back my gift to her, my mother bought her a replacement ring with a ruby the size of a dot. Aunt Alice's ring was returned to her by mail, registered and insured, because my mother said, "Alice wouldn't think twice about lying, claiming she never got it. Now do you understand why my cousin Danny is the way he is?"

Although I didn't want Aunt Alice's ruby ring enough to keep it in the first place, I nonetheless thought it only fair that I, too, should get a ruby ring from this ordeal.

"And did you?" Henry asked.

"No."

"I suppose that the point of this story is a warning similar to that of one about the Trojan horse."

"Does there have to be a point to a story?" I asked.

"I wouldn't think so." Henry poured us more wine, and when the floodwaters receded, he said, "You know how when there is a blackout, and you're sitting there in the dark waiting and waiting for the lights to come back on? And then they do, but there's that moment when you wish they hadn't? When you wish you could've sat there in the dark a while longer?"

"What of it?" I asked.

"Nothing. Just that there's something to be said for being in the dark, is all."

"You are a funny one."

"Ha-ha funny? Or the other kind?"

"Both," I told him. "You are both kinds of funny."

"We are a well-suited pair, don't you agree?"

Maybe it has something to do with the pull of the moon because, despite the statistical improbability of any two people meeting up, it is inevitable that the tremulous are drawn to the languished, the sick to the broken, the forsaken to the sad, *every pot has its cover* and the funny to the funny ones, too.

The next morning we took a water taxi, our return to the Garage San Marco. Back on the road, we went north, and the Lido was behind us.

.   .   .

Things Had To Go Together: Polka dots were the sworn enemy of plaids. It was imperative to match shoes to pocketbook, scarf to gloves, curtains to carpet, sheets to pillowcases. Otherwise, you had chaos and, even worse: weirdness, and to wear what was not *the* style, that was asking for trouble. On my first day of school, my first day of school as a second-grader, which for me was a year not unlike the Inquisition, I came downstairs for breakfast only to have my mother send me back to my room to change my clothes because I could not wear a purple blouse with a yellow skirt.

"Why not?" I asked.

"Because the colors clash," my mother said, and she said it in such a way as to make "clash" sound dangerous, like "crash." *The colors crash.* "They don't go together."

In the second grade we had desks with hinged lids, and we held them open while Mrs. Milton, a woman with arms too short for her to clasp her hands behind her back because you know she would've if she could've, goose-stepped up and down the aisles peering inside each desk, as if she could see into our minds. Which were either clean or dirty. Mine was dirty. Mrs. Milton came to a full stop. Lifting my desk by two of its four legs, she turned it upside down and shook it the way you shake a garbage can to be sure no bit of trash is clinging to a corner or stuck on gunk. My books, notebooks, pencils, erasers, crayons, paper, dried apple core, troll doll, pencil sharpener, and pencil shavings scattered all over the floor, and I stayed after school to clean up the mess, to tidy my desk to her Teutonic satisfaction. Every day this happened. Exactly this way. Oh, for the grace of first grade, where gold stars were affixed to my every effort. Now, each morning I clung to my bedpost like a baby rhesus monkey to its wire mother, and I begged, "Please. Don't make me go. Please."

The day came. Enough was enough, and instead of going to school, I snuck into our garage and into the back seat of my mother's car. From the rear window, I could see out the garage windows to the street where, at the end of the school day, I would see the other kids nearing home. The way Rosie Ruiz cheated in the Boston Marathon, I would join up with the pack. That was the plan. I had books to read and food to eat. A sandwich, an apple, two Oreo cookies secure in my Josie and the Pussycats lunch box. And it was a good plan, except I fell asleep, and it was dark when I woke, not from a kiss or a light snowfall, but from some neighbor boy yelling, "I found her. I found her." Like I was the Lindbergh baby.

All that changed nothing, and Mrs. Milton, she'd had it up to here *here!* with me, her hand skimming the top of her head. She wrote my mother a letter describing, in stunning detail, my messy desk, my sloppy handwriting, my untidy attire, which Mrs. Milton readily acknowledged, was *not* how my mother sent me off to school, and my overall slovenliness as a human being. My mother was supposed to sign this letter, as if in agreement, "Yes, yes, my daughter is a grubby little ragamuffin who sits in her own waste." I was to return the letter to Mrs. Milton the next day. "And don't lose it." Mrs. Milton licked the envelope, as if she were sealing my fate.

To slide the letter between pages of a notebook was to chance losing it. Better to hold it in my hand, hold it tight between my fingers. It wasn't raining when I left school that afternoon, but it had rained earlier in the day, and no sun broke through the sky to dry the puddles. Against a chilly wind, I walked up Nelson Street, where Alley Bonfiglio lived. Later, when I was in the sixth grade, I was killer-in-love with Alley Bonfiglio. His name alone—Alley—was enough to get me going. Alley. Like a dark alley where danger lurked. Eventually I learned that Alley, the coolest of cool names, was short for Alphonse, which wasn't the least bit of a cool name, but still I adored him because he'd been smoking cigarettes since he was seven, and it was rumored that he had a JD card, that he was a registered-with-the-authorities juvenile delinquent, and if that wasn't enough to make a girl swoon, then I don't know what is. Assuming there really was such a thing as a JD card. We believed that there was, but we believed in all sorts of things that were made up.

My shoes got wet walking through puddles, which somehow my mother intuited because from the living room, where she sat with her knitting, she called out, "Wipe your feet." My mother did not knit baby booties and frumpy cardigan sweaters. She worked with textured yarns, fine wool, and up-to-the-minute patterns.

"You have to sign this," I told her.

"Sign what?" she asked, because all that remained of the letter was the bit of paper the size of a dime held tight between my thumb and index finger. The wind must have torn the body of the paper away, and my hands clamped to my cheeks, my mouth agape, like I was a little-girl version of Edvard Munch's *The Scream.* I whirled in circles and fell at my mother's feet.

Textured yarns, fine wool, stylish patterns, and my mother often knitted matching sets: a blue nubby-tweed hat with a scarf in the same blue nubby-tweed for Joel. I once got a sweater, hat, scarf, and mittens done in red mohair patterned with white snowflakes.

When things don't go together, when they are not uniform, they are therefore irregular, and that which is irregular can become unstable, and instability worried my mother. To ward off the genetic possibility of being yet one more crazy woman in her family, my mother clung to what chimed, as if to relax her grip on that which was without distinction would be to slip out of her color-coordinated outfits and into a straitjacket.

To listen to music, to read books, to go to a museum, those were activities within the range of what normal people do, but to write books, to paint pictures, to play the violin? No. People who did those things were offbeat, Dadaists, freak shows, none of which was good to be. All artistic inclination was to be squashed like a bug underfoot. Except for crafts because crafts were not art. "Arts *and* crafts," my mother explained. "Like night *and* day." Crafts were hobbies, something you did in your leisure time, as if macramé were racquetball for the athletically disinclined. Moreover, crafts, or at least the crafts my mother did, begot goods of a practical nature. Her knitting—the hats, scarves, and sweaters—we wore. The ceramic pots she glazed were used as fruit bowls, and there was nothing eccentric about needlepoint throw pillows.

At age twelve, I asked if I could take piano lessons. Try as she might, my mother could not come up with a sound reason to object other than the truth, which was that my grandmother and each of her three unbalanced sisters were accomplished pianists, although only my grandmother was truly gifted. To articulate that objection, to say that to play the piano was to sign on with the crazy women, would be to cast aspersions on her own mother, and you just don't do that. Not ever, and so the lesser of two evils prevailed. It was a Thursday afternoon when an old man with tufted nose hair, whom I thought to be Swiss because he had a Middle European accent and there was a cheese smell to him, came to our house to give me my first piano lesson, which was not at all as I'd imagined it would be.

Our piano was in the family room, which used to be the basement until my mother had the walls paneled in oak. The floor was oak, too, but much of it was covered with an area rug. The family room was where we kept the television and a Ping-Pong table for Joel, which were things my mother wouldn't allow in the living room because they didn't match the early American furniture. The piano might have matched, but regardless, it was stashed with all else that was unsightly.

Mr. Wolffstein, the piano teacher—his name really wasn't Wolffstein but it should have been—sat beside me on the piano bench where, with each key I hit, he winced as if an F-sharp were a pin I'd jabbed into a voodoo doll that was stuffed with his toenail clippings. Some sixteen thousand hours of piano lessons later—what seemed like sixteen thousand hours of piano lessons, given the veracity of the observation that time flies when you're having fun—I had all but mastered a hunt-and-peck rendition of "The Song of the Volga Boatmen" and no more *Yo, heave ho!* than that.

At that lesson's end, the piano teacher spoke to my mother in private, but I heard every word because this was after the time when I was pretending to be deaf. "Mrs. Landsman," he said. "I hope you do not take offense, but you are wasting your money on me. Your daughter has no gift for the piano. Worse than no gift."

My mother did not take offense.

My mother put effort and forethought into it, into situating herself in the center of Normal, but she needn't have bothered. Plain and simple: the crazy gene passed her by just as the gift for the piano did not attach itself to me.

Because what is and what is not passed along in our DNA is pretty much of a crapshoot, it's my good fortune that Huntington's chorea does not run in my family, nor any of those Hebraic glitches that result in diseases common to Jews—sphingolipid disorder, Fanconi anemia, Bloom syndrome, Tay-Sachs disease—or any kidney disorder, either, because if I ever did wind up needing a new kidney, I'd be shit out of luck waiting for Joel to cough up one of his. We do, in my family on my mother's side, have that predisposition for coming apart at the seams, and there is the ovarian cancer, but other than a shared smile, I look nothing like my mother, which allows me to trust that what's on the inside is equally dissimilar. Her hair was black, her skin was an opalescent white, and she had cheekbones that were like doorknobs. I most resemble my father's mother. Although she, too, died young, no one knows from what, and I am free to believe it was tuberculosis or salmonella, something she picked up rather than something she passed along.

Henry couldn't say which side of his family he resembled because when he was days old, he was adopted. "I don't know who I favor," he said. "Being adopted wasn't something we discussed. Like there was something untoward about it all. Now that I'm thinking on it though, in my family no one talked about anything much but for golf and weddings."

Most everyone loves to talk about weddings, but they don't talk so much about marriage.

He and his sister both were adopted. His sister is, or was, six years older than Henry. *Is* or *was* because Henry had no idea if Taylor was dead or not. Taylor, that was his sister's name.

"My sister," he said. "She was the prettiest girl around, and at school every year she was voted Best Dressed. She and my mother would go on these weekend-long shopping excursions. Come home with a bounty of bags filled with dresses and shoes and those sweater sets that girls wore back then." In her senior year at high school, she was voted Best Dressed, Most Popular, and Prom Queen. In 1966, this was to hit the trifecta," Henry said. "But she wasn't stuck up. She was nice."

"How is it that you don't know if she's dead or not?" I asked. "What happened?"

More often than not we don't know what really happened, and what we say happened is more likely to be a reconstruction of events rather than a restoration. We imagine as much as we remember. If we remembered everything, all of it, the thread of the story would tangle in knots and we might never get free of it.

This much was probably certain: In the summer before she was to go off to Sophie Newcomb College, which was the women's wing of Tulane, with a notion to study political science, which was no kind of subject for a young lady, Taylor, Henry's sister and the Most Popular, Best-Dressed Prom Queen, came home with one eye red and swollen half shut. Because she'd had a Tom Collins or two too many, either there was no remembering how it happened or maybe she wasn't telling how it happened. Her red and swollen eye turned a nasty shade of purple and yellow. A week or so later, she came home with a split lip, which also was the result of a mystery. "I don't honestly know," she insisted. "I must have banged into something. Or maybe I bit my lip, you know, in a nervous moment." After she went to bed, Henry, who was still a boy at the time, and a scrawny boy at that, got up and softly, so as not to be heard, walked from his room to hers intending to find out who had done this to her, and he was going to do something about it, too. "I was wearing cowboy-print pajamas," Henry said. "Can you picture it? But when I got to her door, I could hear her crying, and somehow I knew that I couldn't fix anything. Somehow, I had the idea that she didn't want anything fixed. She wasn't crying about the black eye or the split lip. It was about something else, something that I knew was far beyond me, and I turned around and went back to bed."

"We're all guilty of something, Henry," I said.

We're all guilty of something. That much I know.

'It's behind us, Sylvia.'

"Then one night," Henry went on, "maybe two weeks before she was to leave for school, she didn't come home at all. She didn't sneak back in after curfew like she'd done other nights. She just didn't come home." In the morning after breakfast— *"After* breakfast, mind you," Henry said—Henry's mother called all of Taylor's friends, asking if they knew her whereabouts. Some of her friends told the truth. "I haven't seen her all summer, Mrs. Stafford." Others said, "Last night? No, I don't believe I saw her last night."

No one much worries into a knot over a teenage girl who doesn't come home one night. Except her parents. Her parents worry, but law enforcement agencies—the police, the sheriff, the state troopers—they are not inclined toward calling out a search party for a girl who all too likely fell asleep in the backseat of a car with some boy or drank herself sick and was passed out behind a row of hedges, a girl who would surely return home soon enough, but Henry's father, Mr. Stafford, was Judge Stafford, and so a different set of procedures applied.

Four days and nights they searched, and it was just like you'd see in the movies. The troopers and the sheriff and the dogs and who knows how many volunteers, men with flashlights and the Boy Scouts, too, they searched through backwoods and fields overgrown and vacant lots. On the fifth day, the judge got a phone call at home. He said, "Yes. Yes, I understand. Well, I thank you," and when he hung up, he drove to the police station and asked that the search be called off. "It's just too hard on everyone. My wife can't hold up," he said, and Taylor was never heard from again. Some years later, Taylor was declared dead. Legally dead, and who knows? Maybe she was dead.

'She was likely to be dead.'

Ruby's contraposition—a contraposition to common assumption—was that New York was about the safest place in America. "In New York," she said, "if a man pulls a gun on you, he wants your money. You give him your money, and he goes away, and everybody's happy. In rural parts, though, if a man pulls a gun on you, he's going to tie you to a tree and chainsaw off your arms and legs. Like you are a piece of furniture he needs for firewood."

Henry told me that his father was an influential man but not a man well-liked, and according to Henry, his mother wasn't the nicest person you'd ever want to meet either. Aloof, was how she was. His mother was distant. "She did not emote," Henry said. "Especially after Taylor disappeared. Then it was as if we'd all . disappeared. Although that could have been because she took to the drink. For breakfast she'd eat enough Valium to put down a horse. But Taylor, she was nice." Henry pulled over to the side of the road, to a patch of land meant for that, for stopping. He turned off the ignition and let go with a short laugh entirely un-related to things amusing. More like a throat clearing or maybe a way to clear the air to ready us for something wry or ironic or not good. "I haven't talked about her in years. I don't remember the last time I told that story."

But surely he had told that story before. All of us, we tell our stories over and over again. Not in the same way and we don't always recognize them for what they are, the same way we don't always recognize that all creation myths boil down to God and man and a thunderstorm.

"You're easy to talk to," Henry said. "Real easy. I can talk to you. That's something, isn't it?"

I wasn't sure if by "That's something," he meant the story about his sister, that it was something of a story, or "That's some-thing," meaning it was significant that he could talk to me, but whichever: yes, it was something, and from there, Henry and I listened to music until we got to Eisenerz, a town that was on the map, but barely, and Henry said, "We've got to stop for gas. We're about down to the fumes."

Maybe it was a gift he was born with, or maybe it was a skill acquired over time, but either way, Henry had a knack for finding a nice restaurant, and after filling the gas tank, we went for a late lunch at a sweet little place where on each table was a vase filled with fresh yellow roses. The linen napkins were white and crisply pressed. Henry ordered a bottle of a local Riesling, and the wineglasses were crystal. While we waited for our food, he took one of the yellow roses from the vase and sniffed it, just as he did with the wine before tasting. Then he handed the rose to me, as if it were his to give.

I put it back in the vase.

Noodles with butter, that was for me. Henry got pork that came attached to a bone, and the waiter poured us more wine, and when we were done eating, we got coffee topped with whipped cream *whipped cream!* Alongside the cup, on the white saucer, was a piece of dark chocolate wrapped in gold foil. The check came also on a white saucer, and I said to Henry, "Please. Let me get this," but Henry put his hand over the slip of paper as if staking a claim to it. "Absolutely not. The gentleman pays."

"But you've paid for everything."

"Not yet I haven't."

'Oh, but he will. He will pay and pay.'

"It's not right that you pay for everything."

"Yes, it is," Henry said. "As right as rain."

The High Cost of Living: My great-grandfather was a chemist by profession, and in his laboratory he concocted a liquid soap, a gentle, liquid soap for washing hair. Shampoo was hardly penicillin or the printing press, but nonetheless, it was a significant cultural enrichment, and so you could say that it took an astounding lack of foresight to conclude that a gentle, liquid soap for washing hair would be, at best, a fad. But there it was, an astounding lack of foresight, and my great-grandfather exchanged his patent for shampoo for a big box of cash.

For many years, he was rich.

Years passed. Three of his four daughters—Beatrice, Hannah, and Alice—were already married by the time Thea, the youngest sister, left home to attend Vassar, and Thea's tuition pretty much cleaned out the remains of her father's fortune. Where and how he would scrape up money for the next year's tuition turned out to be worry for nothing because two months into her first semester at college, Thea met John, who was a student at Dartmouth.

Young love. Impetuous and half-witted, and in the stealth of a winter's night, John and Thea took a train *Cantaloupe today but I'll marry you tomorrow* to Maryland, where they got married. This marriage was kept secret from John's family for a number of reasons, not the least of which was that Thea was Jewish and John was a Baptist. Or maybe John was a Methodist, although to mix up Thea's John with Salome's John would not be only because of the commonality of the name. That Thea chose to wed one of the Un-Chosen, her parents couldn't have cared less. As for a ceremony on the sly, they were, in fact, grateful. Spared the expense of a wedding, and because in 1934 there was no place at Vassar for a married woman, either, Thea's father got out from under the tuition bill, too.

The newlyweds set up house in a tiny apartment in Greenwich Village. A pair of Bohemian types—John had his aspirations to be a writer, a writer of stories, and Thea painted—they lived off John's allowance, which was a good amount for a student, because as far as his parents knew, that's what John was: a young man completing his education at Dartmouth.

What was a generous allowance for a student was stretched a bit thin for a young couple with rent to pay, and John and Thea found themselves living hand to mouth. These children born into wealth were now, relatively speaking, poor. Poor, but pinch-me happy to be together, to live out their artsy-fartsy dreams: writing and painting by day, and at night they went to cafés and to salons and to Harlem to hear jazz. Whether John had any talent as a writer or Thea's paintings were any good, I couldn't say, but for two years, give or take, John and Thea—young and in love and starry-eyed—resided in the domicile of their artistic inventions where everything was possible, although not everything was considered. Such as: Thea got pregnant. A baby. How were they going to care for a baby? A baby costs money, more money than they had, and could they really raise a child in that closet of an apartment? No. John would have to give up writing stories by day. He would have to get himself a job. A job. Some wretched, meaningless job, and the idea of it caused him to despair. There had to be some other way, and there was. "It's time you met my parents," John said to his young wife, and off they went to West Virginia, which, technically speaking, is not a part of the South, but those of us from the North, we tend to go by the accent and what is considered to be the cracker factor, which is shortsightedness in its own right. John's hometown, the whole town, all of it—the coal mines, the general store, the hotel, the newspaper, and the lives of those who lived there—belonged to John's father, who was some kind of Appalachian Big Daddy.

John held Thea's hand as they walked up the steps leading to the Big House, where a scrawny young woman opened the door. Her uniform was pink, and her teeth overlapped. She wore brown oxford shoes. "They're waiting on you," she said to John, "in the liberry."

"Library," John corrected her.

"That's right. You best go on in."

John's parents stood up. His mother embraced her son, and then John said, "I'd like you to meet Thea. My wife," he added, and before they could so much as properly take in the news of that, that John had a wife, John let it drop, "Thea is from New York." A wife from New York was troubling enough to John's parents; further descriptives were best left off, especially that one his parents used as a verb: as in, You know he's going to try and Jew me down on the price. To divert attention away from geographical disturbances, and to smooth down any ruffled feathers, John rushed to tell them the news. "We're having a baby."

Miffed as they might have been at his springing a daughter-in-law on them, and a New York one at that, a baby fixed everything. A baby. A grandchild. A grandson. An heir ensuring that the coal mines, the general store, the hotel, the newspaper, all of it would stay in the family for generations to come. To that end, to keep the coal mines in the family and the family in the coal mine business, John's parents gave the not-so-newlywed couple a house of their own because it was time for John to come home, where he belonged, and New York City was no kind of place for their grandchild to be born.

That night, in their new bed, in their new house, a house nowhere near the size or stateliness of the Big House, but an impressive house by any standard, Thea wept, "We can't live here."

John held his wife and soothed her. "Just until the baby is born," he promised. "Until then, I don't see that we have a choice."

But there's always a choice.

We make our choice, and then we put the blame on fate.

(to be continued)

The Hotel Sacher was Old World to the gills. Chandeliers galore, Persian carpets, oil paintings and they weren't paintings of lighthouses either. In our room a velvet chaise flanked an antique writing table. The chairs had curlicue legs. The lamps were brass and the bed was huge. A bed the size of a playground, and eventually Henry and I wound up on a bare mattress, the sheets having come undone, and after that moment when you can't talk, as if all you could manage would be garble, or maybe you don't want to talk for fear of what you might say, after that moment passed, Henry said, "A man can't help but be in love with a woman so close to her feelings as you." Then he kissed the top of my head, like dotting an *i* or putting a period at the end of a sentence. The finishing touch to make it perfect and right.

I must have had some kind of look on my face because Henry asked, "You don't believe that I'm in love with you?"

"No. I don't believe that you're in love with me, but if you want to pretend to be in love with me, I'll play along."

Despite my assertion to the contrary, I did believe him. I believed that Henry was in love with me. I believed him because we can believe whatever we want to believe, and I wanted to believe that Henry was in love with me because I needed to believe that such a thing could happen. I needed to believe that there was more for me than yet another pleasant dinner with a perfectly nice man, or another Thursday night having drinks with old friends, or another Saturday afternoon shopping for another new blouse, because coming home from dinner or drinks or shopping, I wasn't able to face that this was the whole of it, what was left. I needed to believe that each and every day to come was not going to be the same as the day before. The same, or worse. I needed to believe in possibilities.

We can believe what we want to believe, but to deny what we know, that's not so easy to pull off.

And yet we go on trying. Figure that.

Here's something I can't deny: love makes a mockery of common sense. There is no effecting a change of heart. No matter a laundry list of fine attributes or the multitude of imperfections flashing before your eyes, just the way life does in that split second before what is another kind of fatal accident. In that way, love is as plain and complicated as faith, and there's no way to explain that either.

I have a photograph of that great-grandfather of mine, the one who invented shampoo, and a matching portrait of his wife. The backdrop to both is a dreamscape on canvas, an enchanted forest *what fools these mortals* under an unnatural sky. In the foreground, my great-grandfather, and his wife, respectively, are seated in high-backed chairs. Somber portraits, although in old photographs, everyone looked as if they were standing before a firing squad. Even children appeared to be getting bad news: Saint Nicholas isn't coming this year, or Papa is going off to war. Smiling for your picture came later. Faster exposure time coupled with modern dentistry netted the doofus with a camera imploring us to say "Cheese."

A photograph might be near to accurate, but "near to" is not "exactly," and in that way, a photograph is like a story. Near to accurate, but who knows wherein is the falsehood? An unflattering angle, an itchy nose, the drifting of an eye, and all you can do is hope you don't really look *that* ugly. Even so, even with the adjustment of the bar for the possibility of a camera's lack of affection for my great-grandmother, she wasn't much to look at. Stiff in a high-necked white blouse under a black jacket with balloon sleeves, and she had bird hair. Hair that was coiled in the back, but up front were a pair of wings, like the wings of a bird that cannot fly, like a kiwi. One on each side of her head, which was as round as a globe. Short, stubby wings ridiculous on women and birds both.

Also, her eyes were set wide apart, like a bird's eyes are on the side of its head, too.

To look at the pair of photographs together, you likely can't resist wondering, What did he see in her? You'd ask because, as if his eyes burned holes through the photograph, holes from which wisps of smoke emanated and sparks flickered, he was that kind of hot.

Love is without answers, but I will say this about Henry: he was the sweetest boy I'd ever met.

'*Boy?*'

Sweet and weak and there was innocence to him, deliberate innocence, innocence that comes from refusing to acknowledge unpleasantries, but an innocence all the same. He never had a job or a worry, but mostly I thought of Henry as a boy because when I was with him, I felt as if I were sixteen. Only not morose, like I really was at sixteen. Sixteen, with a future not yet realized. With Henry, I got to be a girl again.

That was something else he said, that night, in the Hotel Sacher, when he said he was in love with me. "I love how you are all girl. The way you always wear dresses and fix your hair and the way you like boys. You're like the girls I remember. All girl. Frilly. And in close contact with her feelings."

Elinor, I was to gather, was a woman not in close contact with her feelings.

"Or at least not so I'd know," Henry said. "She might enjoy herself. Just not with me."

There is no solid rationale for why we love one person and not another, but they, Henry and Elinor, each had their reason for getting married; a pair of reasons not especially admirable, but virtue is penetrable, not a solid wall, and weaknesses are strong. Even the most uncorrupted of us, good people, are poxed with flaws and failings. It might not have been righteous that Henry married Elinor, but it was understandable, and therefore it was forgivable.

What I didn't understand was why they stayed together. After gaining access to her trust, why not call it a day? "What's in it for her now?" I asked.

"Sport," Henry said. "It's a blood sport. Like bullfighting."

"Bullfighting is not a sport," I said. "The bull has no chance to win."

"Exactly."

"Come on," I said. "Really. Tell me the truth. Why does she stay married to you?"

"Because I'm useful."

"Have you ever considered leaving?"

"Leaving?"

"Yes. Leaving."

"But where would I go?" Henry asked.

I reached around to the floor, where I found the top sheet, and I covered us, as if what had been exposed could be covered that way, and then we slept, which is yet another way to cover things up.

Fat rolls crusted with poppy seeds, yellow pats of butter cut like cookies, raspberry jam, soft-boiled eggs, and while we lingered over the last of our coffee, I said to Henry, "I'll need to find an Internet café. At some point. Soon. Today." A neighbor was taking in my mail for me. All junk to be sure, catalogues and coupon packets mostly, but the box holds only so much. I had bills to pay, and it was probably a good idea to check that nothing urgent needed my attention, although that was unlikely. "What should I tell her? My neighbor. That she should expect me home when?"

"Why not say you will be away indefinitely?" Henry suggested.

"Indefinitely?" I asked. "As in: indefinitely the middle of September?"

"Probably." Henry placed his napkin alongside his plate, and he said, "Let's find you an Internet café, and when you are done with your chores, we can go off and wander aimlessly."

Thirty minutes, if that, at the computer was all it took to send my neighbor an e-mail, pay my bills, and delete the spam. There was nothing urgent needing my attention and no word from Ruby, either. Not that I was expecting to hear from Ruby, but I noticed that I had not. Then I collected Henry and we wandered aimlessly past a cathedral and a palace and across a town square where there was a clock that was famous, although it didn't wow us any. We explored smaller streets, and we climbed a staircase of unintentional beauty. There was a small spring at the lower end of the steps, and huge chestnut trees along both sides formed a canopy. A staircase leading uphill is sort of like a staircase to nowhere. From the top step we could see, off in the distance, the giant Ferris wheel.

From Vienna, we set off for Krakow.

. . .

It won't be for long, John promised. Five months in West Virginia, and my grandmother's sister Thea had her baby, a boy, a *son*, but before John could figure out a way to support his wife and child, which in those days was not so easy even for a man who had marketable skills, which John did not have, Thea got pregnant for the second time. Oh, John did have a job in West Virginia. His father had made him publisher of the newspaper, which was a job that came with an office with his name on the door. Publisher sounds like a significant job, important even, but except for writing the holiday greetings, which was not at all like the writing to which he'd once aspired, it was a figurehead position and the paper came out but once a week. It was never more than six pages thick.

"Shhh." John held his wife in his arms and stroked her back. "Don't cry. We'll figure out something. Soon. Soon we'll leave. I promise."

"I can't stay here, John. I can't live here like this."

Here: Black Lung, West Virginia

Like this: as if they never did live in Greenwich Village, as if she'd never painted and as if John never wrote stories and as if nights in cafés had never happened but were only wished for, and as if she were not Jewish but Methodist all along, as if she'd always played hymns on the piano for the church choir and would do so *Onward, Christian Soldiers* for all of her days to come. She could not live here like this, but if they moved back to New York, John's father would cut them off without a dime. He'd cut them off without a dime if they moved anywhere beyond the perimeters of the town he owned. They lived at his mercy and on his good graces because, for all intents and purposes, he owned them, too.

"Soon," John said. "I'll figure out something."

Another man in this situation, or a similar situation, might have said to his father, "Keep your damn money. I'll manage just fine without you," but John knew he could not manage just fine without his father.

Thea had another boy, which made everyone happy. Everyone prefers boy babies. Except Thea; she wanted a girl.

Not long after the second baby was born, a miracle happened. John's father had a stroke. A massive stroke. A humdinger of a stroke, which landed him in a coma and on a feeding tube.

The doctors were not optimistic. Not at all. "He's not going to recover," they told John. "Now, it's just a matter of time as to when he expires," and it was forgivable that, given the circumstances, John and Thea, they were not all broken up about the lousy prognosis.

"Soon," John promised Thea. "He can't hang on like this for long."

The Cloth Hall of Krakow was the center for commerce in the Middle Ages and is now a market for tourists. There, Henry bought me an amber ring. A souvenir, and after that we walked across the main square and around the Gothic church where the hour is marked by a bugle call, which was unusual. A bugle call instead of a clock chiming or a bell tolling, and Henry noted, "A bugle call to herald the cocktail hour."

"We're closer to lunchtime," I said. "Not that it matters."

Our meal was three courses long, four if you count Henry's martini, which he drank while we looked over the menu. A long and leisurely lunch, and at the start of my second glass of wine, with the unequivocal clarity of a bell tolling or a clock chiming, it struck me: the habit of comfort, the ease of leisure, how uncomplicated luxury can be and so what if there are compromises to be made. Whose life is without compromise?

'All things being relative.'

"More wine?" Henry asked. "Can I pour you another glass of wine?"

"Why not?" I said, and Henry said, "No reason I can think of."

Soon, John promised Thea, soon his father would expire as if he were a carton of milk with a definitive expiration date, and John would inherit most of everything or all of everything because John's father was devoted to the concept of primogeniture. The right of inheritance belonged to the eldest son, even if that eldest and, in this case, only son was unaccomplished. John's mother, she would be well provided for, but the deeds to the properties and the businesses—the coal mines, the stores, the newspaper, the hotel, the houses—those were bequeathed to John, who intended to unload it all; quick as a wink sell everything but the roof over his mother's head, and then he and Thea and their two boys could live in New York or Paris or Timbuktu, and they would never return to West Virginia, not ever again.

While they waited around for John's father to die, John and Thea did as they always did: John went to his office at the newspaper and came home at noon for lunch and then stayed at home. In those hours while he was away, Thea stared out the window. On Sundays, John and Thea and the two boys and John's mother went to church, where Thea accompanied the choir on the piano. After church, John and Thea and their two boys had Sunday supper at the Big House with John's mother, always chicken à la king that was prepared and served by the Help.

What John did not factor into his calculation was this: his father was a man who had a charcoal briquette for a heart. His father was a man who paid his employees substandard wages which, in short order, went back into his own pocket when they paid top dollar for food at the stores he owned. His father was a man who turned his back on anthracosis and rickets and iron-deficient children eating dirt like it was sugar. He was a man who could have, and would have, as fast and easy as a wave of the hand, disowned his only son, his only child, for marrying a Jew, for wanting to live somewhere other than in a coal chute, for wanting to be a writer of stories; and a man like that, a man such as John's father, he doesn't give up the ghost so easy. He'd hang in there just for the spite of it.

In her own house, such as it was her own house, Thea had Help, too. A miner's wife came to cook and to clean, and another one watched over the boys. Thea could not give her sons a bath or make dinner for her family, "Because," John's mother explained, "if people see you working, they will talk."

Time passed and there was no more coal left to mine.

The hotel saw its last guest.

Thea got a little bit peculiar.

One spring afternoon, the windows open, the light breeze lifting the curtains, John's mother sat down to lunch, which was an avocado stuffed with shrimp salad. She picked up her fork, and she said, "My, my," and there at the table, fork in hand, John's mother died. In sharp contrast to his father, she died *My, my* just like that.

More time passed. John's father had been in a coma for almost fourteen years.

The company stores closed up shop.

Thea got very peculiar, and her first son went off to college, to Dartmouth College, without knowing that he was Jewish, which he was for no reason other than the Jewish law of matriarchy. A year later, the other son got a scholarship to the Julliard School of Music in New York City. He also never knew he was Jewish. Only John and Thea knew, and they kept the secret, as if it were a shameful one. That son, the one who went to Juilliard, he had a gift for the piano.

Henry and I had a memorable dinner at a restaurant that specialized in mushrooms, a wide variety of *Eye of newt, and toe of frog* mushrooms prepared in all kinds of ways, and the green cloth napkins on the tables were folded into origami tulips or maybe they were conical hats. Henry had a mushroom and venison stew. I got something similar but without the venison, and the next day we drove from Krakow past fields of bluebells and red clover on our way to Berlin.

Conclusion: Seventeen years after his stroke, John's father died, taking with him the last vestiges of hope Thea and John had left. Seventeen years of intensive care ate up every last blood nickel they had, this family, once rich and powerful but no more. All that remained of the dynasty was the newspaper, that sorry little rag, and the Big House, his father's house, once white and now coated with soot and crumbling, for which they could not find a buyer, and so John and Thea moved in, the way a pair of ghosts would move in. Which is what they were, a pair of ghosts of their former selves. John never did become a writer, no real surprise there, and Thea never painted again, although she did take up crafts. Thea's crafts were not like those my mother did. "Kooky," my mother said. "The things she makes are kooky." To put a positive spin on the kooky factor, it could be said that Thea was ahead of her time, the way she utilized recycled materials: piggy banks from empty Clorox jugs, and tin cans brightly painted and strung into wind chimes. She dyed eggs the way Easter eggs are dyed and crushed the blue and yellow and red eggshells into bits and pieces that she then glued like mosaic tiles to the lids of old cigar boxes. Her depiction of van Gogh's sunflowers in crushed eggshells, although deranged, was masterful in its execution.

$\mathcal{A}t$ a $sidewalk$ $cafe$ on the Kurfürstendamm, which is a broad tree-lined avenue
like the Grand Concourse in the Bronx,
which was where my father grew up, the
summer rain pitter-pattered on the striped
awning overhead, washing the city in
shades of gray. Because a need to give me
things sometimes overwhelmed him, Henry
handed me a packet of sugar from the bowl
on the table.

When my mother understood for real that
she was dying, she and I sat, one afternoon,
on the bed where she and my father slept
and loved. Their bedroom was decorated in

the same style as the rest of the house, early American, with some good antique pieces. Oak chests of drawers and table stands. A handmade quilt for a bedspread. Pottery glazed colonial blue. Nice, if you go in for that sort of thing, although I don't. Dumping the contents of her jewelry box between us, my mother said, "Pick out what you want." On her lap were a pad and a pen. "Whatever is left, I'll leave to Laura."

"I don't want to do this," I told her.

Had her cancer been diagnosed the year before, when it was there but no one knew it was there, it would've been me getting the leftovers because Laura was a dream of a daughter-in-law until she began to show her true colors *sharper than a serpent's tooth* and then there was the incident with the Raisinets and my mother got to thinking that maybe I wasn't exactly the daughter she'd wanted but I wasn't half bad either, which was why here in the last months of my mother's life, I was getting first dibs on the jewelry, although it didn't feel at all good and certainly it wasn't something to make me happy.

"Please." My mother reached out and stroked my hair, and I didn't want to cry in front of her because we'd all been pretending like she was going to recover, so I sifted through the pile of bracelets and rings, and she picked up the pen. On the top of the pad, my mother wrote: For Sylvia. As if "For Sylvia" were the title to something.

"For Sylvia." Henry turned the words over the way a thought is considered. "For Sylvia. Forsylvia. Like a flower. The forsylvia are in bloom." He spooned a dollop of cream from his coffee and put it in mine. "For Sylvia."

At the beginning of the time when there would be no more condolence calls, no one dropping by with doughnuts or cherry pie to assuage grief, my father asked me if I would pack up the things of my mother's life, take them out of the house, somewhere, anywhere, away. My parents were not profound people, but they had a profound love, and it was unbearable for him to open the closets and see her dresses on hangers, the row of pocketbooks on the top shelf, her shoes poised on racks, toes aimed skyward. Her toothbrush, her hairbrush (for when she had hair), her cosmetics, her medicines, her knitting (the back of a sweater that got no further than the shoulder blades), her bottles of perfume on the vanity, all of it, to see these things, things, everyday things, things that remained after she was gone, caused him to be torn apart all over again as surely as the rended cloth of mourning.

Because she was that kind of good friend, together Ruby and I would throw away jars of moisturizers and packets of emery boards and cans of hair spray. Ruby would help me to empty my mother's closets and the evidence of her life because she was that kind of good friend and also because I'd said, "You know, you can have whatever of hers you might want." Ruby and my mother, they wore the same size in clothes and shoes, everything except bras because my mother was ample in that area, whereas with Ruby, it was all Wonderbra and padding. I didn't want my mother's sweaters, coats, pocketbooks, or scarves because my mother and I, we did not share an aesthetic sensibility. Of my taste, my mother mostly said, "You're joking, right?"

My mother wore *This is what they're all wearing* put-together outfits, and she had an appreciation for designer insignia not shared by me, but Ruby, she was wild for labels that read: Unattractive and Yet Expensive.

The Brooks Brothers polo shirts with the sheep for a logo that Henry wore were not all that expensive, and excluding the yellow one and the pink one, too, they weren't spectacularly unattractive either, but it did occur to me that the disparagement I'd cast on designer insignia might have offended him. "I wasn't talking about your shirts," I said. " I like your shirts." Which wasn't exactly true. I didn't like Henry's shirts, but I loved Henry, and everything that made him Henry was just right. Even the things that weren't right. "The sheep," I said, "they are cute."

"No offense taken," Henry said. "I've always worn these, and the idea of change, well, change comes with its fair share of risks, doesn't it?"

"Absolutely," I said. "Terrible things could happen if you put on a shirt of Italian design. You could go up in flames."

Henry laughed. A laugh that sounded as if it were read aloud by an amateur actor who wasn't comfortable on stage. For a man with his own sense of humor, Henry never laughed easily. He laughed as if it were learned behavior and he wasn't quite sure if he did it well.

One afternoon when I was a teenager, I was with my mother, who had to make a stop at the bank. Because, at that age, I'd sooner have put a pickle fork up my nose than be seen in public with one of my parents, I waited for her in the car, staring that vacant stare of the adolescent out the car window, where I couldn't help but notice that most every woman exiting the bank carried a pocketbook of similar, if not the same, design. Some bigger, some smaller, some satchel-shaped, others rect-angular, but all of them were dung-colored vinyl embossed with mustard-gold Roman numerals: fifty-five. These bags must have been a giveaway from the bank, to entice you to open a new account, and what some people won't do for free crap. I debated with myself, was it or was it not worth the initiative—never my strongest suit, taking initiative—to get out of the car to ask my mother to open a new account to get one of those free pocketbooks. Six seconds into it, I concluded: no; but now in my mother's closet were two of those Louis Vuitton bags, and Ruby held them up as if they were a pair of bowling trophies. "Really truly, I can have these?" she asked. "Both of them? Two Louis Vuitton pocketbooks? You don't want one?"

"I don't want one," I said.

"You're sure?"

"I'm sure."

Snazzy in one of my mother's Princess Diana sweaters—Princess Diana was known to wear sweaters with that kind of sleeve—Ruby took one of the pocketbooks with her to the mir-ror. At her reflection, Ruby cocked her head as if she were study-ing someone else, someone to emulate, someone she wished to be. I hated seeing that, that she wished to be someone other than herself.

In the oak chest of drawers was where my mother kept her underwear, some of which, we discovered, was sexy. Nothing that would've insisted I reevaluate the world as I knew it, but she had some frilly silk and lace things that you don't necessarily think about finding in your mother's underwear drawer, if for no reason other than how often do you think about what's in your mother's underwear drawer?

"Oh, good God," Henry said. "Never," and as if the mere idea of it, of his mother's underwear drawer, were enough to throw him for a loop, Henry signaled the waiter and he ordered himself a cognac.

Magazines by the bed—*Woman's Day, American Crafts,* and *Martha Stewart Living*—I tossed in the trash, while Ruby unzipped a garment bag she got from the closet and behold! A mink coat. A mink coat that was maybe six or seven years old already, but never worn because after nearly a lifetime of being an ardent lover of animals—my mother never met a dog she didn't want to kiss on the mouth, and that included the great salivators like Saint Bernards—she finally made the connection between her succession of mink coats and the minks who'd had the coats before her.

My mother was not the first or hardly the only person, myself included, unable to or unwilling to conjoin the contradiction: love thy dog and thy cat and thy parakeet and thy veal and thy *some pig* sausage and thy Cornish hen stuffed with wild rice.

Easter time when I was five or six years old, my father took me to the big toy store near where we lived. It wasn't a chain store, the big toy store, not a Toys "R" Us kind of place; it was owned and operated by a pair of timid twin brothers who wore horn-rimmed glasses and Hush Puppies on their feet, and though they did look like a pair of perverts, they weren't, as opposed to my great-uncle Nathan, who *was* a child-molesting drunk.

That's the kind of Jews we were, that come Easter time, Joel and I got chocolate bunnies. One year I got a sugar egg with a peephole looking onto a bucolic scene of a cottage, which I preferred to save rather than to eat; to have it, for always, and I hid it in a drawer, under my pajamas. Putting away the fresh laundry, my mother found it and she threw it in the garbage because sugar would attract bugs, which was the same excuse she gave for throwing away the maple candy pressed into a mold the shape of a pilgrim and squirreled away in a shoe box in my closet.

At the toy store, on the counter near the cash register, were two boxes. One was filled with pink and lavender chicks made from cotton pom-poms; the other with the more expensive yellow ducklings, which were real ducklings that had been gutted and stuffed, or maybe they were freeze-dried. I got a duckling, which I hugged, and I stroked its yellow down, and I might have named it, too, just as if it were alive and a pet, and it never dawned on me, or not until years later, that it *had* been alive and murdered just in time for the holiday season so that bratty kids such as myself could have a toy that looked exactly like the real thing, a toy that *was* the real thing, except now dead.

Prior to my mother's epiphany—which came with the news that those cheap fur-trimmed parkas imported from China, that was dog fur—she would get a new mink coat every three or four years. It was only days after coming home with her last mink coat that the dog fur story broke. Why my mother didn't return the mink coat to the store to trade it in for something nice in cloth, I don't know. That it was still there, in a garment bag in the coat closet, came as as much of a surprise to me as it did to Ruby, although for me the surprise wasn't especially pleasant, but Ruby, oh Ruby, her words held tight in her throat, like a groan, the sort of groan that emanates from a primal desire, like sex. "A mink coat," she said.

I try to be a fair and open-minded person, but it isn't always possible and I do take issue, serious and scornful issue, with women who wear fur coats. As for a man who wears a fur coat, well, go ahead and shoot him square between the eyes because a man wearing a fur coat is the most jerk-off thing ever, but we can't always live by our convictions. It was the way Ruby—wistful, lonely even—cuddled with the fur as if it were a kitten, that's what broke me. "You can have it," I told her. "On one condition. You are never, ever to wear that thing around me."

"A mink coat? You're giving me a mink coat? I can't believe it. This is a dream come true," Ruby said, which should have been a tip-off, and then she asked me, "How could you not want any of these things?"

But I did want a few things. Such as: the black silk chemise with the flesh-colored lace at the bodice.

The same black silk chemise that, as fate would have it, I was wearing that afternoon, at that sidewalk café on the Kurfürstendamm where Henry and I sat at a small table under the awning while it rained. I leaned forward for Henry to peek down the front of my dress, and I said, "See? Pretty, isn't it?"

"Spectacular," Henry said, and he signaled for the check, and in the rain, sharing my umbrella, we hurried back to the hotel, to our room. There, Henry slipped one strap of the black silk chemise from my shoulder and he kissed where that strap had been, and from outside, the nasal *we-u we-u* of a police car transported us to another time, as if we were characters in a John le Carré novel, as if the *we-u we-u* were music, an overture to another time, to a darker Europe.

'*Like* The Spy Who Came In from the Cold. *That one starred Claire Bloom and Richard Burton.*'

Then Henry did the same with the other strap, slipped it from my shoulder and kissed that spot, and then he kissed my neck, and the black silk chemise must've wound up under the bed because two nights later when I next unpacked my suitcase, it wasn't there.

It could be that I am unduly harsh when I refer to Uncle Nathan, Aunt Hannah's husband, as a child-molesting drunk because I couldn't say if he diddled other little girls, and with me there was only that one time. But the part about him being a drunk, there's no wiggle room to that fact.

A Sunday afternoon. Or maybe a Saturday early in winter. Or maybe late in winter. But winter for sure. Aunt Hannah and Uncle Nathan had come for lunch, to spend the day with their family, which was, by then, pretty much just us. There were no leaves on the trees, and the sky was an icy slate-gray sky just before snowfall, but never mind the cold, I wanted to go out and play. Maybe not play exactly. Ten or eleven I was then, an age well beyond the thrill of the swings and the purpose of a sandbox. Most likely I wanted to go out only to futz around, get away from my parents and Aunt Hannah, all of whom were still seated at the table, lingering over coffee. Joel had gone off, probably to pop his pimples, which, to be honest, were few. Uncle Nathan was in my room, where he was passed out. To get to my closet without waking him necessitated that I tiptoe around the bed, but I wasn't even halfway there when he roused from his bourbon-induced stupor. "Hey," he said. "Come mere an give your old uncle a kiss." Given a choice, I'd have opted to eat bird shit rather than kiss Uncle Nathan, but I wasn't afraid to kiss him because I knew him. People we knew did not, could not, do bad things because we knew only nice people. Strangers were capable of doing bad things to us, and we were never to get into a car with one, and we did have to throw away loose candy collected on Halloween because of the old woman who put razor blades in apples. Apocryphal as that story is, we believed it, or some variation on it having to do with rat poison. I, a great fan of candy corn, especially the brown ones, did not throw them away. Willing to play the odds that these candy corn, my candy corn, were not laced with Drano, I ate them before I went home, where my parents would have confiscated them.

Holding my breath because he was sure to stink, and with all my attention focused on that, on holding my breath to stave off olfactory inhalation, I wasn't paying attention to other matters, which was how Uncle Nathan got his hand up my dress and his fingers into my cotton underpants. His fingers, probing.

For how long? Five seconds? Fifteen? A half a minute tops, before I pulled away and ran off and down the stairs and out the door without my coat, which is likely why I remember thinking it was going to snow, because I was cold and I was shivering and there was no sun to warm me, but still I stayed in the yard until I saw Uncle Nathan and Aunt Hannah get in their car and drive away.

It goes without saying, I should think, that Uncle Nathan's fingers latching on to my prepubescent snatch was one gross-o-rama moment, but as entirely unpleasant, nauseating really, as that encounter was, I cannot, nor will I, say that Uncle Nathan damaged me for life or damaged me in any way, because it would not be true, and what went on at my friend Carolyn's house, which was not something that I could name, *that* was far more disturbing by a factor of ten. Uncle Nathan did not damage me, nor was this a memory that got repressed, a memory I repressed only to recover it later like those other people did. Those other people who, as children, got molested and worse but then they forgot all about it until 1994 when snap! they remembered the whole thing and all the ensuing sicko details. The way that happened, the way they all remembered pretty much all at once, was like how a plague sweeps through or like the ripple effect of a stadium wave. Many of them with the recovered memories got to tell their stories on television to Geraldo Rivera, who applauded their courage and hugged them.

After dinner, I found my mother alone in the bathroom, where she was brushing her hair, and I told her, "Uncle Nathan stuck his hand into my underpants."

There is portent to a pause because so often pauses precede wisdom and storms, things worthy of our attention; and after such a pause my mother said, "Are you sure?"

"Yes." I was sure. I was very, very sure.

She was holding her hairbrush aloft, like a gavel to bring down as sentence was pronounced. Or maybe the hairbrush was held aloft to gauge which way the wind was blowing, to determine on which side she ought to come down. "Well, then. Take care not to be alone with him again. Not under any circumstances," she warned me, and she went back to brushing her hair. My mother had no stomach for confrontation, which was why she never told Uncle Nathan to keep his pervert hands off me, and why he and Aunt Hannah still came to our house for barbecues and birthdays and Thanksgiving, the same as always. In this way my mother fell short as a parent, which was something I had to learn to accept because it's how she was, and either you accept people as they are or you turn your back on them and walk away. Those are the choices: forbearance or flight, although that philosophy was slow in coming to me, and for many years, I expected more from people than they could give.

The thing that struck me most about the onslaught of recovered memories was how often the memories recovered included peanut butter as a detail. Peanut butter, yet no one died from eating the peanut butter, which is something I mention because a few years after all those memories came flooding back, out of nowhere and all of a sudden, every other person you met on the street was allergic to peanuts and would die within ten seconds of being in the same room as a peanut. Peanut butter sandwiches were toxic. Which was interesting because when I was a child we ate peanut butter sandwiches with impunity. Although there was that song, "Found a peanut / Found a peanut / Found a peanut last night," and it was a rotten peanut and the peanut eater did wind up dead and in hell, so there was a time when I would eat a peanut only after it was fully scrutinized for rot, a thorough examination that irritated my mother, who snapped, "For crying out loud, Sylvia. Eat the damn thing or throw it away."

What Went On at Carolyn's House: The onset of summer, and we were thirteen, a pair of junior high school babes, out shopping for new bathing suits. I got a hot-pink bikini that had a bow on the top part where there should've been cleavage. Carolyn had cleavage. Not astounding cleavage, but noteworthy. She was forbidden to get a bikini, but she did find a more modest two-piece that wasn't entirely feeble because it was a Hawaiian print. Carolyn had long blond hair and a nose like a rabbit's and all the boys were in love with her.

Back at her house, we sat on the green plaid couch in the living room, where her father was reclining on a Barcalounger, watching television. His shoes were off, but he was wearing socks. Navy blue socks. Her mother was in the kitchen, making us something to eat. At the commercial break, Carolyn's father nodded at the bag by her feet. "You got a bathing suit?" he said. "Let's see it."

Baseball. That's what he was watching on television, a ball game.

Carolyn got up from the couch. She went to the guest bathroom, which was off the dining room, and she came back wearing her new bathing suit just as her mother emerged from the kitchen with a tray of ham sandwiches and three glasses of 7Up. Carolyn's mother was the spitting image of exophthalmic—bugeyed—mega-dork Joanie Cunningham, from *Happy Days*, the television show; not the Beckett play, although there was something of that, the Beckett play, about her too. She put the tray down on the coffee table and sat beside me on the couch, and the two of us sat there as Carolyn stood before her father.

"Lean forward," her father said, and Carolyn did. Then he said, "Turn around," and she did that, too. "Now, bend over. More," and she bent over more, and her long blond hair swept over her shoulders, and then she had to face front again and arch her back, and all I knew was that this taking measure, unseemingly algolagniac and creepy, wasn't right, but I sat there. Sipping my 7Up, trying to pretend it was normal.

I wanted the boys to be in love with me the way they were in love with Carolyn, but they weren't, and had I been asked the question, Is it true blondes have more fun? I'd have said yes. Yes, blondes do have more fun, and maybe the boys would be in love with me if I had blond hair like Carolyn's, as if love were ever so simple.

But love is not simple, and Henry agreed. "If only it were," he said, but I didn't ask him, What then? What if love were that simple? Because it's not.

.   . .   .

.

Vincent and I celebrated our fourth wedding anniversary, and then a few weeks went by, uneventful weeks, and on a Wednesday when I came home from work, Vincent was already there, sorting through the mail. I opened a bottle of wine, and I said, "Vincent, we need to talk." I motioned for him to sit down, and he sat on one end of the couch, which was a small couch, really more of a love seat. I handed him a glass of Merlot, and I sat at the other end of the couch, and he asked me, "Is this going to be bad?"

Is this going to be bad? And I feared, What if he never gets over me? What if, devastated, he becomes a shell of a man, eaten away by heartache the way maggots do to a corpse, which goes to show how very full of ourselves we can be, to imagine we can have such an effect. I so very much did not want to hurt Vincent, but like the best way to tear off a Band-Aid, fast and all at once, I said, "Vincent, I adore you, but it's not what it should be. I don't want to be married to you anymore."

He swirled the wine in his glass, watched it eddy. I waited, but he didn't say anything. Nothing, and I sat there until it was too weird and then I said, "What are you feeling?" and Vincent said, "Relieved." Which cracked us both up, and when we finished laughing, I asked Vincent, "You want to go over to John's for a pizza?"

"Sounds good," he said, and that's what we did. Vincent and I, we went out for a pizza. Half mushroom, half roasted peppers, and we did get a little bit sad because the end, the end of all things—a book, a life, a summer, a marriage, the last bite of cake, the last of innocence lost—is always sad, at least a little bit, because it is the end; it is the end of that.

7

To keep for myself, I took my mother's black silk chemise, a red satin slip, a pair of gloves, and her perfume to have, to dab on my neck and on my pulse points. Pulse points, where you can feel the way your heart beats. Her perfume was Shalimar, a perfume that was also significant of an end of an era. "And," I told Ruby, "I want her camel hair coat."

"What camel hair coat?" Ruby said. "I haven't seen any camel hair coat."

"Check the closet in the hallway. There's a burgundy scarf in one of the pockets."

Also in the pocket were a silver compact mirror and a diamond necklace.

The coat was not in the closet in the hallway, and then Ruby and I went through every closet in the house before we went back and looked again. "It has to be here somewhere," I said.

My mother's last and final birthday came the day before she died, which I have since heard is not uncommon, that people often die on or around the anniversary of their birth. A lot could be made of such a coincidence, much of it under the rubric of Spirituality, but that is not a path I care to walk.

On that day, her birthday, my mother wasn't much conscious, the morphine drip was working double-time, but my father wanted to make her a party, so we—my father, Joel, Laura, my mother's best friend Helene, Vincent, and I—gathered together in the hospital room. My father bought three helium balloons, all yellow, at the hospital gift shop, and he tied them to the foot of her bed. We got a chocolate cake with butter-cream frosting, but my mother couldn't swallow so much as a crumb without puking it back up, and none of us had any appetite, either, and even if we were hungry we weren't about to eat cake in front of her. Vincent brought the cake to the nurses' station, for them to have with their coffee. I don't know if they ate it or just threw it in the trash. They probably got a lot of cakes that way. Cakes from the dead and the dying.

My mother did come out of the morphine stupor well enough for the opening of the presents, but because she did not have strength enough to tear away the paper, my father did that for her. Having seated himself alongside her, on the edge of her hospital bed where the faint smell of decay was not masked by the odor of disinfectant, he opened the box and held out the heavy silk scarf for her to see. "This is from Sylvia and Vincent," he said.

To talk was an effort. Slowly, gently, softly one at a time, my mother unpacked each word as if each word were an egg to be transferred from the carton to the molded cups in the refrigerator next to the butter. "It. Goes," she said. "With. My new. Camel. Hair coat."

The previous March, four months earlier, when for a few weeks she'd rallied before the cancer went on its last and final tear, my mother went to Saks, and in a whirlwind of optimism at an end-of-season sale, she bought herself a camel hair coat. "To put away for next year," she said. We knew that she would die well before the coming autumn, that she would not live to see another winter, to see the deep violet twilight of another November sky, to see snow fall once again, to watch her breath come out in a puff of frost, but why deny her hope? Why deny her the imaginability of a future? Let her have hope that maybe she could have more time, which was why I picked out a scarf that would accent her new camel hair coat, the coat that she would never get to wear, because why should anyone have life without the possibility of what *might* be, what *could* be? Tell me what is so essential about facing the fact that your time is up? Is looking at death head-on going to save you? No. And call it what you want, there *is* such a thing as a miracle, and I wanted my mother to spend her last hours contemplating the coming winter, wondering, Will we get much snow this year?

As if her room at the hospital didn't already look like a funeral parlor, what with the floral arrangements abloom on every flat surface, Joel and Laura gave my mother *Say it with flowers* pink roses for her birthday because that is the sort of thoughtful people they are. The silver compact mirror, one that would slip neatly into a purse, was from Helene, and it was a fitting gift for a woman such as my mother because she was beautiful and vain. Even throughout the chemotherapy, when she got onion-skin paper thin and all her hair fell out so that, as she put it, "Naked I look like a plucked chicken," she kept herself up, wearing a wig and false eyelashes, and for a woman who was two steps from dead, she was still something to whistle at.

A token of love comes in a box because love itself cannot be contained, and the box that contained my father's token of love to her, his wife, was a black velvet box with a hinged lid, and he opened it to reveal a necklace. A diamond. A solitary diamond, maybe three-quarters of a carat, maybe more, I really don't know how to determine such things, set in gold and hanging from a beaded gold chain.

To speak again required more strength than she had, but my mother had something to say, and she was a determined woman. "That. Is. Not." She stopped to rest, the way we do near the end of a long day that is not quite yet over. "That's not. The. One. I. Want. Ed." That's not the one I wanted, which was a pretty funny thing for her to say, and you could tell she thought so, too, because there was that smile of hers, coy and sardonic in one go, a smile with the tail bit off.

"You do that same thing," Henry said. "That naughty-girl smile of yours. Half of a smile makes you look like you're a girl not wearing underpants."

"Maybe I'm not," I said, and Henry slid a hand up my skirt, and I told him, "Both hands on the steering wheel, and eyes on the road," and I smiled.

"See," Henry said. "There it is, that half of a smile, giving me ideas." Ideas such as, "How far are we from someplace civilized? Someplace where we can get a nice room?"

"That depends. What country are we in?" I looked at the map as if next to a red circle it would read: You Are Here. Map-Quest was not a feature of Henry's car.

Despite the ease of a common currency and no longer having to line up in wait at Passport Control, Henry had nonetheless lamented the formation of the European Union, how it blurred the lines, made fuzzy that which had once been distinct. Henry wasn't one to warm to progress. Until now. Now the lack of boundaries, our having lost track of time and place, was its own kind of wonderful. "It's almost like we are a primitive people," he said. "Leaving aside our modern conveniences—the automobile, the dry martini, electricity—we're like a pair of hunter-gatherers going any which way in search of berries and walnuts."

"So that's what we're looking for?" I asked. "Berries and walnuts?"

There was nothing modern about Henry's martinis. You wouldn't catch him ordering the likes of an apple martini or one with pomegranate juice in lieu of vermouth. Even a vodka martini was a crime against nature. Gin. Always gin, and gin is practically absinthe in the way it, too, speaks of an earlier generation of the soused and the pickled.

After we'd all quit laughing at what my mother had to say—That's not the one I wanted—my father took the diamond necklace, the one my mother didn't want, and the silver compact mirror, and the silk scarf, and he told her, with all of us there, that he would take the gifts home and put them in the pocket of her camel hair coat. "Don't forget," he said to her, his wife whom he loved, loved so keenly, so deeply. "I'm going to put everything in the coat pocket. It'll be there. Waiting for you, when you come home," but my mother had already drifted off to sleep, never to wake again. So, "That's not the one I wanted" were my mother's last words, a doozy of a thing *Either that wallpaper goes or I do,* to say at the end. Words—That's not the one I wanted—easily interpreted as tragic and horrible, but because I'm pretty sure she was talking about the necklace and not about her life, it wasn't horrible.

Her death was horrible though. Painful and ugly, and I was glad for her that she wasn't anywhere near conscious at the end because her wig was askew and sea-green gunk was coming from her nose and her mouth as if her insides had rotted the way fruit does and all the rot was leaking out. My father, sitting beside her with a box of tissues in his lap, mopped it up, and the three yellow helium balloons tied to the foot of the bed swayed like hula dancers.

An End to Another Era: Pierre-François Guerlain was a man with a nose for perfume, and he wasn't wrong either on the subject of that which endures and that which does not. "Glory is ephemeral," he said. "Only renown is long-lasting." His renown, the House of Guerlain founded 1828, is still going strong as we speak.

Pierre-François was perfumer to the stars, whipping up fragrances for Queen Victoria and Queen Isabella; his son Aimé created Jicky, the first modern perfume, which he named for the girl who broke his heart, but Guerlain's Golden Age of Perfume began in earnest in 1919, at the end of World War I, when grandson Jacques introduced another perfume, Mitsouko, which was bright, lighthearted, and smelled of peaches. Mitsouko was the antidote to the war, a gay perfume to aid and abet in forgetting, a fresh and happy start to a new era.

Later, in a year between the world wars—1925, to be exact, a year to remember in perfume history—Shalimar made its debut. Shalimar became the flagship perfume of the House of Guerlain, and it still is. Playing into the Western stereotype of an exotic and erotic orientalism, the perfume was named for the Shalimar Gardens in Lahore in Pakistan, which were built in 1641 by the emperor Shah Jahan as a tribute to his favorite wife, and she must've been something, that wife of his, because the Shalimar Gardens have three levels of terraces, four hundred and ten fountains, five water cascades, and trees bearing figs, plums, mangoes, apricots, cherries, oranges, and that's just for starters. Shalimar, the perfume, was amber; deep and dark and musky, with a base note of vanilla. Across the ocean, in America, Shalimar reached its height of popularity in the 1950s, although women of refinement shunned it as it was too overtly . . . well, it had a whiff of sex about it.

Not all the perfume created by the House of Guerlain was inspired by love. Before Shalimar and before Mitsouko and before World War I, in 1912 Jacques launched L'Heure Bleue. A dusky scent with a hint of almond and redolent of melancholy, it was as if L'Heure Bleue, or as translated into English, the Blue Hour, foretold what was soon to come, as if the thick perfume was to herald the scent of the scarlet poppies of Flanders Field.

In 1994 the House of Guerlain was acquired by LVMH, the conglomerate of Moët Hennessy·Louis Vuitton, and Shalimar was reformulated. It's similar to what it was, but it's not the same.

Ruby and I made one more sweep through the closets without finding the camel hair coat, and then I went out the back door to the yard, where my father was sitting in a lawn chair. Shaded by a maple tree, he was staring off into the distance, as if something out there confused him. My father is more than six feet tall and he is broad-shouldered, but that afternoon he gave the impression of having shrunk. I half expected him to be demented, too, such was his grief.

For more than a year after my mother died, I thought my father would never again quite rejoin the living, but then he hooked up with Joyce, and he was the same as he'd always been, until his accident, when he became different.

"Dad." I touched him lightly on the forearm, as if a firm touch would have spooked him, set him off like a car alarm. "Dad," I said, speaking softly, too. "I can't find Mom's camel hair coat."

"It's in the hall closet," he told me, but he did not look at me. "With the winter coats."

For the record, camel hair is not fur; nor is the camel shaved embarrassingly bald as is a sheep. Camel hair is gathered in the warm weather when the camels molt, so, as far as the camel is concerned, it's no different than scooping up its poop for fertilizer. That said, the camel hair coat was not in the hall closet with the other winter coats. It wasn't anywhere in the house, and Ruby asked, "Other than your father, was anyone ever here alone? Because it looks to me like someone stole that coat."

My mother was pronounced dead, in the afternoon, sometime around three. Maybe it wasn't an official pronouncement, but the doctor said something like, "That's it. Be glad for her that it's over."

My father put his head in his hands and he wept.

Absences are generally felt; something or someone is missing, not there, and we might feel the loss as acutely as if it were a phantom limb, but the absence of life is an absence you can see. My mother looked dead. Which was to look like a facsimile of herself, as if you could have propped her up in a chair at Madame Tussauds, put a pair of knitting needles in her hands, and she'd have blended right in with the other wax figures: Queen Victoria, Winston Churchill, Ringo Starr. I could see the absence, the absence of her life, and then I could look no more.

I left my father alone with his grief because we grieve alone, yet in the corridor Joel and Laura were huddled together. Not for comfort, but in cahoots like a pair of snotty little girls. I got the cold shoulder while they worked out a tactical plan. It fell to Laura to pick out a nice dress for my mother to wear, as if to be buried was the same as to go someplace swanky for dinner. From there, from my parents' house, Laura would go to the funeral parlor where Joel would be making arrangements. That much decided, they left with not so much as a backward glance, and I had no idea what to do next.

It's not often I have something nice to say about my brother, but it was good of Joel to organize the funeral because had it been up to me, my mother, she'd still be in a refrigerator in the hospital basement.

We were not a religious family, but—like the Marranos of Spain and Portugal, without really knowing why, what any of it meant—we adhered to a handful of customs and rituals of the faith: Joel was bar mitzvahed, and surely he was circumcised, although just as surely it was done at the hospital by a doctor without friends and family gathered around to watch the lopping off of a foreskin, as if it were an experiment in a high school biology lab. But the vast majority of the rituals we observed—the grand total of which was maybe nine— were death-related. A last-minute just-in-case-you-never-know. The plain pine box, closed; the absence of flowers; the week of mourning at home; Joel and I named in memory of the dead; and my mother's funeral was on the first new day after her death. Which didn't leave much time to dillydally over picking out a coffin or choosing the outfit she'd wear for all eternity. "Maybe my sister-in-law had my mother buried in the coat?" I offered up that possibility, but Ruby wasn't buying it. "In July?" she said. "Who gets buried in a camel hair coat in July?"

On the last go-round through the closets, Ruby found, tucked away in the back, a shopping bag. Not the coat, but a white linen skirt, the tags attached, and she said, "You know I don't want to make accusations, but don't you think it's strange? The coat isn't here, and no party-type dresses either. Your mother had all these nice outfits for every day, and yet nothing to wear to a wedding? Or for New Year's Eve? She had a busy social life, so where are the party dresses? I'm not talking for myself, mind you," Ruby said, "but it is downright funny that you have the coat gone and we didn't find any party dresses and no one was ever here alone except Laura. Who looked to me to be the same size as your mother, too."

"Are you implying that my sister-in-law stole party dresses and the coat with the diamond necklace in the pocket?"

"Yes." Ruby stepped into the white linen skirt. "That is precisely what I am implying."

"Why would she do that?" I asked. "It makes no sense. They have piles of money. She can buy her own dresses and her own coat. And her own diamond necklace."

"Yeah, rich people never take what isn't rightly theirs," Ruby said, as if that settled that.

Henry wanted to know if we ever did find the coat. "Because your friend," he said, "she's not wrong. About people. How we sometimes take what isn't rightly ours. Just because we can." About people. Henry left off the adjective *rich*, as if it were human nature, common to all people to steal a coat from a dead woman's closet. "Sometimes," he said, "we think that everything belongs to us, the way a king had domain over all he could see, and we take what isn't rightly ours."

Rightly ours, as if what is meant to be will be ours.

As if all things rightly belong with whoever wants them most.

.

.

$\mathcal{I}t$ *was too easy* to visualize my father spending the rest of his days alone in front of the television, a drool cup strapped to his chin, which explains why, on Friday evenings, I took the train to Pound Ridge, which was not my idea of a whoop-de-do way to spend the weekend.

Pound Ridge is a suburb of New York City on the commuter line, and the house had central heating, central air-conditioning, filtered water, and a refrigerator that made ice cubes on demand, yet my father fancied himself to be staking out virgin territory, as if to live in Pound Ridge were something like camping out under the stars in Montana, and he marveled, "It's something up here in the country, isn't it?" A perspective not entirely without logic because my father grew up in the Bronx, and Pound Ridge zoning laws being what they were, he now lived in a house where his neighbor's house was beyond his field of vision, except maybe with binoculars. Deer came into his yard and munched on his flowers. Where else could he be except in the country?

I arrived in time for dinner because it made me sad to think of my father cooking for one, and he made us spaghetti with meat sauce from a jar, Ragu maybe, so I ate mine dry with some grated cheese for flavor. We had salad, too. Then we went to the family room, all keyed up to watch a rerun of *Law & Order*.

My father settled in on one brown leather armchair, and I curled up on the matching one—identical chairs, but the one I took was smaller. Like a Papa Bear and Mama Bear pair of chairs, and I was sitting on something else, too. Something hard and small, and from under the cushion, I pulled out *a plum and said* a Matchbox car, a metallic blue Matchbox car, and I handed it to my father as if he'd know what to do with it. He turned it over and then spun the wheels against the palm of his hand. "I love those kids so much," he said. His grandchildren. My brother Joel's children. I forget their names. Alistair? Anastasia? Gucci? Some kind of embarrassing, knock-off-snooty names like that.

Then my father said to me, "Maybe I wasn't a very good father to you," and his words sat there between us like a bad smell no one would own up to and we were waiting for it to dissipate, and it was awkward. "It was different when you and Joel were little," my father said. "Back then, a father's job was to provide for his family and see to it that you had things, and . . ." and he was spinning his wheels just as surely as he did the wheels on the toy car, and it wasn't going to get us anywhere, either, so I put a stop to it. "You were a good father," I said. "Really. You were," and maybe that was stretching the truth, but he wanted to be a good father, and he wasn't a bad father, and there was nothing to be gained by making the man feel lousy about something that was long past when there wasn't a damn thing to be done about it now. I picked up the remote control. "Come on," I said. "We don't want to miss the opening."

That was pretty much what we did on those weekends together. We took meals and we watched television, and there was the occasional outing to Waldbaum's to pick up some groceries, and once we went to Home Depot to get new screens for the living room windows and the thrill of it nearly did me in, so I'll own up to more than a modicum of self-interest here when, one morning while my father and I sat at the kitchen table, I suggested he take a trip. To Florida. We were eating the sesame seed bagels I'd brought with me, bagels from H&H, with cream cheese, and we were drinking coffee and looking out the picture window onto the yard. The trees were bare now, and the lawn was patchy and the color of hay, the way it turns after the first frost. "Down there, the weather will be warm," I said. "You can swim, take up golf, see some old friends. You're healthy, you're handsome, you can drive a car, and you have hair. The widows will be all over you. Who knows, maybe you'll meet someone you like."

"No," he said. "I could never forget your mother."

"Of course you can't forget her. But that doesn't mean you can't meet someone new," I told him. "Just to keep company."

"It wouldn't be the same."

"No. It wouldn't be the same. It would be different, but still it could be nice."

"I could never forget her," he repeated.

Unforgettable. That was my mother's favorite song. "Unforgettable." She was a big fan of Nat King Cole whom, for quite some time, I had mixed up with Old King Cole *a merry old soul, a merry soul was he* and it took some doing to convince me that they weren't even related.

A great fan of Nat King Cole and mad hot for Frank Sinatra, and when she was twelve or maybe thirteen, my mother went to see Sinatra in concert. "And all the girls were screaming, 'Frankie! Frankie!' and I screamed, too," she told me. Later, when she was no longer a girl, she no longer needed the release that came with screaming, "Frankie! Frankie!" but *The best is yet to come* let her catch a line of song and she was gone, whisked back in time, back to wearing bobby socks and her hair in a ponytail, back to that night when *babe, won't it be fine* she saw Sinatra in concert because no matter where our taste in music goes, how our ears and our sensibilities evolve, the pop music that first rocked us will forever elicit that Pavlovian response, set our heads bopping in time, and if no one is around, we'll sing along, too.

"In my youth, " Henry said, "I was quite partial to the Bee Gees."

'Oh, my Lord. The Bee Gees?'

"Henry," I told him, "don't ever repeat that to anyone."

"It is mortifying, isn't it?"

"Worse than that. I hurt for you," I said. But in the spirit of You Show Me Yours, I'll Show You Mine, I owned up to the year of Blondie on my answering machine. Instead of, "At the sound of the tone," I'd recorded Debbie Harry singing, "Don't leave me hang-ing on the tel-e-phone," and I asked Henry, "How goofy is that?"

And Henry said, "Very."

"But not as goofy as the Bee Gees," I noted.

'Nothing is as goofy as the Bee Gees.'

"No. Not as goofy as the Bee Gees," he agreed, and then as if he needed to prove himself somehow not entirely ridiculous in that regard, Henry said, "Why don't we put on some music?"

Henry kept the CDs mostly in the glove compartment, although some were tossed onto the backseat. I don't remember what we listened to on that afternoon, but it seems, in retrospect, that always the Brandenburg Concertos were playing, as if I remember it from a bird's-eye view: a car, a forest-green Peugeot, coursing along a mountain road, the route depicted in Morse code–type dots and dashes, and then the music comes, the melodic garlands woven from the first oboe and the violino piccolo, and then that violin joins the first horn for an exuberant allegro.

My father took my advice, and one week in Florida, in Dade County—six days after having hooked up with Joyce—he bought a condominium in a retirement community. "In Delray Beach," he told me. "We'll come back in May. For the summer."

It was a blessing, his picking up with Joyce, although it would be inexact to say that Joyce was a new girlfriend because she was a retread. From long ago. From the Bronx, the old neighborhood. Joyce and my father grew up in the same building on the Grand Concourse, or maybe she was from the building next door, but either way, he knew her forever, and they had been high school sweethearts up until the start of the Korean War when my father was drafted and shipped overseas but not to Korea. My father lucked out; he was stationed in Germany, to be part of the occupying forces, which was not a danger to life, limb, or mental health.

Sandwiched between the glory of World War II and the fury of Vietnam, the Korean War is a war we tend to forget. *Oh, yeah. Right. Korea. Did we win that one?* Like the War of 1812. Oh, sure. We know *when* that war happened, but who we fought or why? No. World War I is remembered because there was a World War II, with its colorful cast of characters, and the ever-present cloud that there *could* be a World War III, even though—another thing we tend to forget—World War I was supposed to be the war to end all wars, and clearly that didn't go as planned. It was in World War I that my grandfather was wounded. His leg and more.

Out of sight, out of mind, with my father off in the American zone in Berlin doing who knows what with his nights, Joyce got herself knocked up by Abe Feingold, a boy also from the neighborhood who was 4-F because he was flat-footed or maybe he was half blind. Abe and Joyce got married, and they moved to New Jersey, and my father came home from his stint in the army to find himself without a girlfriend, which was not a crushing blow. My father was a handsome man, and, during his time in the army, and then after, at City College, where he got a degree in accounting, there were not a lot of lonely nights. Not lonely, but not complete either until he met my mother. Although I could see how it might look that way, my father did not marry my mother on the rebound from Joyce. He did not dream and scheme for the day when he and his high school honey could reunite, even though that's what happened, just what they did.

My parents, their love for each other, it was significant.

As if my father's part of the Bronx, the Grand Concourse, were similar to a small town in Ohio or a secret society at Yale, my father's boyhood friends, they all kept in touch so that over the years my parents saw the Feingolds at anniversary parties, weddings, bar mitzvahs, and the occasional funeral, too. And each time they saw the Feingolds, they would come home and the first thing my mother would say was "I cannot stomach that Joyce Feingold." To convey the full extent to which she could not stomach Joyce Feingold, my mother would screw up her face, stick out her tongue, and make her eyes go crossed, at which my father laughed as if my mother were being adorable. It wasn't that, in and of itself, the face she made was funny. Although my mother was to be admired for her willingness to make such a face, because beautiful women don't often screw up their faces like that, as if they fear it might stick. Like in that episode of *The Twilight Zone* in which the people wore masks of ugly faces that stuck. What was funny about my mother's making the face was the predictability of it, which I chalked up to the fact that it's a rare woman who has fond feelings for her husband's former girlfriends. No, my father did not carry a torch all those years for Joyce Feingold. He hooked up with Joyce again because she was familiar to him. He knew her. He knew her well. He and Joyce had their history together, common ground.

"A shared history isn't love," I said.

"No," Henry agreed. "It's not, but it can be good enough."

'Good enough for what?'

Joyce spared my father the hoopla of dating, and she saved him the time it takes to get to know someone new. As if, as we age, we are no longer able to think in the long run of years or months even. We come to afford only smaller and smaller measures of time, dealing in the nickels and dimes of weeks and days and growing more miserly with each passing hour. How much of what's left are we willing to spend on chance?

And my father did seem to be enjoying himself, which is more than most of us get to do, and once a week I called him there, in Florida, to say hello, and the same as always, it was Joyce who answered the phone. "Hi, Joyce," I said, "This is . . ." but before I got the chance to finish, "Sylvia. How are you?" Joyce said, "Hang on. I'll get your father." The same as always, and I had to appreciate the invariability, the inevitability, of it. "Hi, Joyce. This . . ."

"Hang on. I'll get your father."

Never otherwise. No surprises. I liked that about her, about Joyce. That she never threw me a curve ball.

My mother screamed for Frankie, and that first night they were on television, on *The Ed Sullivan Show*, I screamed for the Beatles, but my mother said, "No. You couldn't have. It's not possible. You must've seen the film footage of that later. You remember seeing film footage of other girls, the girls in the audience, screaming. You were an infant then, when the Beatles were on *Ed Sullivan*. Or maybe you weren't even born yet." Just as my mother had not yet been born when King Edward VIII walked off the job to marry Wallis Simpson, but *Unforgettable* that didn't stop my mother from remembering it all. A fool for love songs and a sap for love stories, for cheap love stories, fourteen dozen thousand times my mother told me the story of King Edward VIII abdicating the throne to marry the woman he loved. She knew the abdication speech by heart, which she would recite while vacuuming the carpet, pushing the vacuum with one hand, the other hand beseeching, as if she were on stage, "But you must believe me when I tell you that I have found it impossible to carry the heavy burden of responsibility and to discharge my duties as king as I would wish to do without the help and support of the woman I love." My mother's hand turned at the key phrases "must believe me" and "heavy burden," and when she got to "the woman I love," her voice quaked and her arm shot up in triumph, her fingers splayed and then pulled into a fist, as if having caught a fly. My mother told me how she sat by the radio, not daring to breathe, bearing witness to what was the most romantic story in modern history, which she no more bore witness to than I bore witness to the Beatles on *Ed Sullivan* or John F. Kennedy's assassination, for that matter.

The Scenic Route

the anniversary of his death or perhaps Jacqueline Kennedy was about to become Jackie O, when on television I watched a replay of the Zapruder film. I was eating Oreo cookies as I watched as the president's head exploded and a piece of his brain went flying and Jackie scrambled across the back of the car.

I do remember when John Lennon was killed, and I mourned his death even though I didn't know him personally.

Tangential to 9/11: If the word *friend* is used loosely, like a knot coming undone, then Jillian Faber was a friend, but I'm not inclined to use the word *friend* in such a relaxed way, and so Jillian was someone I knew. When she moved to Arizona, we lost contact, and I was not sorry. Jillian fancied herself an artist (collages) and a writer (prose poems) and a potter (she once took a ceramics class), and an herbologist (as opposed to an herbalist), and still she had time left over to be a free spirit. Her apartment reeked, like a gift shop in New Hope or Saratoga Springs, of scented candles and sachets of dried orange rinds. Instead of furniture, she had pillows everywhere. In her living room, on the mantel, on display, were a statuette of the Buddha, a seashell, and an old snapshot, yellowed at the edges, a nude, of herself seated in a high-backed chair, her legs spread—think when the dentist says, "Open wide"—like that. You could say who am I *People in glass houses* to talk because there could be any number of such pictures of me floating around, and not all of them tastefully done, but here's where I see the distinction: I don't keep one front and center in my living room, and while surely Jillian's beaver shot of herself was a little ray of sunshine for the plumber who came to unclog her kitchen sink and a once-a-month jolly for the ConEd meter reader, for everyone else, it was just painful to look at. Not because she was unclothed; it was the raw nakedness of putting such a picture out there, making such a show of it, what *that* said about her, what she *wanted* it to say about her, and the poor production quality and the yellowed edges, that hurt, too.

February 2002, and I was waiting to cross *at the green, not in between* Sixth Avenue at Thirteenth Street when I heard someone calling my name, and there was Jillian, hurrying toward me. It was safe to assume that Arizona was home to her still because she was all gussied up in Navajo Reservation Gift Shop finery: dream-catcher earrings, a beaded headband and matching beaded moccasins, a turquoise squash-blossom necklace, turquoise rings on seven out of ten fingers. Her coat was made from a striped blanket, like those blankets that, in an early go at germ warfare, the white man contaminated with smallpox before giving them, as gifts, to the natives, but I've also seen those blankets in the Orvis catalog. Maybe it was from the exertion of running to catch up to me or maybe it was from the February cold, but Jillian's face, a shade of pale prone to sunburn and carcinomas, was now piglet pink. Her hair hung in two braids tied at the ends with leather cord and bird feathers, and you might think, what else is there to say about her, except there was more.

"Oh, Sylvia." Her breath was labored. They must not do much rushing around in Arizona. "I'm so glad I found you," she said. "I've come to warn you. To warn everyone. You have to get out. Leave New York. I had a vision."

"A vision?"

"I'm one of the Gifted," she said. "The Navajo consider me to be . . ." and she ended the sentence with a word I didn't know, which she translated. "It's Navajo. For Visionary."

Dollars to doughnuts, it was Navajo for Chucklehead.

"It's going to be bad, Sylvia. Another attack. Flames everywhere." She gestured wide to indicate the city as a whole. "Building after building is going to fall. Much worse than 9/11. Please, Sylvia," Jillian placed a hand on my shoulder, as if to steady her gaze, "you have to promise me that you'll leave."

"Let me ask you something." I took a step back so her hand fell away. "If you hadn't run into me just now, would you have called me, to warn me? If you hadn't run into me, were you going to let me go up in flames?"

It was as if I'd slapped her hard across the face, and as if stunned by the violence, she took a moment to respond, and when she did, she lied.

"Unforgettable, that's what you are," my mother sang, sang songs long past their day on the Hit Parade. "Unforgettable though near or far," she sang while she polished the dining room table or changed the bed linens or sat in the armchair by the window with her knitting. "Answer me, oh my love." Nat King Cole, Sarah Vaughn, Dinah Shore, and Frankie! Frankie! "When somebody breaks your heart like you broke mine," my mother sang as she wiped down the kitchen counter and I, apparently a confused child, recently acquainted with the phrase "scared to death," which scared the piss out of me, inquired, How *exactly* did this happen? How does somebody break your heart? How does a heart break? And my mother explained, "It doesn't really break. It's just a figure of speech," but *Oh, I am nursing a broken heart* I could not imagine a heart breaking any way other than the way a plate breaks—either shattering into pieces or in half, along a clean line. Never mind coming to know that, for a fact, the heart, as an anatomical organ, has no place in the affairs of its namesake, that the medieval notions of blood, black bile, yellow bile, and phlegm coming to bear on love, anger, joy, or melancholia might be rich in explanation, but physiologically wrong. Love, anger, joy, and the beleaguered sadness of being—it's all in our heads. Yet even now, I can't help but picture a broken heart-shaped plate. One half in each hand, and even if it could be glued *All the King's horses* together again, there would be a piece missing, a piece never to be found, and where that piece should be, desolation will reside, and then Henry said, "I have a confession to make to you."

I wasn't sure I wanted to hear this confession, but once that door opens, there's no closing it. "It's not worse than the business with the Bee Gees, is it?" I asked.

"Is there anything worse than that?"

"No. I suppose not."

"When we first met," he said, "and I told you I was nursing a broken heart? That wasn't entirely true. What I was doing was trying to recall all that. Just before you sat down at that café, I was trying to recall what it felt like to be silly in love. What it felt like to get your heart broken, because it had been such a long time since all that, and there I was trying to conjure love and loss, and I was wondering if it was possible to have that again, and if not, what then?"

'You begin.'

Henry said that he was sitting there trying to make sense of that kind of empty.

That kind of empty; when hope is no longer deferred but evaporated, and try as you might, and you do try, you can't find the pleasure in the little things. A fine meal, good music, a breathtaking view of a landscape, the smell of the ocean, snow falling, it all adds up to a storehouse of memories and regrets, and you can't imagine there's a perchance left to be had. "And then," he said, "I looked up and there you were. At the next table. Wearing that white dress. So pretty," he said. "So pretty, and I thought to myself, She's going to drink that coffee, and then she's going to walk on off. And I'd have let you walk on off because I wouldn't have been bold enough to stop you. I was thinking about how it would've been over before it began, and how sorry I'd be."

It's only the music *Unforgettable, that's what you are* that does it. Expecting to be delighted anew with other forays down memory lane, you are likely to encounter disappointment, and if you don't believe me, try eating a Hostess cupcake, the kind with the chocolate frosting and the vanilla squiggle on top, ambrosia to the kindergarten set. It will not taste good.

'A Moon Pie neither.'

It will taste nothing like the memory of it, but I cannot predict what will happen two or seven years from now when I turn on the radio and hear any one of the Brandenburg Concertos.

9

Prague was our destination, but the route we took to get there, the scenic route, loop-de-looped like a skywriting plane scripting out a message *Drink Pepsi Surrender Dorothy* in puffs of white smoke on blue sky. The scenic route, only we didn't catch sight of much scenery other than déjà vu–type sensations of evergreen trees and garden gnomes, because of how fast Henry drove. Loop-de-loop and fast, as if we were in hot pursuit of a horsefly, as if he thought he could lose himself in the chase.

'*Or spin himself into another shape. Like the tigers in* The Story of Little Black Sambo *and how they turned into butter from running fast in a circle.*'

Outrun himself, leave himself behind.

'We're not supposed to reference Little Black Sambo *nowadays, are we? I didn't think so, but I was crazy about* Little Black Sambo *and those tigers.'*

Then we came to rest *a body in motion* in Karlovy Vary, where we stayed in a hotel that looked like an old-fashioned valentine. In the morning, we walked through the Mill Colonnade, which spanned five mineral springs and was Neo-Renaissance. Upstairs, on the balustraded terrace, was a café where we had a snack and a drink before setting off again on the road to Sázava, which was in Moravia, which would get us to Prague after we circled back around.

My first semester at college, and one night a group of girls was sitting around a table. We could have been in a dorm lounge or a cafeteria or a coffee shop, but we were in a dive bar on Amsterdam Avenue. Half drunk or all the way drunk and earnest, we were talking about books the way college girls do, books that changed our lives because we were that kind of young, when a book could change your life. Most of the girls in that group got sloppy over *Little Women*. Louisa May Alcott's *Little Women*, how they identified with, were inspired by, Jo's independence and her plucky spirit, and how because of Jo, they wanted to be writers, too, but I wasn't so keen on *Little Women*, and if I saw myself in any of the sisters, it was Beth, the one who did nothing except die.

"I never read it," Ruby said, which no one believed—how could you not have read *Little Women?* Everyone read *Little*

Women—until Ruby explained, "Why would I want to read about a bunch of Yankee girls during the Civil War?" and what could we say to that?

Later, on another night, when we were sober, Ruby told me that she'd never read *Romeo and Juliet,* either. "I asked my mother what it was about, and she told me it was about two teenagers who disobeyed their parents and wound up dead because of it."

At the time when she told me about her mother's synopsis of the play, I thought it was too funny for words. "But now," I said to Henry, "now, I don't think it's too funny for words, although I don't have words for what I do think about it, either."

.

Candy: During the time when we knew my mother was dying, my father gave candy to his grandchildren, which, it turned out, was an unutterable sin, malfeasance for which my father should've rotted in Willy Wonka hell, where rats would've fed on his chocolate-coated liver. Joel and Laura gave their children celery for snacks because they didn't believe in sugar. That's how Laura said it. "Joel and I don't believe in sugar," she said, as if sugar were something you could *not* believe in, like angels or astrology. Joel and Laura decided that the appropriate—their word, *appropriate*—response to my father giving candy to Hollingsworth and Camilla was to forbid my parents to see their grandchildren. My father did not understand the error of his ways. "Raisinets," he said to me. "I gave them Raisinets. What was so wrong with giving them Raisinets?"

Nothing was wrong with giving them Raisinets. What was wrong, wrong in its most basic form—the profound lack of compassion—was to deny a dying woman the pleasure of her grandchildren. They denied her that pleasure and they denied their children the pleasure of their grandmother, who would soon be dead, and all because of a handful of Raisinets, which barely qualify as candy because they are mostly raisin.

(to be continued)

Mostly Raisin *and* an American Institution: It was in 1911, in the city of Philadelphia, the City of Brotherly Love, that the brothers Blumenthal started up a business importing chocolate and cocoa. They must have done okay for themselves, those brothers, because a dozen years later they branched out with their own line of candies: Sno-Caps, which were followed by Goobers. In 1927, they introduced Raisinets to the line, and, well, Raisinets speak for themselves. Between those years—1911 and 1927—other things happened, too. Take 1914, for example, which was when Meyer Blumenthal met a young woman named Sara Hoexter just weeks prior to her graduation from Hunter College, a milestone to be followed by Archduke Franz Ferdinand of Austria getting himself assassinated by Gavrilo Princip, a Serbian nationalist often described as crazed. On that day, June 28, 1914, the day that the archduke got picked off like a duck at a shooting gallery, Sara Hoexter wrote in her diary, "Mama bought me jeweled slippers from the Perugia shoemakers. Frightfully expensive. I love them madly," which might not be what she wrote verbatim, but ·

it was something equally lame along those lines, as was her diary entry for April 6, 1917, the same day that the United States tossed its hat into the ring of carnage by declaring war on Germany and thus joining in on the massacre that was World War I: "Row with Mama over the gown. She is scandalized because my ankles show." The gown was her wedding gown, and whether Mama's decorum prevailed or Sara shocked the world by showing some ankle, I could not say, but regardless, Sara Hoexter and Meyer Blumenthal got married, and by the time November 1917 rolled around, Sara was pregnant and the Bolsheviks had seized power in Russia. Although there is no mention of the Russian Revolution in Sara's diary, as there was no notice of the fall of the Eastern front, Sara did write extensively about the strand of black Tahitian pearls Meyer gave to her for her birthday, and she wrote about hats a lot, too. Much was made of going to the theater and to concerts. Ticket stubs and programs were affixed to the corresponding pages. After World War I—a mishap that got zippo airtime in Sara's diaries of those years—she and Meyer had two more children. Three children total, and then Meyer got himself a girlfriend. Then, sly dog, he got himself another girlfriend, and another.

A few months after Black Tuesday, 1929, he and Sara separated. During those mean years of the Great Depression, countless businesses bit the dust, but Blumenthal Brothers Chocolate and Cocoa Company was not among the gone. Savvy or lucky or both, the brothers had themselves a deal with the movie industry, and as we know from history books, going to the movies and/or hitting the hooch, whichever, was the refuge from the day-to-day sorrows of poverty and loss. Sno-Caps, Goobers, and Raisinets were sold exclusively at the concession stands in movie theaters, which were often like palaces, with circular staircases and crystal chandeliers, and for the Blumenthal brothers it was *Pennies from Heaven* raining money.

Sara, now divorced from Meyer, relocated to New York City, where she lived in a suite at the Salisbury Hotel, which was, and still is, located opposite Carnegie Hall. Her New York diaries chronicle afternoons spent shopping, lunching, and playing cards, and many pages are devoted to the attention she received from men. The diaries from her later years cover mostly loneliness. In 1969, the Blumenthal family sold their Chocolate and Cocoa Company to the Nestlé Corporation, and to this day Raisinets are a best-selling candy.

It's bittersweet, that story of Raisinets.

The week that followed my mother's death brought friends and relatives and neighbors coming to pay their respects. They came with fruit pies and butter-cream frosted cakes and bakery cookies in white boxes tied with string, as if death brings on a sugar jones. A significant number of the people who came to the house—the house that had in one, alas, not so swift, moment of death become my father's house, his alone—were people I hadn't seen since I was a child. They, these people, could not get over it—their words, not mine—how my niece, Joel's daughter, looked so much like me. "I can't get over it," they said. "Look at her. Exactly like Sylvia at that age," to which my brother and his wife gripped the armrests of the chairs where they sat, gripping so hard that their knuckles turned white and their faces red. A prick of a pin and Joel would've blown like a tire.

"I'll bet you were cute as a button." Henry took a sidelong glance my way. "One of those real adorable little girls. The flirty kind."

"Maybe. But I also picked my nose and wiped it on furniture."

"You are a complicated woman," Henry said.

My niece must have been about three or four then, when the dining room table was the repository for all those cakes and pies and cookies. Her brother was a year older, which means they are teenagers now, and there's a rosy thought. Cakes and pies and cookies and doughnuts, and someone even brought petits fours, and is there a little girl out there who doesn't ache at the sight of a petit four? Those too-cute-for-words, all-you-can-do-is-squeal, teensy-tiny cakes iced with pink and white frosting and purple rosettes. The little girl who looked like me, all doe-eyed and solemn with the woe that comes from wanting desperately that which you can never have, she was eyeing those petits fours with a heavy heart, and no child should know despair. I cut a slice of apple cake for myself, and I put it on a plate with five or six petits fours and a few of those butter cookies with the dried maraschino cherry dead center like an engorged nipple. With a tilt of my head I signaled my niece to follow me into the kitchen, where she stuffed the sweets into her mouth faster than she could chew, looking like a hamster, its cheek pouches filled with hamster feed. The apple cake was, I admit, nowhere near as tasty as the infantile pleasure of undermining my brother and his wife. It's nothing to brag about, but I am not above the occasional bout of petty behavior.

I didn't really forget their names, my niece and nephew, and on more than one occasion, I'd thought about being their aunt, separate from the accident of birth. Assuming Joël and Laura would have allowed me that. Which they wouldn't have, but had I the chance, wouldn't I have been oodles of fun? I'd have given them all the things forbidden but dearly coveted: plastic vomit, Slime, cubes of sugar. That's what I'd imagined, but whenever I tried to add on to the story, I'd get no further than finding myself in FAO Schwarz with two children who were no more specific than Dick and Jane *See Spot run* let loose to pick out a dream toy. The girl would choose a preposterous six-foot-tall Steiff giraffe, and the boy would go for a train set with a locomotive that runs on steam and comes with your very own conductor's cap, which are not even the sort of toys children like anymore. I would pay for these things, and there the fantasy faded out. I could take it no further, and those children, they might not even know they *have* an Aunt Sylvia. After all is said and done, who remembers some woman you met nearly a dozen years ago when you were still so small you had to be lifted onto the toilet, even if that woman did sneak you a plate of petits fours because your parents equated sugar with crystal meth, because every little girl ought to have a petit four at least once in her life. A teensy-tiny cake iced with pink frosting and purple rosettes, and after that, I never saw those children again.

My father had been in Florida for all of three months when he called me, which was two surprises in one: (a) he never called me, and (b) he was calling from Pound Ridge.

"I thought you weren't coming back until May," I said.

"I came back early," he told me, "because I sold the house."

Make that three surprises.

He loved that house. His house in the country. Now he intended to stick around long enough only to dispose of the contents before heading back to Florida. "So if there's anything you want from here," he said, "you should come get it."

In the two days that went by before I could get there, the house had been pretty well picked clean. Joel and Laura must have ripped through the place like a pair of tornadoes, carrying off most of the furniture. Which was okay by me, because I didn't have room for the big oak pieces and I didn't much like them, either. Not that the colonial American furniture was necessarily to their taste, either, as I recalled Laura saying they did up their prefabricated balsa-wood *huff and I puff* mansion in a Southwestern decor; a little bit of New Mexico right there in Pleasantville, although she did not refer to their house as a balsa-wood mansion. But that's what it was. Huge, and glued together from a kit, like a Sears house or a model airplane.

Pleasantville, as if that will make life so.

The next night I met up with Ruby for dinner, and I said to her, "I'll bet you anything Joel and Laura carted that good oak furniture straight from my father's house to the nearest auction house."

"There's a thought," Ruby said.

"That, or else they sold it to some antique store."

This was something I came to regret saying, not because it was a crummy thing to say about my brother but because it put an idea in Ruby's head—an idea that took off and spun out of control, but that happened later, and you can't always know how things will turn out until after the events unfold.

Because most all of the furniture was gone, my father, Joyce, and I stood there, three points of a triangle in the living room, and I kept expecting Joyce to offer me something to eat or drink, which was sort of weird on my part because it wasn't Joyce's house.

"The people who bought the house, a young couple," my father said, "they never even set foot inside. All they want is the property. They're going to tear down the house and put up a new one."

"They're going to tear down the house?" I asked. "Why?"

"It's too small for a family." Joyce folded her arms across her chest, as if taking a stand on capital punishment. "A young couple just starting out. They're going to have children soon enough. They'll need room "

"This house has three bedrooms. Isn't that big enough for a family?"

Joyce gave me a look, a "Sure, if you're willing to settle for less" look, and she said, "They want a big house."

"So," I asked, "if they wanted a big house, why didn't they *buy* a big house?" This, I was to gather from Joyce's expression, was the kind of question only a simple person would ask. Sure. Why not buy a smaller old house with sky-lit bedrooms and a brick fireplace and oak beam ceilings, only to raze it to the ground to put up your huge new house that is both flimsy *and* a blight on the landscape?

"People don't like old things," Joyce said, but some people do like old things, and from what remained of the contents of what had been my parents' house, a house furnished entirely with old things, I took a few old things for myself: a cranberry glass vase, two paintings—scenes of the Hudson Valley in oil that were my grandfather's, by which I mean he was the artist—and the one thing I wanted most, which was a seashell.

The seashell, a cowrie shell, was carved the way a cameo is carved, with my grandmother's name "Beatrice Adler," which was her maiden name and beneath that "November 1909," the year she was born, and there were some swirls and flowers along the shell's edges. It could have been a gift commemorating the occasion of her birth, like a sterling cup. Or something she got later. A memento, a souvenir, from a girlhood holiday at the seashore, from a funfair at Brighton where she skipped along the Palace Pier eating pink candy floss. Which was highly unlikely because who would have crossed the Atlantic *now ready for boarding* during the time of the Battle of Ypres or at any other time, either, when there were plenty of amusement parks close to home? Maybe she got the shell at Asbury Park, where there was a Ferris wheel and, in the background, music from a calliope, as if off in a dream. Men in boater hats and women in their summer whites strolled the boardwalk, where alongside the vendors selling frankfurters, salt water taffy, and cotton candy was a man who carved your name and birth date on a cowrie shell. It could have been like that.

Or not.

"That's all you want?" my father asked. "You're sure? Because I'm not taking anything. We've furnished new. From scratch."

When I got home with the two paintings, the cranberry glass vase, and the cowrie shell in a shopping bag, I told Vincent, "He's not taking one thing from that house. He loved that house. All those things he and my mother bought together, things from her family and his. You'd think he'd want to take something to remember it all by."

"Some people don't like to remember," Vincent said.

"Not even the good things?"

"Especially not the good things," Vincent told me, and he picked up the *TV Guide* from the coffee table and headed off to the bedroom.

There is cruelty to memory, the way there is an ache after a dream. Yet to remember the days, I keep an amber ring from Krakow, garnet earrings, a pinecone, a bit of the Berlin Wall encased in Lucite, a snow globe, a Cinzano ashtray to remember *I won't forget* Fiesole, and a necklace made of glass beads from Prague.

.　　　.　　　.

It was soon after my father and Joyce went back to Florida that Vincent and I separated. When he moved out, he didn't take much of anything with him other than his clothes and his books. "Don't you want anything else?" I asked him. "Something to remember us by?"

"You keep it," Vincent said, and he took my hand in his and gave it a squeeze, and said he had to go now.

10

Such a sucker for love stories, never would my mother face up to the fact that the Duke and Duchess of Windsor were a pair of cold-blooded snakes, that Edward no more wanted to be the king of England than he wanted to be an ass wiper for a living. No matter how jazzy it is to be a king, there was a heavy responsibility to it in 1936, as the skies were growing dark and the winds were shifting and people talked in hushed voices and no one knew whom to trust. Edward hardly wanted to be the one to set a good example. Edward, he wanted to whoop it up in the Bahamas while England prepared for war, and that's just how it was.

"Come to think on it," Henry said, "I probably might have abdicated, too."

'Probably? Probably might've abdicated?'

"You think?" I said.

"Are you being snide?"

"Yes."

"Are you hungry?" Henry asked.

"I could eat."

The way a divining rod locates water underground, Henry found us a lovely restaurant in what had once been a wine cellar in a Moravian village without a vowel to its name, and we looked over the menu by candlelight. Henry ordered a roasted partridge that was stuffed with apples and walnuts, and I got white asparagus and a fried potato ball. For dessert we had sweet wine, and we shared a pancake filled with ice cream and chocolate sauce, and then Henry had a cognac.

Also, Henry favored sheets with thick thread counts.

Steadfast in his refusal to let me pay for so much as gas or so little as coffee, as if my money were no good, as if my money were the currency of some defunct country and as worthless as the pretty postage stamps from Persia and Abyssinia and Zanzibar, which you'd think would be valuable to philatelists but instead are priced at pennies, Henry took the check. "It's nothing," he said.

"It's not nothing. It's like sixty-five-gazillion kron."

"Yes," said Henry, "but in euros, that is no money at all. It's free."

"Nothing is free."

'But you know it sure can seem free at the time. No money down.'

It wasn't what I'd said but how I said it, as if I were rubbing it in, as if Henry didn't already know perfectly well, all too well, that everything and everyone comes at some cost. "I'm sorry," I said. "I didn't mean it the way it sounded."

"No need to apologize for the truth." Henry put down a credit card, a silver-colored one. The waiter picked it up and turned it over to look at both sides, and as if charmed by it, or smitten, he said, "Oh. Plat-tin-um."

'Uranium is more like it.'

"Were you always like this?" I asked him.

"Like what?"

I meant sad or maybe pathetic, but I didn't say that. Instead, I said, "Lonely."

"Au contraire." Henry told me he is often the life of the party, as if he didn't already know that to be the life of the party is the most sad and pathetic of all the things to be.

There was another love story that my mother liked to tell again and again. The one about her aunt Semille, who was related by blood, although the path of that bloodline was convoluted or unknown, but she was family of some kind or other, and so my mother called her Aunt Semille.

A woman alone and a refugee from the hate and havoc that was Europe in those days, Semille fled from France, having to get out of Paris as surely as if it were Dodge, and like a flea she jumped from place to place to yet another place until she got to Cuba, and from there eventually to New York, where she had family. In 1946, without two nickels in her purse, and all her worldly goods in one very small suitcase, she turned up on my grandparents' doorstep.

"One very small suitcase?" Henry said. "Family of yours with one very small suitcase? I don't believe it."

"Are you being snide?"

"Probably."

· My grandparents' doorstep happened to be an upscale doorstep because my grandfather was not only a misanthrope; he was also a man with an eccentricity or two. Such as: he, too, rarely had a pair of nickels to rub together, but he insisted on living on one of the swankier blocks in Manhattan, one where the fallout of the Crash of 1929 did not come down in a rain of ash to darken the landscape. It could not be said that my mother's earliest years were spent in squalor because there was no squalor on that run on Riverside Drive, but there were no little extras for her, either, like a new dress for her birthday or an orange. The way my mother told it, she was a little girl whose only toy was a piece of string tied to an empty shoe box. "I dragged that shoe box around by the piece of string," my mother said, "pretending it was a doll carriage." The Little Match Girl herself, but true enough, a roof overhead did not always allow for food on the table. To put food on the table while at the same time affording her husband his dignity, my grandmother periodically rose up, like the phoenix, put on her hat, her white gloves, and on the sly, she walked across town to Third Avenue to pawn a piece of jewelry so she could buy eggs and bread and milk. They mostly had eggs for dinner not only because they were poor but because my grandmother, she could do that; she could scramble an egg and make toast. In the weeks following, if she wasn't able to scrimp together enough money, she had no choice but to go to her sister Hannah to borrow what she needed to redeem her ruby earrings, to get her gold watch out of hock.

But no matter how little you had in those years, you didn't turn away family. Semille spoke French and she knew some Russian and Romanian, and in nearly perfect English, she told my grandparents that she'd once had a husband but he died, and there was nothing new to that story. The world was thick with widows back then, but how exactly did Semille's husband die? And where? And when? She didn't want to talk about it, and given what had gone on, who could blame her? No, no children. There were no children. Just the husband, now dead, and everyone else, all the family there, they were gone, too.

Many years, twenty-nine or thirty-one of them, after Semille got to New York, a cousin of my mother's—*cousin* being the other catchall word for "related somehow," related somehow but not old enough to be an aunt—came to visit. From France, and so some of Semille's story about how in Europe she had no one, not one relative there and alive, didn't add up, but stories, when closely scrutinized, rarely hold together. Always there are gaps, holes, questions, lies.

This cousin, Eliane, she was dreamy French-y French, and I wanted to be just like her, with her Pepe Le Pew accent and her shoes with spiked heels, and the way she wore her hair up in a *French* twist was so very ooo-la-la. Eliane, my mother, and I went shopping at Lord & Taylor, where Eliane sniffed and said, "What is wrong with American women is you wear what is in fashion and not what is lovely." A truism that I never forgot, which was why in later years I did not succumb to jackets with outsize shoulders pads or anything in spandex or dung-colored vinyl pocketbooks, either, and there's another coin in the bank of contradictions: I am particular that what I put on be lovely, but once I'm dressed, all efforts give way to ennui. Hems come undone, seams open, buttons get lost, and I shrug as if these things can't be avoided, as if to lean into the wall alongside the sign that reads Wet Paint is an inevitability.

I have no idea how Eliane survived the Holocaust, and I never asked anyone because I could not imagine her—Franco-snooty and elegant—having any connection to those people whose pictures I had seen: the hollow-eyed, the emaciated, the dead inside.

My mother was eight years old when Semille came to live with them. Eight years old, or maybe nine or ten. My mother fudged her age; for three years running, she was thirty-four, but regardless, she was a child then, and while some children might have resented having to share their bedroom with a refugee, my mother adored Aunt Semille, who died years before I was born. The bloodline is sufficiently distant that any genetic material I might share with Semille must have been sprinkled over me like fairy dust because there are traits of hers that now are mine.

It's a Hebrew name, Semille, or rather a Frenchified version of a Hebrew name that means "heard God." I was named *for*

Semille, in her memory, but I was named Sylvia, "Because," my mother explained, "I was afraid if I named you Semille, the kids at school would call you Smell, and that's hard to live down."

Point well taken.

Smell is a nickname not easy to escape.

In addition to being "sensitive" and "delicate," my grandmother was sweet and kind and gentle and good, and of course Semille could live with them, but my grandfather, he wasn't so cold that he'd put Semille out on the street to fend for herself, but, one way or another, she had to go.

There was help to be had. It was what they did, the dogooders from the Ladies Auxiliary and from Jewish Relief; they assisted refugees, widows and children, and soon Semille was ensconced in a small apartment of her own. Once every two weeks, she got a check in the mail. Money for food and other needs for living. For Semille, other needs for living were longplaying records for the phonograph and necklaces made of glass beads, as if these things, these *douceur de vivre*—cheap jewelry and good music—were the necessities. Always she wore four or five strands of glass beads around her neck, and on those last days before her next check came, Semille ate crackers for dinner and nourished herself on opera.

Most days, after school let out, my mother first stopped to visit with Semille before going home. Sometimes my mother gave Semille an apple not eaten at lunch, an apple deliberately saved for that purpose, although more often it was a banana.

.   .   .

In Prague, the Most Legií was the bridge known only for being a bridge that was not the Charles Bridge. The Charles Bridge, one of the many jewels of the city, was agog with tour groups and street musicians and artists set up to draw your portrait in charcoal on paper and pickpockets and some doofus on stilts and lots of tourists wearing hats like those worn by court jesters. With all the action concentrated there, on the Charles Bridge, Henry and I got to have the Most Legií all to ourselves.

Because the Old Town Square was a dead ringer for the set of *Cinderella,* the Disney version, it was easy for us to imagine that the profusion of people were extras milling about on an old movie lot. Extras in movies are like background music, and in that way, they did not intrude on us, on how we kept alone to each other. At the Clock Tower, a huge crowd was clustered like metal shavings on a magnet because in ten minutes, give or take, the hour would strike and the animated figures would get set in motion. Raucous enthusiasm for time passing makes me anxious, so no, I didn't want to stick around to watch the mechanical skeleton kick up its heels. We walked back and around the Town Hall to the market stalls, where you could buy raspberries that were nearly the size of plums and precious red strawberries no bigger than candy-coated almonds.

"Wait here," Henry said. "I'll be back lickety-split." *Lickety-split!* and while he was off and I was standing there looking at the fruit and the candy, three young women approached me. College girls maybe, American for sure. Their bellies spilled over the waistbands of their stonewashed jeans, jeans so tight as to accentuate their pudenda, which is never a good look *not what is lovely* and the boldest of the three, she stepped forward. "Excuse me," she said, but she spoke with caution, as if expecting me to be surly or dangerous. "Do you by any chance speak English?"

I nodded my head, yes.

She brought forth her camera and held it out, as if it were an olive branch. "Would you mind taking a picture of us?"

"Sure thing," I said, and for no reason that I could see, the three of them found this, "sure thing," to be hilarious. When they finished laughing themselves sick, the bold one explained, "You sounded just like an American when you said that," to which I said, "No shit," and at that, they nearly busted a collective gut.

I was about to tell them that I sounded like an American because I *was* an American, but then it hit me: if I told them, I'd be ruining their story, the story they'd tell when they got back to Akron or Pittsburgh or wherever they were from, the story they would tell about the Italian or Czech or French or Spanish woman, whatever they thought I was, and how she said "sure thing," and "no shit," as if she were one of us.

When you keep to yourself, when you don't reveal who you are, often people will invent a story for you and you can let that story become the whole of it because you can't be bothered setting the record straight, or you can't tell the truth because it's too late for that, to offer up facts not in evidence is to risk something, the opening of a door to an uninvited guest.

The three girls bunched up next to a stall selling those moronic jester hats and marionettes and *say cheese* they smiled broadly and I snapped the picture of them with the puppets. I gave them back their camera, and there was Henry coming back to me. In league with a leopard's inability to change its spots, there was no mistaking Henry for Italian or Czech, and I did have to wonder where in Paris was he able to buy Topsiders, or did he have those boating shoes shipped to him along with his polo shirts? The *Herald Tribune* was tucked under his arm, and he had something for me, too. "A souvenir," he said, and into my hand he let fall a necklace made of Bohemian glass beads.

Purple glass beads *glass beads!* that were so dark as to almost be black. Each bead was cut like a mirrored disco ball. Glass beads like those Aunt Semille wore.

Hooking the clasp from behind, I patted the necklace against my breastbone, as if to keep it put. "What do you think?" I asked. "Do I look like a refugee?"

Henry kissed me, and when he broke away, he studied me, and he said, "Smell. My Smell. My sweet, stinky Smell," and *memoria in aeterna*, I was grateful for my mother's prescience. Had she named me Semille, I would have been Smell forever.

An old-fashioned tram ran on wooden tracks up Petrin Hill, where there were gardens and a replica of the Eiffel Tower and a Mirror Maze where Henry and I were replicated: four, five, nine of us unfolding in mirror after mirror, until we were at the vanishing point. At which point we went back to the hotel, and we stayed there, in our room, our splendid room, losing ourselves that way until it was the cocktail hour, and over drinks, Henry asked, "What shall we do tomorrow? Move on, do you think?"

"I don't see why not," I said, but before we did that, before we checked out of the hotel, Henry offered a suggestion: to put all the things that I am using on a regular basis in one suitcase, and what's left can go in the second suitcase. "And that one," Henry said, "we can leave in the car."

"Very sensible," I noted.

"Yes," he said. "Yes. It is," and for a moment it seemed like neither of us was comfortable with that, with that which was sensible, but the moment passed and I said, "Okay. Let's do it."

Henry helped me sort out what was needed from that which caused him to scratch his head and wonder. "Elmer's Glue?" he asked. "Why would you pack Elmer's Glue in your suitcase?"

"Because things break," I said.

"Yes. Things break," he agreed. Things break, but nonetheless, Henry put the glue in the suitcase with the books I was not currently reading, the first-aid kit, the two heavy wool sweaters I'd packed in case it got cold, which it didn't, and my cell phone, which was not a global phone and therefore didn't get reception in Europe. Hair dryer, travel iron, and sewing kit were amenities provided by hotels, thereby making mine redundant, and one umbrella was deemed sufficient.

Some years went by, but still, my mother, on her way home from school, continued to visit Semille. Maybe not every day, but two or three days a week, and it was on one of those days, one of those last days before the relief check arrived, while they ate crackers and drank water, that Semille told my mother a story. "When I was not so much older than you are now," Semille said, "I went to a gathering of young people." A party of some sort, or a salon, and there Semille set eyes on a young man. "And it was like a key in the door. The lock tumbled and the door opened and the room was flooded with light. In that instant, we fell in love. But my parents did not approve of him." Semille never said why her parents disapproved of the young man she loved. Maybe his family was a humble one. Too humble. Maybe he had a clubfoot or a congenitally withered hand. Maybe it was some Jewish version of the Montagues and the Capulets, a European Hatfield and McCoy–type family feud. Or maybe it was that Semille's parents were people of their word and a marriage had already been arranged for their daughter. The wedding was in the works when she found her true love. Not everyone is fortunate enough to find her true love.

"Or is it misfortune?" I asked, and Henry said, "Jury's still out on that one."

Night after night Semille slipped away from her parents' house, and she and her true love came together in secret. Hand in hand they walked, and they talked about everything under the sun, and under the moonlight they kissed, night after night, and then Semille did a terrible thing: she obeyed her parents' wishes. She married the man they chose for her, the man for whom she felt nothing and that, feeling nothing, grew, grew solid and strong, so that you could've driven nails through Semille's heart and she wouldn't have blinked. "My husband didn't die," she told my mother. "Maybe he is dead now. I don't know.

But I left him. I ran away. Years ago. Before the Nazis, we were living in Lyon, and one morning I got on a train to Paris." She told this story to my mother, who was then maybe thirteen or fourteen and already a sucker for love stories. "I got to Paris, and I said I was a widow, and I took a job in a dress shop." Semille told my mother what she had never told anyone else. "I hated the man I married. I hated him with an all-consuming hate. He wasn't a bad man, but he was not my true love, and for that I could not forgive him. I could not forgive."

Semille's favorite opera was *Carmen*.

"Yes," Henry said. "I see how that could happen."

"How what could happen? Which part?" I asked.

And Henry said, "All of it."

11

If sorrow is a hollow, like a bowl, then it stands to reason that a flat-screen TV or a pink iPod or a pair of Perugia slippers will alleviate the symptoms of the void, the way food will, for a while, satisfy hunger. "Buy yourself a little something," my mother used to say. "You'll feel better," and she would tell me about my grandmother, about how buying herself a little something let her feel better. For a while.

My grandmother was the fifth child born to her parents, but the first three were stillborn, so they didn't really count, and the fourth one lived for only a few days, which wasn't enough time for anything. When I'd first heard of this, of how my grandmother had lived but the other babies didn't, I obsessed about that, about dead babies, until I hit upon a rational conclusion: there was a cutoff point. If you made it as far as three years old, you could not die after only a few days; you could not suddenly wake up to find yourself dead, and if you lived longer than a few days, you could not be stillborn, either. Thereby, I kept myself safe from death until I was eight and a boy who lived on the next block from ours got a brain tumor. He died and I developed headaches.

As pretty as a Madame Alexander doll, with green eyes and soft corkscrew curls, my grandmother was as spoiled as curdled cream. She had a Steiff bear, a Steinway piano, and in the winter of her fourth year, she wore a white ermine coat with a matching white ermine muff to keep her hands toasty-warm, which is yet another example of connections not made, because my grandmother also had Queenie, her adored Persian cat, whose fur was white just like the ermine's, except Queenie got to keep her fur.

The baby Dalai Lama didn't have it so soft as my grandmother did, and she and her three subsequent sisters and the brother, too, lounged on the velvet-cushioned and fully staffed lap of luxury until all the shampoo money was used up and nothing was left except nice manners, an appreciation for music, Wedgwood china, a few pieces of jewelry, and my grandmother's inability to fend for herself. Too delicate to learn how to cook a meal, yet she suffered the loss of wealth with dignity and generosity. She did not succumb to resentment or envy or self-pity; never wept over what was gone, although she did sometimes weep for no reason at all, and the weeping would give way to the urge to buy something, something pretty. This urge would swell the way love does, and the way desire becomes necessity; with no pause for thought, she'd go directly to the five-and-dime store, to Notions, the aisle of small and useful items. Nearly half of Notions was devoted to sewing supplies, and there she'd take an hour or more, deliberating over which spool of thread to buy, as if a spool of thread were something rare and exotic, from India maybe. There were rows and rows of them, and in such pretty colors from which to pick but one. Pretty, pretty colors, and the spool of thread was a luxury, too, because despite its utility, it was, for my grandmother, useless. She didn't *do* anything with the thread. She didn't know how to sew or embroider; it was an object, a pretty colored thing to buy, to have, to lift her spirits. A spool of thread cost a penny back then.

Treat yourself to something pretty. A little indulgence to quiet anguish is not unlike an offering to the gods, and maybe it will make you feel better. For a while.

It's an option, although one not applicable to Ruby. For her, pretty things, useless things, luxurious things, were a consequence of happiness. New shoes would not put Ruby in a good mood, but a good mood could set her skipping off to buy new shoes. Or a washer/dryer.

Or fresh orchids to put in a vase by her bed.

Or a new car.

Ruby shopped when happy. Very happy. Too happy, if you can believe that there is such a thing as too happy.

"Too happy," Henry said. "I should hope there's such a thing."

"Something to strive for?" I asked.

"Isn't that what I'm doing?"

Spring time, when hope is eternal, a good mood is pervasive, and everyone is foolish; it was early, very early, on such a spring morning, a Saturday, when Ruby called and asked, "I didn't wake you, did I?"

"Yeah," I said. "You did."

Ruby half-assed apologized for that, for waking me, and then she told me to be downstairs, outside, on the street, in ten minutes. "Because I'll never find a parking spot near you," she said, as if that were an explanation.

Ten minutes?

Downstairs?

Parking spot?

The crack of dawn, pale pink and yellow and barely an inch thick, was parallel to the horizon, and the toot of a car horn does not make music. "Over here," Ruby called out from the window of a black car parked at a fire hydrant. "Come on, come on. Get in," she said, "before I get slapped with a ticket."

"I need coffee." I reached around for the seat belt. "Whose car is this?"

"Mine. It's a Saab Turbo sedan, and don't bother asking because it didn't cost me a dime." Ruby pulled out and cut across Eleventh Street, making for the West Side Highway.

"Not one dime?"

"No money down," she said.

It is worth mentioning that Ruby was, at that time, working for Chase Bank. To be sure they never let her anywhere near the till; she was in Manuals and Documentations, writing up the brochures for retirement accounts, home equity loans, reduced mortgage rates, but Ruby knew perfectly well that no money down did not mean free. "And I got a deal on it," she told me, "because it was the floor model."

Ruby bought the floor model because had she opted for a blue car instead of a black one, if she'd sat down with the salesman, a former college linebacker named Chick who still had the thick neck but now had a pot belly, too, and if Chick had shown her pictures of fancy tire rims or rhapsodized on the fun of a sun roof, if she'd sprung for the portable navigation system, it would have meant waiting for delivery, and that she could not do, because later she might not be in the right frame of mind to appreciate the kick of a new car.

The Henry Hudson Parkway took us to the Cross Bronx Expressway and from there to the Cross County Parkway to the Post Road, where I again, for the third time, reminded Ruby that we needed to be on the lookout for a place to stop. "I'm going to die without some coffee," I said, although I did neglect to mention that we were a half mile from an all-night diner because we were headed in that direction anyway, and my familiarity with this area was something about which I preferred not to remind Ruby. Had she realized how near we were to Leland Road, she would've insisted we go there, because when infused

The Scenic Route
159

with zip, when she got invigorated in this way, she derived a particular pleasure from unearthing the past, as if people you knew twenty-five years ago were like geraniums, easily dug up and repotted.

From our house on Leland Road, you could spit from the window and hit the house next door; the premium on property being greater than that on privacy, which was reason enough for my parents to move to Pound Ridge. "With more land," my mother seemed to think this move needed justification, "we could put in a pool with a deck and have a big garden, too."

"Sounds good," I said.

"You're not upset?" My mother was vaguely insulted. "This is your home. All your fond memories from childhood took place here. In this house. Joel is very upset."

Joel was happy, as happy as Joel could ever be, on Leland Road. Happy to ride his bicycle in the street, to play Little League baseball, to join the Dweeb Scouts. He fit in, whereas I didn't quite.

Oh, I had friends; I was popular just enough to entertain the possibility that maybe, just maybe, I'd get invited to our high school prom, which, at the time, mattered. Three boys had asked my friend Carolyn to the prom, and like Portia with her three suitors, Carolyn took her sweet forever deciding on one, while I entertained further possibility that maybe, just maybe, one of her rejects would invite me in her stead. That didn't happen, but I did go shopping with Carolyn to help her pick out the perfect gorgeous gown. I stood by while she made appointments to get her hair styled and her nails polished. I sniffed the stinky purple orchid corsage that came in a plastic bubble box. I offered my opinion on Pink Blush of Spring lipstick and pearl earrings, as if I gave a shit.

"I gave my prom date a gardenia," Henry said, "and she wore it in her hair. Although at Camden Military Academy we referred to our prom as a cotillion."

"You went to a military school?" I was surprised by this because of the blurry quality to him, because I could not picture Henry wearing sharply creased khakis or giving a crisp salute with sincerity.

"Four years' worth," he told me. "Along with a classical education, I was given valuable training in the Four Ps," and he ticked them off on his fingers. "Precision. Promptness." He did this while driving. "Propriety. And pride in my country."

"So you flunked out?"

"Don't I wish," he said. "Didn't I try."

He couldn't get booted out of school no matter which rules he broke because he was a legacy, although in his grandfather's day it was called the Carlisle Military School.

Henry's date for the Camden Military Academy cotillion was a girl named Emily Lynne Bartlett, who had a lazy eye. Emily Lynne had black hair, and when they slow-danced *Climbing the stairway to heaven* Henry smelled the sweetness of the flower, and that, the sweet smell of the gardenia, almost let him forget how her eye was turned inward, like it was a pigeon-toed eye.

Rather than locking myself up all alone in my room where I could feel gloriously sorry for myself on that night, the big night,

I met up at the elementary school playground with Janice King and we could feel sorry for ourselves together. Janice King was not invited to the prom because she was good at sports. She played basketball with the boys. Early in June, it was warm out. We didn't need jackets or sweaters, and we sat up against the chain-link fence. Janice passed me the bottle of rum she'd pilfered from her parents' liquor cabinet. "It's not true, you know. I'm not a lesbian," she said. "They think I'm a lesbian because I'm an athlete."

"And because of marching band." I took a swig from the bottle and spazzed a little from how bad it tasted. "You're in marching band. That's a lesbian thing. The uniform. And the tuba."

"Trombone," she said. "I play the trombone."

"Why do you think no one invited me?" I asked.

"Because you're weird."

"Weird? How am I weird?"

"I don't know." Janice took the bottle from between my knees. "You just are. You're weird. Everybody says so. Don't feel bad about it. Being weird doesn't make them hate you. They like you okay. They just think you're weird."

"Like the way they think you're a lesbian," I said.

"Exactly. Except *you* really *are* weird. And I'm really *not* a lesbian."

The next day I dyed my hair blond, but it turned out more copper-colored and also there was a green tint to it because that's what you get when you don't know what you're doing. I came out of the bathroom with my hair the color of a new penny, and I ran smack into my mother, who took one look at me and said, "What is wrong with you?"

On Sundays, my family took trips to the city, to the Museum of Natural History or to the United Nations or to Chinatown, but always we had to go home. My father driving, my mother next to him, Joel and I in the backseat, we'd be going down Ninth Avenue when the light was pink and violet and slate gray, and I would be overwhelmed with a fierce longing, a piercing love, for the buildings, for the streets, and for dusk on Ninth Avenue, which could not have been a real memory because at dusk we would've been going north on the West Side Highway or the FDR. We would not have been going down Ninth Avenue, but still that's what I remembered.

One thing I liked about Leland Road was the scent of freshly mowed grass in summer. Keeping your lawn trim was a priority there, so you got that smell a lot. Flower gardens of rosebushes and morning glories and pansies proliferated, and in early autumn there were mums and marigolds, and on the first weekend after the leaves fell, all the dads were out there raking those dead leaves into piles. Cars were parked in driveways and not on the street, which for some reason mattered a great deal to my mother. The same as it mattered to her that for the Christmas season no one went overboard with the lights or the plastic Santas. "And fireflies," I remembered. "When we lived in the house on Leland Road, on summer nights, I caught fireflies and kept them in a jar."

"Fireflies," Henry said. "Lightning bugs, we called them. I never see lightning bugs anymore."

Leaves, autumn leaves, were not alone among the dead on Leland Road.

"Me either," I said. "Maybe they are an endangered species, what with all those years of kids catching them and keeping them in jars where they died overnight."

Among the Dead:

(1) My turtle was from Woolworth's Pet Department, where they also sold parakeets. Some of the turtles sold at Woolworth's had pink or yellow flowers painted on their shells, and there were six hundred and fifty-two thousand turtles both with and without flowers piled high in a fish tank like junked cars: limbs tangled, toes jammed in eyeballs, tails bit off, necks twisted like rope as mouths went like fish mouths for a gulp of air. We're talking about depraved indifference on the part of Woolworth's management.

He, she, my turtle—these creatures are born, live, and die gender-unidentified, whichever—it dwelled in a plastic pool the size of a football but shaped like a kidney bean, which had a dry dock and a plastic palm tree. It seemed happy enough to swim in the bean-shaped pool, and it slept under the palm tree as if at the turtle version of the Chateau Marmont. Nonetheless, despite the heavenliness of all that, I thought my turtle might enjoy the warmth of the summer sun on its back and a walk on the lawn, solid ground beneath its feet, and that's where we were: a summer morning and I was stretched out in front of our house on Leland Road, elbows to the grass, my arms like posts, my chin resting in the palms of my hands, watching my turtle have itself a field day, when Sean Ryan crossed the street, and he came and sat next to me. I ignored Sean Ryan because that's what my mother had told me to do. "Ignore him and he'll go away," she said, and so I did and so he did. He went away, but like a bad penny, there he was again, kneeling beside me, holding a hammer, which in one swift move, he brought down, hard, on my turtle's shell. The turtle splatted, and what followed is largely a blur because it happened just as fast that I grabbed the hammer and bashed Sean's hand and then he was screaming and then his mother was screaming and then my mother yanked me in the house and I got punished for breaking two of Sean Ryan's fingers with a hammer.

(2) During the time when Sean Ryan, bona fide twisted sicko fuck, lived among us on Leland Road, hating him was something like boosterism in our neighborhood, the way it brought everyone together because everyone had their fair share of Sean Ryan stories to tell.

A Saturday afternoon, late in spring, when Sean was seventeen, a time when he should have been playing softball with his friends, except he didn't have any friends, or working a part-time job as a stock boy or bagging groceries, except no one would hire him, and forget about a girlfriend, that was never going to happen, he was casting about looking for something to do: a window to break or a bicycle tire to slash or a child to torment, when he paused, for a moment, at the Halens' house where their dog, a tenderhearted and trusting collie, frolicked in the yard.

Sean went home for supplies and then came back for the dog. "Come here, boy," Sean called. "Come on. That's a good boy," and Sean Ryan led the Halens' collie, which was a girl, a few blocks away to where six new houses were going up on land that we'd heretofore called "the woods" because it was three or maybe four undeveloped acres of trees and wild blackberry bushes and a small stream. Construction workers kept bankers' hours, and now with the trees and the blackberry bushes cleared away, there was no reason for any of us to go there. The site was deserted, and Sean tied one end of a short rope to the dog's collar and the other end to the frame of one of the six houses under construction. He left no leash room for the dog to roam.

Sean Ryan was murdering his way up the food chain: my turtle, Mrs. Fitzgerald's orange cat, which he choked to death and then hung from the mailbox on her front porch, and now he was going to kill the Halens' dog. From what would be the basement of the next house but for now was just a big hole in the ground, Sean got busy. With Scotch tape, he attached an M-80 to the firecracker on the flimsy stick that was the tail of a bottle rocket. The M-80, the size of a wine cork and encased in red cardboard, was not the quarter stick of dynamite that Sean Ryan believed it to be, but it did have more than enough explosive power to blow a dog to bits. The tail of the bottle rocket went into an empty beer can, like a long-stemmed rose in a vase. The beer can was the launching pad, designed to stabilize the rocket so that it would follow its preplanned course of flight from the trench to the target, which was the dog. All Sean needed to do was to light both fuses and step back. The blastoff would be followed by a whistle, and then: *kaboom!* Sean struck a match to one fuse and then to the other, but the weight of the M-80 was more than the flimsy stick could support. The can tipped over, which was not supposed to happen, and Sean Ryan crouched down on one knee to upright the bottle rocket, and the M-80 exploded and blew off the lower half of Sean Ryan's face. His jaw got separated from his neck, and he bled out.

All that afternoon Darcy Halen, who was five months pregnant, and now frantic, too, searched high and low for her dog, and just before dinnertime, she found the poor thing, shivering and whimpering and tied to the frame of the house under construction. Wondering how this came to be, Darcy Halen nosed around the site, and there, while standing at the edge of the big hole, she discovered Sean Ryan's body. What was left of his face was charred.

Perhaps it was naive of me, but I did expect our neighbors to erupt *Ding-dong the witch is dead* in spontaneous jubilation at the death of the evil that was Sean Ryan. I expected Darcy Halen's collie to be rewarded with chew toys, but no. You could have rowed a boat in all the tears shed. As if Sean Ryan had been a sweetheart as opposed to the creep-a-freak that he was, a boy who would've grown up to be a rapist and after that a serial killer, had he not accidentally killed himself before he got the chance to fulfill his dreams. "It is always, always, a tragedy when someone dies young," my mother said, by way of partial explanation as to why death brings out the hypocrite in us all.

It's as if with death comes instantaneous absolution.

You die, and everyone forgets what is left in your wake. Like when my mother called to tell me that Uncle Nathan had died. Just because Uncle Nathan's exploration of my not-yet-ready-for-prime-time private parts did not damage me any did not mean, as far as I was concerned, that I had to be sorry that he was dead "Good," I said.

"Sylvia. That's not nice."

"*That* is not nice?"

But let us assume, for the moment, that there is something to the coefficient of tragedy between the dead and the young, that indeed it would have been a tragedy had, as a young boy, Pol Pot choked on a chicken bone or fallen down a well like Benny Hoople did. Which might or might not have been a true story, the one about Benny Hoople, but my mother was fond of it as a way to keep track of time, making reference to the same summer Benny Hoople fell down the well, or four years after Benny Hoople fell down the well. Like that. Benny Hoople was from Nebraska or someplace, and he was not someone my mother knew, but his story, a boy falling down a well, made an impression on her, the tragedy of a child dying by misstep. But Uncle Nathan—drunk, child-molesting Uncle Nathan—three to one, cirrhosis of the liver should have done him in long before he did die; what killed him in the end was pneumonia, but better late than never. Underwhelmed with grief, I took a pass on the funeral.

"What will I say?" my mother asked. "What will I tell people, if they ask why you're not there?"

"How about the truth?" I said, and that was the end of that conversation.

It's to be expected that now, these many years since Sean Ryan smashed my turtle to death, I should concede, Okay, I should not have broken his fingers, but I concede no such thing. I am not sorry that I broke his fingers, although I might concede that his death at age seventeen was a tragedy if you subscribe to the idea that maybe, just maybe, a genuine shit of a boy, an apprenticing sociopath, can evolve, can become, perhaps not a full-fledged Mahatma Gandhi, but less of a shit if allowed to live out a full life, and within the framework of that possibility, however slim, maybe it was a tragedy that he died when he did.

As to *how* he died, that was divinely inspired.

(3) The family who moved into our house on Leland Road, not unlike the way a hermit crab moves into an empty snail shell, was a family the same as my own, if you rolled back the clock on us by a couple of years. Except in this family the daughter was two years older than her brother, whereas Joel is two years older than me, which maybe made this family our mirror image. When they bought the house, the daughter was fifteen and the son was thirteen, and after they'd been living there for two years or thereabouts, the mother and the daughter got into an overblown, knock-down, drag-out fight, which was no surprise because of how teenagers are melodramatic. The girl was screaming and crying and carrying on, kicking the walls, histrionics galore, and at the height of it, she bolted from the house. Her mother ran after her, close on her heels so that when the daughter got behind the wheel of the family car, or maybe it was her own car, I don't know, the mother gripped the car door with both hands and she stuck her head into the open window to try

to talk some sense into her daughter. Only the daughter wasn't having any of that. She floored the gas pedal and took off and took her mother's head with her.

What happened to that family after the daughter decapitated the mother, I don't know that either, but whatever happened, it couldn't have been good, and you can be sure none of them will forget, no matter how hard the drink or how deep the sleep. That girl, she slept in the same bedroom that was my bedroom for eighteen years, and in that way we were connected, except I got off easy.

Coda: The Fort Lauderdale airport was a place not unlike Heaven's Gate, and there, like Saint Peter and his sidekick, my father and Joyce were waiting for me at baggage claim. "Why did you bring such a big suitcase," Joyce asked. "You're going to be here four days. How much do you need for four days?"

"Maybe she'll stay longer," my father said, although we all knew that wasn't going to happen.

The parking lot was six steps from the exit, and Joyce said, "I should have waited in the car. I didn't know it was such a hike." My father had a new car, a midnight blue BMW, and I wondered, What's with the Beamer? Always my father drove a Cadillac, which my brother, Joel, referred to as the Jew-mobile. Joel's insensitivity and imbecility aside, a person driving a Land Rover forfeits all rights to judgment on other people's cars. At least the Cadillac was jazzy and never pretended to be anything other than what it was.

The highway from the airport to Delray Beach was lined with weathered palm trees and shopping plazas. Joyce complained that it was too cold in the car, and my father turned off the air-conditioning until Joyce said, "It's boiling in here," and then I got it, that former-girlfriend rivalry was not the impetus of my mother's Joyce-makes-me-barf face. Joyce *was* a pill. A glass-half-empty sort in every regard. Having been married to Joyce for twenty-something years, Abe Feingold went and died from what should have been a routine surgery: gallstones or an appendectomy. My father, he didn't die rather than live out his days with Joyce, but there are other ways to cease to exist.

Down a narrow road we stopped at a security gate manned by three guards in a booth. My father flashed a badge or gave the secret handshake, as if entering the Palm Oasis were the same as crossing Checkpoint Charlie back in the day when there was a Checkpoint Charlie. "Will you look at this place, Sylvia," my father said. "Three times a week, the grass is mowed. Around-the-clock gardeners, they've got here." I kind of wondered why anyone would need around-the-clock flower care, the way you might need around-the-clock medical attention, but the lawns were as perfect as AstroTurf, and the gardens were like those at Versailles. "Two golf courses," my father boasted, although he had yet to play golf. "And the tennis courts. Like Wimbledon. And wait until you see the swimming pool."

"Where are the people?" I asked.

"Indoors," my father told me. "It's too hot out here. Inside it's climate-controlled."

Keeping with the theme of the afterlife, faint strains of Burt Bacharach rearranged accompanied an elevator ride so smooth, as if only my soul and not my body were going up to the fifth floor. At the end of a hotel-style hallway, my father flashed the plastic key card and said, "I bet you never saw this before. Instead of a key."

"Will you look at that?" I said, and my father held the door open. The way a movie camera pans, I took in the living room: two walls of mirrors floor to ceiling, the white couch, the *objets de swans* and other assorted figurines, and all I could think was this: it was a good thing that my mother was already dead because this place would've killed her.

Flush to the wall, the one wallpapered in a coral-on-white diamond pattern, was a narrow table with a marble top and gold legs. A display table showcasing an assemblage of framed photographs. Front and center, that is, the one from which the others spread out like fingers from a hand, was a grainy black-and-white eight-by-ten of my father and Joyce. My father was in uniform, U.S. Army, and soon to be shipped out, and Joyce was wearing a summer frock, polka dots with a ruffle around the neck. Her hair was done up in a glamour-girl style of the day, and my father had his arm around her. They were looking half into the camera and half into each other's eyes. On either side of that one, in matching gold-tone frames, were two more pictures of my father and Joyce, but smaller. Five-by-seven and recent. In one, my father has on a gray suit and a yellow tie and Joyce's dress is red. Her hair, mahogany brown, is now short, but it might have been the same color as it was in the 1950s, thank you, Lady Clairol. Other pictures, smaller, snapshot-size but all framed, were arranged just so: my father and Joyce *then* at the beach. My father and Joyce *now* poolside. Joyce *then* on a bicycle. My father *now* sitting in a golf cart. Joyce *then* perched on the hood of a car. My father *then* leaning up against a brick building. Joyce and my father *now* seated at Table 8, behind an arrangement of red carnations—a Valentine's Day dinner at the Palm Oasis clubhouse—and there was not one picture from the intervening years. Not one picture of the flat-footed or half-blind Abe Feingold and not one picture of the three children Abe and Joyce had together. Two sons and a daughter, and that first son, the one who was the catalyst for the marriage, was supposedly some hotshot adman. There was no picture of Joel—not that I was eager to look at Joel's face, but still—or of me, and no pictures of grandchildren from either side, and there was not one picture of my mother, either.

To look at those photographs was to consider a world in which everything was the same, except a few of us got deleted, as if we were a mistake, an unintended line drawn, and so erased.

Absence creates its own story: Arnie Landsman held Joyce Whosits in his arms as they danced to Russ Morgan, "Sweetheart, forever, I'll wait for you," and then Arnie went off to war, and when he came back, they got married. They did not have children, which was a disappointment to be sure, but they had each other, and together they ran a mom-and-pop business, a dry cleaners or a small shop selling stationery supplies: typing paper, manila envelopes, Ticonderoga number 2 pencils in bulk, that sort of thing. For thirty-eight years, give or take, they lived in Riverdale, in a nice enough apartment, one-bedroom, eat-in kitchen, until they sold the business and retired to Florida, to the Palm Oasis, where everyone is in dress rehearsal for being dead.

I did not ask my father, not then or later, "Hey, what gives?" I did not say anything because he seemed to be enjoying himself there in the Palm Oasis, with Joyce, and I, glad to be done with the dutiful-daughter routine, didn't want to upset the balance. Maybe he didn't want a picture of my mother around because her picture might speak to him, a rebuke: of all the women to choose from, did you have to pick Joyce Feingold?

But still, I should have asked, "What gives? Why don't you have a picture of my mother, your wife, your beloved wife, whose rot you wiped up with a tissue while you wept? Why did you dispose of everything that was hers, everything you had together? Why did you not keep anything?" I should have *would have, could have* asked, "What gives?" and maybe he would have said, "To remember is to grieve, and what good would that do?"

But I didn't ask then, and later it was far too late.

12

The sun was now up, and the diner was empty but for some truck drivers seated along the counter, spaced like ebony keys on a piano. Three teenage girls were sprawled out in the booth across from ours, and Ruby said to me, "Remember being that age?"

"Not if I can help it," I said.

The waitress had circles of mascara smudged under her eyes. Her uniform was salmon, a color that becomes no one, especially under fluorescent lighting. She flipped open her pad, as if it took effort to lift the pages.

"Coffee," I said, "and a bagel with cream cheese."

Ruby asked for coffee, too. "And pancakes with a side of sausages. And bacon. And you might as well bring me a plate of homes fries with that."

After drowning the pancakes in syrup and pouring ketchup over the home fries, Ruby ate a few bites, but mostly she moved the food around on the plate until the waitress came over and said, "Are you done playing with that?"

"What's it to you?" Ruby asked, and I picked up Ruby's plate and passed it to the waitress. "She's done," I said, and it was a good time to ask for the check, before Ruby got ornery, which sometimes happened and it was never charming.

We took Central Avenue, going north, toward Hartsdale, a town most famous for its pet cemetery. It really is something special, that pet cemetery. The first of its kind in America, and it is also the site of the first War Dog Memorial, dedicated to the dogs who served with the Red Cross in World War I. There were rumors that Dumbo the elephant was buried there, or maybe it was Jumbo the elephant, and Clever Hans, who was a horse who could do trigonometry or Euclidian geometry or guess your weight or something like that, supposedly he was buried there, too, and our family dog was laid to rest in the pet cemetery in Hartsdale. Bobo, that was her name. Our dog. Also Hartsdale was famous *if famous isn't pushing it* for being home to the original, the very first, Carvel stand, where we would go for ice cream, although it wasn't real ice cream the way Cool Whip wasn't real whipped cream, but similar and better preserved.

It was a hot day in July when my mother got her new car, an ever-so-sporty convertible, and the first thing she said was,

"Who wants to go to Carvel?" and Joel and I said, "I do. I do." We ran to the car, and the top was down.

The convertible replaced her Studebaker, a 1962 Studebaker Coupe, which was a lemon, which I came to learn did not, in this case, refer to the acidic fruit of the same name. The Studebaker spent more time in the shop getting repaired than it did on the road, but my mother loved that car and my father had to coax her into giving it up, as if it were an irrational fear. The day the Studebaker got sold, my mother locked herself in the bathroom and wept, the same as she did some years later when Bobo died.

Bobo. Tongue-lolling, tail-wagging, racing madly after a leaf, all dopey and sweet, Bobo was not one of your brighter dogs, but Bobo knew love. She was filled with love, she overflowed with love, she was drowning with love, she spun like a top with love for all the creatures of the earth: people, cats, shih tzus, Joel, ladybugs, Bobo's heart held them all. She loved to run, and she loved to sleep, and she loved to be petted and she loved to be kissed, and she loved to eat. Bobo never met a food not to be devoured, and even some things not in a recognized food group, such as my father's wallet and the jar of Vaseline she licked clean. She loved everyone and she'd eat anything, but she had her favorites: my mother and Cheese Doodles.

Bobo's heart was big. Too big. Literally too big, and *nothing to be done, the humane thing now* she was going to die because of it, because of her big heart. We brought her home from the vet to have one more day with her, to love her deeper, with all our might, but I couldn't. I couldn't even look at her, and I stayed in my room, where I hid from the grief.

In the morning, from my bedroom window, I saw Joel sitting on the front steps leading to our house. Bobo sat beside him, and he was feeding her Cheese Doodles. After each Cheese Doodle, Bobo licked my brother's face and he, in turn, kissed the top of her head, on that point of bone common to Irish setters, and then he'd feed her another Cheese Doodle, and he did that until there were no Cheese Doodles left in the bag, and my father came and took Bobo away to be put to sleep, and my mother locked herself in the bathroom.

There it is, the evidence of something else—something more—to Joel, something about him that was not miserable, but something good.

All things considered, and some things to be expected, I'd have thought Henry would be driving a convertible. "A snazzy little sports car," I said, "in a virile shade of Midlife Crisis red."

"Sports cars are too often temperamental," Henry said. "High-strung. On the road, I prefer reliability, and anonymity. A red car calls out for attention."

'Anonymity, there's another way to lose yourself.'

At Carvel, Joel and I got the usual: vanilla custard cones with chocolate sprinkles. Custard, that's what we called it. Custard, although it wasn't custard any more than it was ice cream, and then Joel and I hopped into the backseat of the car. Because this was before children riding in cars were routinely immobilized with the de Sadean system of belts, buckles, pulleys, and locks, before extreme caution reconfigured childhood so that children now suit up in crash helmets, knee pads, and jock straps to take their tricycles for a spin around the front lawn, Joel and I blithely and without reprimand did not sit properly. Instead, we were kneeling, turned around, and looking out to what was behind us, with the idea of watching the landscape recede. We had yet to get in a lick of ice cream before my mother started up the car, and as she drove away, the force of air blew off the sprinkles from our vanilla cones. Chocolate sprinkles spattered on the trunk of the blue car looked like mouse droppings, although I might have remembered the car as a lighter blue than it was. Color, over time, fades because it gets washed out by the sun or dimmed by memory. ·

The pet cemetery, Carvel, and the house with the bay window. Soon after my parents moved to Leland Road, my grandfather bought that house, the one with the bay window, although the proximity to his daughter was not likely a factor in the decision. My grandfather wasn't any more fond of my mother than he was of anyone else. Which is to say: he didn't like her a whole lot, either. The three exceptions to his explicit and pretty much blanket disgust for humankind were: his wife, whom he loved dearly; his one friend, who was Chinese and a pharmacist; and me.

The Chinese pharmacist taught my grandfather the art of Chinese brush painting, which was an art form inspired by nature. As was the Hudson River School of art. My grandfather was a painter of that sort, a Luminist; an artist who, in the contemplation of nature, was perpetually renewed. It was a good thing, too, that he found decency in a tree, purpose in a leaf, tranquillity in a stream, because he sure as shit didn't find anything of value in people or the civilization we made. My grandfather's romantic *I love to go a-wandering* landscapes were not the least bit fashionable in the era of Abstract Expressionism, and they did not sell. To pay the bills, he offended his own sensibilities by painting portraits and taking commissions for works imitative of Degas or Maxfield Parrish, depending on who did the commissioning.

It could have been the housing boom of the 1950s; new houses meant new furniture, and interior decorators were, just like that, in need of reams of landscapes to hang above sofas. Or perhaps it is the nature of all things to be cyclical. All I know for sure was that there was enough of a revival of interest in the Hudson River School that my grandfather's circumstances changed enough for him to buy the house in Hartsdale.

How he came to know the Chinese pharmacist is a mystery to me, but I went there with him once, to the shop on Mott Street, where the shelves were lined with bottles of ginseng root that looked like mutant hamsters and aborted birds floating in formaldehyde. The pharmacist took me to a back room, where he unlocked the closet door with a key on a ring that hung from his belt, and there, in the dark of the closet, looking out at me, was a dragon. *A dragon!* A yellow dragon *and sealing wax and other fancy stuff* with red eyes, and more or less the same size as the Loch Ness monster. The pharmacist was either a very old man and therefore revered or some kind of Chinatown bigwig or both, which I surmised because I assumed that this, keeping a dragon in your closet, one of the big dragons that parade the streets on Chinese New Year, was an honor and not just any old schmo got to keep a dragon in the closet year-round.

Between the ginseng root and the dragon, the trip to Chinatown with my grandfather could have been the stuff of nightmares, but, instead, Chinese New Year feels as if it is my holiday, too.

I was not quite seven years old when my grandfather died, and my heart did not break because, in the same way their bones are mostly cartilage, a child's heart is not yet brittle enough to shatter, either. Instead, I could not keep food down for nine days.

At the Four Corners, which were the gateway to Hartsdale, I said to Ruby, "Take this left, and at the top of the hill, take another left."

At the top of the hill there used to be a farm where pumpkins grew on thick and tangled vines, a pumpkin patch like that from the Alger Hiss story. That farm stand was where we bought our pumpkins for Halloween and apple cider, and they made fresh cider doughnuts, too, which might be why, in memory, it is late October and thermochromatic at peak autumnal hues like calendar photographs of New England, with leaves heritage red and yellow and brown and orange like marigolds; leaves raked into piles that crunch underfoot, and I am four or five years old, wearing a heavy red wool sweater with matching red scarf and mittens, but no coat. In all likelihood my nose is running. Now, where the farm used to be, were, predictably enough, a dozen monstrosity-big replicas of Queen Anne and Edwardian houses, each of which came with a guarantee: your neighbor will be a dipshit.

"Doesn't your brother live in that kind of house?" Ruby asked. "What are they made from anyway, those houses? Particle board?"

"Something like that," I said, and then I directed Ruby to take the next right where sweet green leaves from weeping willow trees swept along the side of the road. My grandparents' house was like a house in a storybook, a house where Pippi Longstocking might have lived, the way it was two parts wonderful and one part strange: it was made of fieldstone, and there was the bay window, a window in three dimensions and shaped like an inlet at the shore, which I suppose is why it's called that, a bay window. On one side of his house, my grandfather planted a garden where he grew carrots and tomatoes, and those baby carrots pulled from the ground flabbergasted me as would any good magic trick. The backyard was level until midpoint, and from there it sloped uphill, and on that incline my misanthropic grandfather, simply but with discriminating sensibility, placed large stones. White stones, and around the large white stones, he planted moss and flowers that grew close to the earth, violets and pansies. At the base of this rock garden, where the ground was flat, was a pond, which was not for swimming but it was home to a pair of bright orange koi, and lily pads floated on the surface the way Jesus walked on water. A Japanese rock garden. Chinese brush painting. Apparently enamored of Asian arts, my grandfather also cultivated bonsai trees, miniature trees that were perfect. Imagine such a thing! Perfect miniature trees. He gave one, a juniper tree, to my mother, and it sat on our dining room table for about three days, which was about as long as my mother could stand looking at a bonsai tree that did not match her colonial American furniture.

Baby carrots pulled from the ground and koi swimming in the pond, and I would grow light-headed from the exaltation of it all. Light-headed and hungry, I'd go inside and ask my grandmother for something to eat, and she would look at me as if I'd just said the oddest thing, and she would have to think about that, as if first she needed to make sense of the words, and then as if to take mental inventory of what she had to offer. Which was also a little nuts because invariably, always, she said, "Would you like a banana? Or a Mallomar?"

Mallomars were marshmallow set on graham crackers and covered with chocolate, and even by the lamentable standards of store-bought cookies, Mallomars stank. Mallomars stank, but the children who lived nearby, they were outstanding children, and I loved them all. Kicky, from across the street, which maybe wasn't his real name, Kicky was towheaded and airy, giving off a glimmer of something like light or hope, and I wanted to marry him someday. At the end of the road, in a house that looked like a red barn, lived a family with five children, all of whom were afflicted. One boy was missing two fingers and his hands were thick with keloid scar tissue. The eldest daughter was blind; another daughter was epileptic; and the next boy, with one leg shorter than the other, he limped. My grandfather, he limped, too, but his legs were of equal distance to the floor. His limp, from World War I, was not precisely a war wound unless you consider everything that happens in a war to be a war wound, the way war breaks people and does irreparable damage. The youngest girl of that family had orange hair and freckles the same shade of orange as the baby carrots pulled from the ground and the same color as the koi in the pond, and they, the girl's orange freckles, were the size of bottle caps. "Which was a tribulation, like a pox," I told Ruby.

"Once, when I was a child," Ruby said, "I was shopping with my mother at the A&P and the woman bagging our groceries was missing an eye. I suppose a glass eye cost more than she could afford. She was wearing a patch."

"Did that make you want an eye patch, too?" I asked.

"Hell, no," Ruby said. "That patch must have itched or something because right after she put our eggs in the bag, she lifted it up to scratch, and there was this black hole looking at me. After that, I wouldn't eat those eggs, either."

"I wanted something to be wrong with me," I said. "Nothing I could die from. But to be afflicted like those children in the red house, I thought that would make me special. I thought they were special."

To be deaf was an affliction, and a proper one, too, and when the school nurse came to our class to administer the hearing test, in our turn, each of us was to put on the headphones. "Whenever you hear a beep," the nurse said, "raise your index finger. Do you all know which one is your index finger?"

Beep. A softer beep. Beep. Beep. A whisper of a beep, and *Where is Pointer* I kept my index finger curled in my fist for the duration of all the beeps. My finger stayed curled in my fist, except at the very loudest of them. Not to have heard the booming BEEP, that would have been overkill.

The school nurse called my mother to tell her I was in need of a hearing aid.

"A hearing aid?" my mother said.

I sat as still as deep waters, focused on the containment of my elation, on the expression of obliviousness, as if I had not heard the news, which I could not have heard because I was deaf.

"She is not deaf," my mother told the school nurse. "She was just pretending to be deaf."

Eventually I got eyeglasses. I wasn't blind like the girl in the red house, but I did legitimately need glasses to see the blackboard at school and for when I watched television or went to the movies. Which did not keep me from wearing my glasses all the time, as if without them, I would have walked into walls and mistook skunks for cats. Later, when I was older, when I was told that I had bedroom eyes, I quit wearing my glasses no matter what there was to see in the distance. A mistake that perhaps reverberated beyond the visual fields.

Emily Lynne Bartlett, the girl Henry took to his prom, the girl with the lazy eye, the eye that drifted inward, she was the daughter of one of the trustees of Camden Military Academy, a man who had himself a string of banks, and you could say that was an affliction, too, that which drew Henry to money.

.   .   .

People Do Find Each Other: On one of those days when my mother, who was by now a teenager in full bloom, stopped in on her way home from school to visit Aunt Semille, she found the door ajar. Semille was sitting in the chair that faced the window, weeping. It was effortless, Semille's weeping, because this sorrow, which she carried with her from long ago and far away, contained no rage and no surprise.

If at some point in her life Semille had ever believed in God, it was a belief she had left behind along with everything else that was lost to her. Nor was she one to partake of ceremony for its own sake, but having heard tell of the synagogue that was like a palace or maybe she'd read of its magnificence, Semille wanted to see for herself this Temple Emanu-El.

The way old ladies dolled up back then—too much rouge and a hat—Semille readied herself for the trip to Fifth Avenue and Sixty-fifth Street, a part of Manhattan that was foreign to her. She also wore four or five strands of glass beads around her neck and a dab of perfume on each of her pulse points.

Out of France, during wartime, and into Portugal and from there to who knows where and on to Cuba and then to New York, where Semille now navigated her way twenty blocks downtown before hopping on the crosstown bus, and there it was! A synagogue not quite as spectacular as the great cathedrals of Europe, but far more grand than any synagogue Semille, or the world, had ever seen, Temple Emanu-El was something like the Vatican for Jews. Semille took in the rows of columns, the stained-glass windows—Louis Comfort Tiffany stained-glass windows! In a synagogue!—framed in marble. The doors to the sanctuary ark were reproductions of the Tablets of Law, and the ark itself, in keeping with the overall motif of the Bible, was an artistic representation of the Torah scroll. At the front of the ark was the eternal light that was God's presence, if you buy into that sort of thing.

It was there, there in Temple Emanu-El at the front of the ark under the glow of that eternal light—it could not be, it was not possible and yet it was—that Semille fell prey *pray* to a small miracle. Her love, her one true love, the young man whose love she had betrayed, he was there, standing there alone under the glow of the eternal light, and the carapace of dispassion Semille had cultivated for those many years, it turned to dust.

Can you imagine such a sweet love story: love that ever-lasted, love that spanned decades, love that survived wars and crossed oceans, and now in their old age *You begin* they could be together. Again.

Telling me this story, my mother would dab at her eyes, and then go back to whatever it was she had been doing: sorting laundry or polishing the silverware or stripping paint from a chair.

The Bedtime Stories My Father Told Me: I was the main character. Like I was one of the Five Peppers or Harold, the bald kid with the purple crayon. A heady experience, being a literary character. Like being famous without having done anything to achieve the fame, which, given my proclivity for doing nothing, appealed to me all the more, and at that, Henry and I exchanged a glance which was not unlike looking in a magic mirror—seeing not ourselves but ideas of who we were winking back at us. While Henry's literary identification was likely of the Lost Generation, the Little Sylvia stories were decidedly Grimm-inspired. A walk in the woods invariably got her lost in the woods. "And Little Sylvia had to eat worms to survive. Fat, juicy earthworms. She opened her mouth wide like a baby bird's mouth, and she closed her eyes tight," but the Little Sylvia stories came to *all's well that ends well* happy endings. Life and limb intact, she would find her way home to the bosom of her family, who had been sick with worry, but along the way she did have some harrowing experiences: snatched by a giant hawk and carried off in its talons; trapped in a cave that was alive with bats; and there was the shipwreck; but most often Little Sylvia was lost in the forest. "And then the night came," my father told me, "and the big moon cast a glow over the treetops. It was cold and the leaves rustled in the wind."

From the living room, where my mother sat in an armchair, her knitting needles working like dueling swords *en garde, touché!* she called out to my father, "Stop telling her those stories. She's going to have nightmares."

Coconspirators, my father and I, and he lowered his voice because you can't leave off a story just at the point when, from off in the distance, Little Sylvia hears the howl of the wolves, which took me from one primal scene to another when later the forewarned-of nightmare woke me. My heart banging against my chest as if banging on a locked door, desperate for the way out. I scrambled from my bed to my parents' bedroom, where my mother, like Eve covering her nakedness, pulled up the blanket, which left my father, for all of a moment, but a moment was plenty, without means for modesty. Having had a gander at my brother, I wasn't entirely unprepared for what was there, but the *size* of what was there, that was mind-blowing. A torpedo. Later, after a series of, not disappointments exactly, but let's call it expectations diminished, it occurred to me that what looked huge to a little girl could well have been average, and I readjusted my scale accordingly.

"Well, there's a load off my mind," Henry said.

To which I said, "Boys. You're such a silly bunch."

Once upon a time, Little Sylvia was abducted by an old crone who planned to make soup from her, as if Little Sylvia were a lamb shank. She was kept in a cottage, locked in the root cellar along with the turnips, potatoes, and beets. The cottage had a thatched roof and a crooked chimney and red flowers flanked the path, and so it was something like a dream come true when winding our way through the Bohemian Forest, Henry and I happened upon a guest house with a thatched roof, crooked chimney, and red flowers flanking the path. "Henry," I said. "Stop. We have to stop here."

'Oh, just like the young Natalie Wood in Miracle on Thirty-fourth Street *when she sees the house with the swing in the yard.'*

This guest house was nothing like the hotels Henry favored; it was lovely in a whole other way, but before he would agree to stay for the night, he had to see the accommodations. "We can't have you sleeping in a root cellar now, can we?"

We were greeted at the door by a pretty woman with a broad face and blond hair thick like hay, and not an old crone who resembled the beggar woman in my book of illustrated folktales, the way my father's grandmother, his *bubbe,* resembled the beggar woman. This pretty woman with the broad face was wiping her hands on the white apron she wore over blue jeans and a yellow blouse, and she spoke to us in what I assumed was Czech. Henry had a gift for languages, and he managed a smattering of most all of them, enough to get by, although he was fluent only in English and French, and now that I think of it, maybe he wasn't fluent in French. Maybe he knew only enough to get by there, too. I looked to him to translate, but he said to me, "I have no idea what she's talking. Maybe some kind of dialect."

Cobbling together bits of Czech with German and a few words in Italian, and topping off the linguistic mishmash with the universal gestures for sleeping and eating, we followed her up wooden stairs that were not rickety to a bedroom that glistened, it was that kind of clean, and even though there was no minibar, which did cause Henry to hesitate, he, too, thought it was the right place for us to stay the night. In pantomime, the pretty woman held up a spoon and brought it to her mouth. Then she tapped at the clock. Dinner at seven.

The mattress on the bed was filled with feathers, and when we fell on it, one feather escaped and floated up where it was caught in the soft breeze. The feather sailed away.

The Bronx is a place I think of as dark. In memory it is always gloomy, as if I were never there when the sun was shining, as if I can remember it only in twilight in winter, but I know it was morning, a Sunday morning, when my father and I stopped at what he called the Appetizing Store, where he bought pickled herring in a jar and three smoked whitefish, which was not food we would eat, but it was food to bring to his *bubbe*. I don't recall having met his grandmother prior to that day, but children at that age, three or four I was, often can't remember what happened an hour ago. At this Appetizing Store I got a candy, the likes of which I'd never seen before. Or since. A confection, caramel or apricot. The color has stayed with me, but the taste of it has not. It was the size of a walnut, or maybe bigger, and it was filled with marshmallow or a white sugar paste. Wrapped in wax paper, it had no label like a proper candy, like a Snickers bar or a box of Raisinets. Over the years, I have looked for that candy, but I never did see it again, or maybe I did see it but didn't recognize it.

In its glory days, the Grand Concourse was middle-class grand and immigrant rich, but those days were over, and the blond Art Deco building, with its casement windows and roofline crenellated like a castle, had frayed. That my father had keys to this building disturbed me slightly, as if he'd been keeping a secret, as if he had a whole other life, separate from the one with us. In the lobby I was met by a smell, decisive but of unknown origin, just as the smell of the doctor's office was distinct and easily recollected but impossible to identify. The floors were marble.

My father was a boy, not quite twelve, when his mother died. With his father busy making a living, and his sisters married with families of their own, and his brother Eli off fighting the Japanese in the South Pacific, where, he wrote home, he'd captured a submarine with one hand tied behind his back, *Bubbe* stepped in to cook meals, to keep house, to care for my father, to care about him. Eli, according to my father, never told the truth when there was a good story to be had. "But everyone liked him," my father said. "He was a charmer." During the war, Eli met—for real—a young Australian woman *go waltzing Matilda with me* who, in some capacity or other, supported our troops. Maybe she worked the concession stand at the USO show, selling cigarettes or Raisinets to the boys in uniform. Eli told the Australian girl that he and Bob Hope were thick as thieves, and what girl's head would not have spun at that? Eli married this Australian girl who fell for his bullshit, and they moved to New Zealand. "Like you," I said to Henry, "he never did return home, either. Not for so much as a visit or a funeral."

Eli's wife, though, she did come to New York, but only after Eli had died, and I gave her, this Australian woman, many points for being a good sport, how she thought it was slam-dunk funny when she learned of the lies Eli had told her, the lies she fell for, as if it were all a jolly-good practical joke. And why not? Where was the harm in it? To believe what is not true, how different is that from remembering what is gone?

Soon after my father got married, his father died, leaving *Bubbe* in an apartment far too big for one old lady. Too much to keep clean, and she could get lost in there and who would find her? And so she moved two flights up, from the fourth floor to the sixth, to a one-bedroom apartment. French doors with glass knobs separated the living room from the dining room, and from there I followed my father into the kitchen—a very small kitchen with the floor tiled in black and white—and in that small kitchen, at a small stove, my father's *bubbe* was bent over, stirring a wooden spoon in a pot. She, too, was small, no bigger than a girl, and no doubt she suffered from osteoporosis, or else she was born a hunchback. She wore a navy-blue dress with a white lace collar and black stockings and orthopedic shoes, and her face was wizened like a dried fig. She let go of the big wooden spoon, and she held her arms open wide, and her smile was like that, too. Open, and I scurried to hide behind my father's legs. My father tried to bring me around, to get me to go to her, to give her a hug, but I held on tight to his left knee because of how she looked like the beggar woman in my book of folktales and she didn't speak English, and I was afraid of her.

Yet another thing I did not do, that I did not do and later wished I had. Another slice from the pie of time I now wish I could put back and do over. Do over, the way little children play games by their own set of rules—rules that include the do-over, the second chance. Drop the ball and do over, trip on the rope and do over, pin the tail on the donkey's ear and do over, and then one day someone says, "No. No do-overs," and in its place is the void: if only.

How it must have stung to know that her wrinkled face and her humped back scared the piss out of her great-granddaughter, as surely as any nightmare. She, who with devotion and with a surfeit of love stepped in to care for my father, a boy without a mother, she would never again know the feel of a child's arms wrapped around her little-girl-size waist, a child's hands pressed against her hump.

Do over.

As we lay on that feather bed, my head resting on Henry's shoulder, I asked him, "If you could do your life over, do you think you'd do everything the same?"

"I'd like to say no," he told me. "I'd like to say I'd do plenty of things different, but I can't say that because I need to believe otherwise."

"You *need* to believe otherwise?"

"Exactly. I need to believe in predetermination. If I acknowledge free will, I'd have only myself to blame. And who could live with that?" he asked.

If only.

A stag's head was mounted on the dining room wall as decoration, and an iron cauldron hung from a crossbar in a fireplace made from a pile of rocks. I managed to achieve a meal of cheese, bread, and an apple for myself, and Henry got meat that might have been wild boar, and it came with potatoes. He was pleased enough with that, although it did take him a few minutes or maybe longer to recover after the proprietress woman came to our table with a carafe which she filled halfway with white wine and then to the top with Coca-Cola. No ice. It fizzed when she stirred. Her smile went as broad as her face, and I gathered that this was a local specialty. An Eastern European sangria, and I was game enough to try it, but for Henry this particular spirit of adventure was irrelevant to travel. Maybe when in Rome, we should do as the Romans do, but with something as significant as wine with dinner, Henry followed another golden rule: better safe than sorry.

'Safe and sorry, that happens, too.'

By pointing at the sullied carafe and then touching the strap on my dress, which was red, Henry was able to get red wine to go with his boar meat, and when he tasted the red wine he got, he said, "Well, this isn't half bad, either." He rested his goblet on the table, which was rustic and made of thick, dark wood, and said, "What do you think? Can you imagine living out your days in a place such as this? With Snoopy and Happy and those other five dwarves living down the road?" .

"Sneezy," I said. "Or Sleepy. Snoopy's a dog, not one of the Seven Dwarfs."

"Right. Right you are. " Henry took another swallow of wine, and then another, and then he asked, "Can you picture it? Living in a rural sort of place? Small town nearby? A simple country life where you don't speak the language but you do sleep on a feather bed?"

'Simple? Small town? Country life? There's nothing simple about it. Although, speaking the language, that does complicate matters some.'

The pretty woman returned to the table to refill my glass, a second helping of the wine and cola mix.

"Does that taste as vile as I suspect it does?" Henry asked.

"Pretty much," I said.

"Then why are you drinking it?"

"Because she is proud of it, and it does me no harm."

"You are a brave woman," Henry said.

"No. No, I am not any such thing."

·   ·   ·

A Simple Country Life Where You Don't Speak the Language: Maybe it was the image of the crumbling mansion or maybe it was their story coupled with other stories I'd read and loved, but my grandmother's sister Thea and her husband, John, who they were and how they lived, they often came to mind whenever I found myself drifting off from the task at hand, which was pretty much always. I'd pictured their town in West Virginia as Hooterville Gothic. Flannery O'Connor does *Petticoat Junction* or William Faulkner's take on *Mayberry R.F.D.* And this was something I wouldn't have minded seeing for myself.

My mother was loading the dishwasher when I sat back down at the knotty pine kitchen table and asked, "Do you think I could work at Uncle John's newspaper for the summer? To learn stuff? Like an internship? I could stay with them. They have a big house, right?" I made this sound like a reasonable idea. "I was thinking maybe I want to be a journalist, and this could be good experience."

Now that I'd brought up an ambition to be something other than a bump on a log, my mother rushed to keep the dream alive. "That's a wonderful idea," she said. "Let me finish up here, and I'll give Thea a call."

The phone in the kitchen was a wall phone, and it was yellow. A muted yellow, and it matched the calico curtains. After the pleasantries were done with, my mother told Thea, "I'm calling because Sylvia is extremely interested in journalism. She'd like to spend the summer with you and John, to work on the paper. To learn."

From the basket of dried gourds on the table, I picked up one of those warty green ones. Decorative dried gourds in a basket looked prehistoric, like Fred Flintstone's fruit bowl.

"She knows that," my mother said. "She understands."

I rubbed my thumb over the nubs of the gourd.

"She doesn't expect to get paid, Thea. She wants the experience, is all."

My mother had another basket in the living room; one that was filled with dried corn, which was mostly brown.

"She wouldn't be any more bored there than she would be here."

An antique butter churn stood in the corner of the kitchen. It was just for show. We didn't use it.

"Even now? Still?" my mother said. "In this day and age? Who would care?"

The spinning wheel in the living room, that was just for show, too.

My mother hung up the phone, and she sat in the chair beside mine. Taking the gourd from my hands, she put it back in the basket and said, "That's not a toy. Thea says you'll be bored down there."

There was a brass eagle on our mailbox. Laura Ingalls Wilder would've been at home in our house. Betsy Ross, too.

"I wouldn't get bored," I told her. "And if I did get bored, I could always come home and be bored here."

"Oh, what the hell," my mother said. "You're not a child. The real reason is she thinks that if you come down there, people will figure it out. That she's Jewish. She's afraid of that. Of the truth coming out. After all these years."

"I wouldn't tell anyone," I said, as if to keep such a secret would damage nothing and no one.

"You wouldn't *have* to tell anyone." My mother tapped the bridge of my nose, which was a stupid thing to do in its own right, but mothers are no better and no worse than other people.

"I love your nose." Henry ran his finger along the length of it. "It's strong. And sexy."

"Well, it's mine," I said, which might seem like an obvious thing to say, but that's not something I'd take for granted because in my high school class, there were a whole lot of girls whose noses were not their own. Like rows of buttons on a card, they were all the same, those noses. The fixed noses. Fixed, although they weren't broken or malfunctioning, but fixed the way you say a dog is fixed when you mean that the dog has been neutered, because, in that way, a fixed nose has been neutered, too, rendered neutral. The way beige is neutral.

I say this about fixed noses not from a position on a high horse because while it is good to pay lip service to the earnest and decent sentiment—it's what's on the inside that counts—it's not true. Oh, the inside counts, it does, but the outside counts for twice as much, which is not a fine thing about how people operate, but that's nature, and not just human nature either. Think peacock, and how the one with the most magnificent tail gets the hen every time, and an antelope born with a gimpy leg is left behind for lion feed when the herd moves on. When it comes to the compositionally disfavored, nature is ruthless, children are cruel, teenagers are savage, and while adults are polite, all studies reach the same conclusion:

tall people get higher-paying jobs, beautiful women get better service, and if you are missing teeth they won't put you on television.

If you think your nose is diminishing your quality of life, by all means go fix it, and you won't hear sanctimonious crap about it from me. My gripe, such as it is one, with the same-nosed girls was that often the noses they started out with were good noses; some, in fact, were magnificent, but in vainglorious attempts at the banality of perfection, flared nostrils were tamed, the distinguished became diminished, and what was the glory of Caesar was sanded down to cute. Plus, the copycat factor. Looking through the high school yearbook, if you deleted the names and the extracurricular activities beneath the pictures, you might think one girl's photograph got repeated like an Escher print. You might think this was Julie Baumgarten, again and again and again.

All in one go, during the spring break of our junior year, Julie Baumgarten got a nose job, chin implant, breast implants, and her braces came off. Contact lenses replaced her tortoise-shell glasses with the google-eyed lenses, and her hair was dyed to the color of honey, or maybe that was a wig, because it was soft and glossy hair, too. That year, first period of the day, I had Twentieth-Century World History, and when some Junior Miss America contestant walked into the room, Mr. Cooper, our teacher, got a bounce in his step. "Oh," he said, "we have a new girl in class," and Julie Baumgarten said, "No. It's me. Julie Baumgarten."

It could be that if you live a lie long enough, tell it often enough, repeat it again and again, time and repetition might make it real enough. The same goes for hiding the truth. You don't forget all of what's true, but you no longer know precisely what the truth is or who you really are. I don't know why John and Thea kept such a secret for so many, many years, but surely keeping such a secret had much to do with the lonely lives they led and the absent people they became.

To walk through the forest at night has got to be the surest way to get lost, and although it was only in the metaphoric sense that Henry and I were already plenty lost, we nonetheless kept to the perimeter, to the fringes of the Bohemian Forest. The only light came from the moon and the stars, stars like Roman candles that burst and Catherine wheels frozen in place and time, as if place and time were frozen, too, as if there would not be a next day or a coming season. Sweeping across the sky that was infinity made visible, the Milky Way looked to be a path of broken glass that was mostly dust.

I felt around the forest floor for a pinecone, and when I found one, I put it in my pocket to keep, and Henry said, "Oh, my cherry."

Or maybe Henry was saying "*Ma chérie*" and it just sounded like "My cherry." Whichever, he said, "Oh, my cherry. I have compromised my life."

"Your life isn't over," I noted.

"My life isn't over," he said, as if that were a surprise, unexpected, the way Lazarus must have been surprised when he realized that he was back from the dead. Maybe Lazarus rose up and said, in that same way, just as Henry did, "My life isn't over."

"Not yet, it's not," I said. "You've still got some good years left."

"Some good years left," Henry repeated, although for us both it was a matter of emphasis, what we meant by "good." Years that would be good ones? Or simply a goodly number of them? And which is more dreadful? A long stretch of years that bring nothing remarkable? Or happy years but few in number? Then Henry asked, "What shall we do for now?"

For now.

The past is done; the future has yet to be. The present, the here and now, exists, except to exist in the present is impossible; the very split second you say "Now," now is gone for good, and yes, I am acutely aware of the existential drivel factor here, but I have no other way to explain how, on that night, we had "for now." For now, there was no past, and without the past, there was no future for us to consider, either.

There was no future for you to consider because he was a middle-aged, unemployable man married to a rich woman, and you didn't have a job either.

"For now," I said. "Let's do nothing."

Sometimes, doing nothing is the same as doing something shameful but not always, and that night we did nothing but take in the stars all the way to the event horizon, which we could not see beyond because what was there had not yet time enough to reach us.

$\mathcal{T}$he old mountain pass was as wide as wire, and it was desolate. Henry had his foot heavy on the gas pedal while I conducted the stringed instruments—the violins, the violas, the cellos—to the joyous third Brandenburg Concerto. As we neared the summit of the second Alpine ridge, a fox darted between the trees, and it began to snow. *Snow!* A summer afternoon, and it was snowing.

Henry pulled off to the side of the road, and we got out of the car and turned our faces to look at the gray sky, to watch the fat snow-flakes come down with the fury of a blizzard. A snowstorm in summer, and there we were like two little plastic figures surrounded by little plastic fir trees in a snow globe.

In the same way that it had begun to snow, without warning, it stopped, and out came the sun and *the eensy-beensy spider* the sky was blue again.

On the other side of the ridge, Henry noted that we were low on gas. Most always, Henry delayed stopping for gas, as if to wait it out might change the circumstances.

"How low is low?" I asked.

And Henry said, "Empty."

It was lucky for us that there is such a thing as Newton's laws; fueled by the gravitational force, we coasted down the mountain and into a filling station. There, I asked Henry to get me a liter of Perrier water or whatever water they had from the convenience shop.

"Sparkling?" he asked, and I said, "Sparkling," and when he got back in the car he handed me the bottle of water, a green bottle, a bar of chocolate, and a plastic snow globe. Inside was a mountain range and some fir trees, and I shook it and then held it still as I watched the fat, white flakes come down.

Henry bought me snow in July.

There's nothing out there that can't be bought with some money.

"To remember the day," Henry said, as if I would forget.

Our room at the Antiq Hotel was a Superior Double, which meant it was a suite and we had a sleigh bed, and the walls and the sheets and curtains and chairs and rugs were all shades of red wine and burnt orange. Also, there was cable TV and a minibar. The courtyard where we had breakfast featured marble statues of cherubs, each playing the violin, and after breakfast we walked to the old town center.

Ljubljana put me in mind of Florence, the way the streets were narrow and cobblestoned and lined with cafés. Old buildings buckled as if burdened by the weight of time. There was a river, too, and just like in Florence, markets stalls were set up along the banks but instead of selling tacky trinkets and knock-off Pucci scarves, these stalls were rife with fresh produce and fresh flowers and bread fresh from the baker's oven.

'Really? You could buy faux Pucci scarves in Florence? Were they nice ones?'

"Don't you think so?" I asked Henry. "That Ljubljana is a lot like Florence?"

"Yes," Henry said. "But there are no tourists here. Or art, and isn't that nice?"

It wasn't that Henry had no appreciation for art; he did appreciate art, and he even fancied himself something of an amateur artiste, with a camera. His camera was not a digital one but an old-fashioned 35-millimeter Minolta, which did require that you know something about lighting and f-stops. He took photographs, shooting exclusively in black and white, of subjects such as a close-up of a leaf, an old woman on a park bench, bales of hay, tasteful smut shots of me, but this reach for artistic expression was, as Henry was, capricious, and mostly he left his camera in the car.

What Henry didn't appreciate about art was having to stand in line to see it, and how the obligation to see it made it something like work, a job you had to go to. "And it always takes you out of your way," he said, which was funny, given how Henry did nothing *but* go out of his way, and yet out of his way from what? From where?

At the market, Henry bought blueberries that were not blueberries as we know them. These were much smaller and they stained our hands and our mouths a dark blue, and they were sweeter, too. Or maybe I just remember them that way. Sweeter.

"You know, I do love you," Henry said. "And I'm not talking casual, either."

"Casual?"

"Casual, the way people love Picasso or figs or blueberries."

"There is nothing casual about my love for these blueberries," I said, and I said no more than that because I didn't dare . . . didn't dare what?

I might like to believe that every day, every hour, every minute of every hour of every day with Henry was *not* the happiest time I ever knew. I might like to believe that I am remembering it that way only because the happiest time ever makes it a better story. Because that's all you have left after people are gone from you, some things and some stories.

But the blueberries *were* sweeter, and Henry's blue mouth kissed my blue mouth, and after that blue kiss, he said, "This would be a nice place for us to live. Don't you think? We could stay here. In exile. Like refugees."

Us? We?

"You want to run off to Ljubljana with me?" I asked, and Henry said, "Yes. I'd like to stay put here in Ljubljana with you."

Those are not the same. To run off requires action; it is to do something. To stay put is passive. Nonetheless, the way tectonic plates shift—one small step to the left and the ground shakes and then it settles—Henry and I had shifted. Just that little bit but enough to entertain maybe, just maybe.

One more blue kiss and Henry asked, "You about ready for lunch? That place across the street there looks to be worth trying."

The place across the street had deep green walls with gold-leaf trim. Henry looked over the menu and decided on the braised rabbit. With a boiled potato.

Venison and mushroom stew, a stuffed partridge, and now braised rabbit. Thumper with a boiled potato, and I asked him, "Are you aware that you've been eating your way through the cast of *Bambi*?"

"Does it offend you? I'll get something else if it offends you."

"I don't know that I am offended exactly. Perplexed, maybe."

"You don't grow tired of the vegetables?" Henry asked. "You're never tempted by a steak?"

"I get tempted," I said, "but then I think about it, and I can't go through with it."

"Ah, that's where you trip up. Thinking on things, that'll stop you every time."

I ordered grilled beets with goat cheese, and Henry, sweet Henry, he passed on the rabbit and got some kind of cassoulet. It might have had lamb in it, but I didn't want to know about that.

On our way back to the hotel to collect our luggage, we paused at a Realtor's office where, in the window, apartments for rent and houses for sale were posted in Slovenian and in English, too. "This one looks nice." Henry liked the dark wood house, more than two centuries old, but the kitchen and the three bathrooms were newly remodeled.

"What would we do with four bedrooms?" I asked, and Henry said, "Same as we'd do in one bedroom."

Four bedrooms, three bathrooms, a kitchen the size of Belgium, and Slovenia was a prosperous nation in the European Union. They weren't giving houses away. I did calculations in my head: sell my apartment in New York, and how long might that money last us in Slovenia? Or Bohemia? Or Tuscany? Two years? Maybe three. And then what? How would we live? Were jobs teaching English really to be had, or was teaching English like being a scribe or a taxi dancer, a career from an earlier era?

There is money to be made in dancing, Sylvia. You thought I was crazy saying so, but for some people, it was true.'

"Do people give English lessons much anymore?" I asked Henry. "As a way to make a living?"

"I wouldn't rightly know," he said.

"Let me ask you something. What do you do there with yourself? In Paris. How do you fill the days and nights?"

"With an active social life."

"You have lots of French friends, do you?"

"No. Just a few French friends. Mostly English friends who live in Paris, and some American friends, too."

"Your own kind."

"I suppose so."

"I'm not one of your kind, am I?"

"No," Henry said. "You're not one of our kind. You're better than that."

To which I said, "No. No, Henry. I'm not that, either."

Because shampoo turned out not to be the craze of its day but more like bread or shoes, a product in for the long haul, had my great-grandfather not sold the patent for his gentle liquid soap, I'd have been the Doris Duke of shampoo. A woman with bundles of money—money to buy that house in Ljubljana or a cottage in the Bohemian Forest or a little apartment on a narrow side street in Florence or Prague, with enough left over for blueberries at the market, and a nice bottle of wine to have with dinner because Henry did care about that, he cared that the wine be nice.

'And who says you can't buy love?'

Rich. One more thing to add to the list of things *our kind* I never much wanted to be. In some circles and circumstances it is admirable, the choice not to pursue wealth, although those were not my circumstances, so it's not like I'm going to congratulate myself for it.

With Ljubljana behind us, I unfolded the map, looking for a direction for us to take.

Except There Was This: Holding a lock of my hair in one hand and scissors in the other, Denis—one *n*—said, "If they were all like you, Sylvia, I wouldn't go home with a headache. You, you read your magazine, and I can focus on my work. The rest of them, yap, yap, yap." Denis snipped, snipped, snipped the air with his scissors, lending embodiment to the "yap, yap, yap," as if the scissors were a puppet talking.

Flipping through the pages of *Vogue* or *InStyle*: Lancôme eyeshadow. Mascara by Clinique. A four-page Ralph Lauren spread, as if anyone looks good in jodhpurs. Factoidal fluff—90 percent of Americans wash their hair every day—hardly something you *need* know, but I didn't mind knowing it, so I read on: John Breck developed and introduced the first liquid shampoo in the United States.

John Breck?

It does happen, and not as infrequently as we might think, that the same invention is twice realized at the very same time. Identical, or nearly identical, discoveries made more or less simultaneously, each unbeknown to the other until one of the discoverers cries, "Fraud! Theft!" Consider the radio. Edison? Marconi? Tesla? It's still up for grabs as to who got there first. Isaac Newton and Gottfried Leibniz, they went at each other like a pair of girls fighting dirty—hair-pulling, shin-kicking fights over which one of them discovered the calculus. Mathematical historians give Newton the credit, but they concede that Leibniz's discovery was an independent one, and he *did* publish it before Newton, so the way I'd call it, Leibniz got screwed. And my great-grandfather, was he the Leibniz of shampoo? Always I believed that shampoo was my great-grandfather's invention, but there it was: John Breck developed and introduced the first liquid soap in the United States.

The power of mind can compensate for loss. We can experience pain in a leg that has been amputated; we can rationalize the death of boys in battle as noble; we can forget what we lost. Or we can do as I did and put faith in semantics: my great-grandfather *invented* shampoo, sold the patent to John Breck, and John Breck *developed and introduced* shampoo into the marketplace. That was plausible. Developed, meaning "new and improved." I could believe it, and where was the harm in that?

'There was no harm, but there was no house to be had from it, either.'

"Have you ever considered a more modest life?" I asked Henry.

"Define *modest*," he said.

"Oh, I don't know. A house with one bedroom instead of four?"

The mind can compensate for loss.

'But not always.'

Ruby pursued money, doggedly chased after money, as if money were a hat carried off in the wind, and you could think she was equally determined not to catch any. As if an infusion of cash were a slightly fucked-up version of Next Year in Jerusalem, as if it were the *idea* of coming into a chunk of money that kept Ruby going, the *idea* that if she could get her hands on more money than she earned, then the Rapture would come. "Ten thousand dollars," she would say, "and everything would be perfect." Other times, fifty thousand would do the trick. Or twenty-five. Or seventeen. The amount was irrelevant because even if she did come into an extra ten thousand dollars or ten-hundred-zillion-thousand dollars, Ruby would spend herself into debt, and her mother would bail her out of debt because that's the way they did things.

About that, about her mother bailing her out of debt, each round, Ruby would say to me, "I know this is going to cost me a pound of my flesh, but I don't see as how I have a choice." That's what Ruby said, but I didn't pass along that part of the story to Henry. I did tell him that Ruby was a woman of many abilities but that she did not have good entrepreneurial skills. "Not everyone has a talent for making money," I said.

"Spending it, though," Henry noted, "that's something we all can do, although some of us do it better than others."

"Define better," I said.

A head for business is a gift, like a gift for playing the piano or knowing how to pick out a ripe melon.

A Horatio Alger Story, Sort Of: When he was a very young man, but the eldest of six children or seven of them, my father's father left home, which was someplace like Fiddler-on-the-Roofville, Poland, with a handful of zlotys in his pocket, and all alone he set sail for America on a ship where he bunked with the goats and a cow.

On his first day in New York City, America, or maybe even his first hour, my grandfather got himself a pushcart, which he loaded up with fruit and vegetables, his stock-in-trade, and in almost no time at all he'd saved enough money to secure passage to New York for the next of his brothers.

Max, too, came through Ellis Island, and my grandfather got him a pushcart, and with the two of them selling fruit and vegetables, they put their money together, and twice as fast, the third brother made the crossing, and such is the way dynasties are built. Three brothers and three pushcarts and in the blink of an eye, their mother and their youngest brother joined them in America. The two or three sisters stayed in Poland, having married local boys, none of whom had much get-up-and-go, which turned out to be a worse thing than they could have imagined.

The youngest brother, they also got him a pushcart, but at the end of the day, he had sold not so much as a banana. His brothers gave him tips. "You have to call out," Max said.

"Offer a bargain," Jacob told him. "Two for the price of one and a half."

"Flirt with the women," my grandfather suggested. "Especially the fat ones."

"The very skinny ones, too," Jacob added.

Again, the next day, the youngest brother went off with his pushcart, calling out, offering bargains, flirting with fat women with moles on their faces and with skinny women with no curves at all, and still, he sold nothing. Five days went by like this, and the three older brothers conferred and concluded: the youngest brother did not have good entrepreneurial skills; maybe he was a scholar, and they sent him off to school, where he studied optometry. He got married, and he and his wife moved into a spacious apartment because they wanted to make a family. For a long time, she could not get pregnant, but then she did and they danced for joy, right up until the moment when one of her fallopian tubes exploded and she died. Then he became quiet and kept mostly to himself.

Of the brothers, only Jacob lived long enough for me to have met him. What I remember of him best was his wife, Leah, who had two gold teeth that I thought to be elegant; an opinion that, when articulated, caused my mother to convulse with laughter, but then she quit laughing to let me know this was serious. "Only peasants have gold teeth," she said.

There are no photographs, or none that I ever saw, of this grandfather as a young man, but I do have one of his wife, my father's mother, when she was a young woman—a girl, really. In this photograph, the children stood in a row; the mother and the stepfather were seated on either end, as if all together they were an accordion. My grandmother, the only daughter and the eldest child, she looked more Romany than Eastern European. Thick black hair, marcelled into waves, framed a full face. Eyes dark and as deep as the unknown, and a mouth like a plum. She resembled her own mother, although her mother did not exude the same steamy quality. Her mother's strength was harnessed into the personage of her bosom and the set of her jaw, definitely not a woman to fool with. Her mother's husband, a second husband and not the father of any of the five children, had a full beard, and his skullcap, shaped like a pillbox hat, topped off a pair of ears, each like the handle of a teapot. Seated in the chair, his black coat reached to his feet, but his feet did not reach the floor. He was that short, a pipsqueak, and by all appearances, he was something of a *schmendrick* too, but a woman with five children couldn't be picky when it came to getting herself a second husband. The two boys in the middle looked to be twins, and the youngest boy was clutching a violin. The eldest boy, not much younger than his smoldering sister, was wearing a Western-style suit. Not Western European but Western style as in the American West, which was not exactly a cowboy outfit but something like Wyatt Earp or Maverick might have worn, a fitted suit with sharp lapels and a bolo tie. This family looked like a circus act, the Tumbling Kapinskys or the Flame-Eating Lefkowitzes, and my grandmother, she could have been the one who read palms and tea leaves.

Shortly after this photograph was taken, my grandmother and her brother, the one in the Doc Holliday costume, came to America. The brother went all the way to California, where he worked in Hollywood as a film editor. The rest of them, I assume, came to the sad end that was Auschwitz, and for their sake I hope those boys were not twins but just two brothers who looked a lot alike.

My father's parents met at a Settlement House mixer, which was like a sock hop for immigrants. They married and from the bounty that was the Promised Land, there came that old story, not a myth of the gods, but a folksier tale. From a pocketful of seeds grew a store of his own, a green grocery on 171st Street. My grandfather's shop was renowned for having the juiciest oranges, the sweetest beets, and fresh, always fresh. Less grandiose than Horatio Alger and his rags-to-riches yarn, my grandfather lived the smaller and truer dream: from tenement to middle class, which was how my father, the last of four children, came to grow up on the Grand Concourse, the Champs-Elysées of the Bronx, instead of in a shit hole on Ludlow Street.

La-di-da bourgeois, and such a palace paid for with money made from selling apples and horseradish root. Wasn't America something?

And wasn't it progress, too, that this grandfather of mine, who made his place in the world from selling fresh fruit and vegetables, should come to have grandchildren who were raised on perfectly cubed carrots from a can, Dole's fruit cocktail, and potatoes factory-cut, pre-crinkled, and ready for frying? Although familiar with the figure of speech "as alike as two peas in a pod," it wasn't until after I'd left home that I encountered a pod or the bright green peas contained therein. Canned peas are a drab olive green. My first brush with brussels sprouts on the stalk, as I had no reference point for such a thing, resulted in my assumption that it was an exotic flower, like a bird of paradise.

Without much to recommend it except for a big lake and the Alps, this resort town in Austria, Klagenfurt, was no place to live, but it was a perfectly good place *as good as any* to have dinner, to spend a night or two. The restaurant we went to specialized in fish, and the tables were set up lakeside.

Here was a part of the world where, during summer, nightfall came late, almost like midnight sun, the way it was after nine in the evening and the sunset was mirrored on the snow-capped mountains above the tree line, turning the slate to a deep mournful purple. The reflection of the Alps shimmered on the surface of the dark of the water. We took a table in the garden shaded by foliage from an old linden tree, and smack dab in the middle of this paint-by-numbers setting was a bathtub-size fish tank set on a wrought-iron stand, and it was filled with carp.

"My brother once put a fish in my shoe," I told Henry. "Which might be the biggest adventure Joel ever had for himself."

"What kind of a fish?" Henry studied the wine list.

"A guppy," I said.

"That's about right."

"Right for what?"

Henry looked up and, as if stating the obvious, said, "Right for the sort of thing a boy would do to a girl."

"Did you do things like that to girls?" I asked.

"No. But the other boys did."

A guppy that might or might not have been dead already, but for sure it was dead after its insides, fish guts, oozed between my toes. It took years to get me to swim in a lake or a pond for fear of fish-to-body contact; but I don't eat fish for the same reason I don't eat meat.

Henry ordered a trout, and it came whole on the plate. The whole fish. Head and tail and fins. The skeleton was intact, and the skin, too. I don't know how Henry or anyone else could eat something while it's smiling at you.

After dinner, we walked back to our hotel which was on the corner of the evocatively named streets: 8.-Mai and 10.-Oktober, the latter commemorating a post–World War I referendum whereby the people of Carinthia voted to remain part of Austria rather than attach themselves to Slovenia.

-

'There was a mistake. They should have gone with Door Number Two.'

The Eighth of May Street honored—no joke but a magnificent display of a collective whitewashing—the Allied victory in Europe. Quick as it took to get out the ladder, down came the sign for Hitler Street and up went Hooray for Allied Victory Road. It took nerve to pull off a revision such as that one.

In the elevator going up to our room, Henry and I weren't revising history so much as we were reclaiming it, carrying on like teenagers—sixteen, but without the anguish or the acne—the way we were making out, as if we had no self-control and no place private to go. By the time we got to the sixth floor, to our door, my blouse was more off than on, and Henry's jeans were unzipped, so it made perfect sense how at first I thought it was us, our doing, the way the sky lit up.

A flash of yellow light, and then the storm took on a zealotic intensity. Fusillades of thunder heralded great cracks and booms. Lightning, forked and flicked like serpents' tongues, broke apart the night, and the sky went incandescent white, as if bombs were bursting and the ground were exploding and soldiers on the battlefield would be praying. I held on to Henry as if he and I were huddled in the trenches. We waited. And then, as these things—storms and battles—are wont to do, it went quiet. Quiet, as if we would venture out to find the landscape littered with the dead and the wounded and the shell-shocked made mute.

. . .

Electroconvulsive therapy, the scientifically and politically correct terminology these days for shock treatment, tends to get lumped together with the lobotomy as a cure more insane than the disease. It's true about lobotomies. Drilling a hole in a person's head to release the voices or the sadness bottled up, you know that's got to have a high rate of failure and worse. Shock treatment, though, that can do the trick. Well enough, which I knew because of my mother's aunt Hannah.

It was something to see, Hannah with her elbows bent at her sides, her fists clenched, as she walked, round and round, from our living room to the kitchen and then on through the dining room, a route that was more of an oval than a circle, but that's a detail not particularly germane to the story. What matters is that she was walking like that, fast and determined and going nowhere. Whatever it was that had, all these years, kept Hannah together was now unraveling like a bandage.

Each time Hannah whipped like a sharp wind through the kitchen, my mother begged, "Stop. Sit for a minute. Please."

My father was at work. Joel wasn't at home, either. Hannah's drunk husband was passed out on the couch in the family room downstairs, while my mother and I watched Hannah crack like a fried marble. Something with which I was familiar, fried marbles and how they cracked, because at that time I belonged to the Craft-of-the-Month Club, and marbles, fried until they cracked from the inside—which was how Hannah cracked, too, from the inside—red marbles, cracked and set in brass findings to create a beautiful necklace, had been the craft of the previous September.

My mother called for an ambulance.

Maybe it was the same night the men took Hannah away in an ambulance, or maybe it was another night soon thereafter, that I heard the words manic-depressive and electroshock and I thought they were saying *maniac*-depressive, and I pictured electroshock to be like a scene from *Frankenstein*, the movie. I pictured a laboratory in the cellar of a Gothic castle, Aunt Hannah strapped to a gurney, a crisscross of wires attached to electrodes that looked like suction cups stuck to her head. A maniac scientist with wild hair and eyes that spun pulled the lever, while his assistant, who had an onion-shaped head, danced like a crazed marionette. A bolt of lightning flashed in the sky and tributaries of electricity cracked and snapped and Aunt Hannah jolted upright.

The imagination of a child might not have been entirely off the mark.

The First Dr. Frankenstein: It was, as the story begins, a dark and stormy night, in the year 1786. Luigi Galvani, a great man of science, was in his laboratory in Bologna, where he was dissecting a frog. At the exact moment that his scissors inadvertently touched a nerve in the frog's spine, a bolt of lightning flashed and the very dead frog kicked, *boing!* as if it were bounding from a lily pad into the pond for a swim, as if it were alive. Alive! Now there was a temptation from which a madman could make some hay, but Professor Galvani was not a madman. Instead of racing to resurrect the dead, Luigi Galvani went on to study and to document the electrical nature of the nerve-muscle function. With the help of his assistant, Giovanni Aldini, who was also his nephew, because nepotism is nothing new, Galvani pioneered the nascent field of electrophysiology.

This nephew, this assistant, was not a hunchbacked fly eater, but he was not the modest man his uncle was either, and Giovanni Aldini took the show on the road, and what a show it was! All over Europe he toured, and huge crowds gathered to witness the electrifying of the dead, to watch as eyelids snapped open like window shades, as mouths twitched and chins quivered as if detached heads were trying not to cry.

George Foster, a convicted murderer who, as sentenced, had been hung by his neck until dead, presented the most dramatic of these extravaganzas, well worth the price of admission. With a pair of conducting rods linked to a battery, Aldini touched strategic parts of the corpse. George Foster winked at the audience; his nose wiggled as if he were about to sneeze; his hand clenched into a fist and the fist shot up into the air—Yes!—as if George's team had just scored a goal. When the conducting rods moved to George's nether regions, his entire body convulsed, and it sure did look as if he'd been reanimated, just like Frankenstein's monster, as if he were going to jump from the table and make a run for it, and who would not have done the same if an electric prod was nosing around his genitalia?

Although this theory was later proved incorrect, Giovanni Aldini was sure that electrical impulses would have no effect on the heart, but he was among the first of the experimental scientists to use electricity to treat melancholia. The idea being this: a shock to the brain would induce seizures, and the resultant spasms would shake off the blues, much the way a dog shakes off water after a swim. Twice Aldini had success with this experiment, inadvertent success, because the thesis was wrong. Early into the twentieth century inducing seizures was again tried as a treatment for mental illness. During World War I, they gave it a serious go, prompting seizures in soldiers who were suffering from emotional breakdowns, although these seizures were provoked not by electrical current but as the result of deliberate infections of malaria or the byproduct of insulin injections. They did, during the Great War, sometimes use electricity as a cure for shell shock, but those jolts of electricity were not routed through the brain. Rather, the current was applied directly to the area of the body where the shell shock was manifest. For example, if a man were rendered mute from the horrors of war, his larynx or his tongue would receive the electrical shocks. Mostly this wasn't effective at all. Another remedy at that time for shell shock was to execute the poor, broken fuckers on the charge and conviction of cowardice. Three hundred and forty-six British soldiers were shot because they shook uncontrollably or because they went mute or they couldn't stop crying.

During a time between the two world wars, another Italian scientist, Ugo Cerletti, observed pigs being anaesthetized with electricity on their way to slaughter, which gave him an idea. It took ten sessions of administering brutal shocks to the agitated and delusional man, but by Jove! Cerletti got it. The schizophrenic schnook became normal. Or at least he was quiet.

Seven years prior to Cerletti's discovery, Clara Bow, already a big movie star, became known as the *It* Girl, the consequent of the eponymously titled film—*It* being the magnetic force of sex appeal—but soon thereafter her career was over. Blame it on the talkies, although the talkies weren't to blame. Clara was the problem. Crisis-a-Day Clara, she was a nutcase, and although she did eventually receive electroshock therapy, who knows what, if any, good it did. In 1965 Clara Bow died alone.

It was a tribute to modern, or rather not quite modern, medicine the way Aunt Hannah defied the Humpty-Dumpty rule. Broken but put back together again. No more walking in circles, she now walked only to get from here to there, a deliberate destination. Lucid, and able to carry on a conversation, Hannah was her old self again. Which was never much of a big personality, but she was the same. Except for the memory loss. Which was insignificant, the proportion of things erased to those remembered, and it was to be expected as a side effect to sizzling a piece of her brain, that she would forget something. A small price to pay for sanity, and Hannah was no longer crazy. Or at least she was no longer crazy until the next time she snapped like a dried twig, but by then I was older, out of the house more, and not especially interested in batty Aunt Hannah or her drunk child-molesting husband.

What Aunt Hannah forgot was her field of study.

After her electroconvulsive therapy, Aunt Hannah could recall most everything. Names. Dates. Places. Her childhood. All there. As surely as if it were last week, she remembered going off to college, the friends she made there, the class she took in American history. Ask her who was the twenty-third president of the United States and, without missing a beat, she'd tell you, "Benjamin Harrison, who was the grandson of William Henry Harrison, our ninth president, who died after only one month in office," but pose the question, Is a subordinating conjunction set off with a comma? and she'd look at you as if you were speaking Friulian. What she knew best, that was gone.

The other thing Hannah could not remember for the life of her, no more than she could remember what to do with an em dash or a semicolon, was this: Was there ever a time when she loved Nathan? "Did I ever love him?" she asked my mother, who did not know the answer or how to answer. If Hannah did once love Nathan, she forgot, but maybe that had nothing to do with the electroconvulsive therapy and everything to do with wanting, needing, to forget.

Henry wanted to again eat a fish, which was why on our second and last night in Klagenfurt we returned to the fish restaurant on the lake. We took the same table as we had the night before, and again Henry ordered the trout, and again I got dumplings. The sun was setting and the mountains were reflected on the water and the water reflected on the mountains; everything was the same except the fish tank. On this night there were no fish in it. My question—Where are the carp?—although unuttered must have been written across my face because the waiter told me, "The tank was hit by electricity. From the storm. It killed all the fish." He snapped his fingers to demonstrate an instant; an instant was all it took. Snap, *Crackle, Pop* like that. Gone.

Wiped out, wiped away, deleted.

That's how it was with my father's memories, too. Wiped out, but in his case, there was no electricity involved, not before or after.

In his case, it was an accident.

"We're at the hospital," Joyce called to tell me. "Your father had an accident and now something is seriously wrong with his brain. They don't know what exactly, but whatever it is, it's not good." Joyce was not one to sugarcoat, I'll say that for her. "They've got all kinds of specialists here looking at him because his brain is very messed up."

Most accidents happen at home, and that's where my father and Joyce were, at home, having just returned from a vacation, a fun-filled Caribbean cruise. Joyce said she and my father had had a ball. "A ball, I'm telling you."

Water sliding on deck, luaus in the tiki room, karaoke in the lounge, all-you-can-eat buffets, disco dancing, and every which way you turn, new friends are to be made. I know there are worse ways to spend your leisure time, but I can't come up with one. "Two days," I said to Henry, "Two days before I'd throw myself overboard. What about you? How long do you think you'd last?"

'Seems to me, the both of you were already sunk.'

"I couldn't rightly say. I could see having myself a fine time." A leaf fell from a linden tree, and Henry picked it up from the table and gave it to me. "A real fine time," he said, "right up until the very end."

I closed my hand around the leaf.

Back home, at the Palm Oasis, Joyce and my father unpacked their luggage, and my father went to take the suitcases to the basement, to the storage area. "Why he took the stairs instead of the elevator, I have no idea," Joyce said. "Who takes the stairs?"

Henry and I again took the elevator to our room, again smooching our way up, and everything was the same as the night before, as if moment by moment were the same thing as word for word, and all we had to do was memorize it. As if by memorizing it backwards and forwards, memorizing it by heart, we could have it all over again. And everything was the same as the night before, except on this night, the sky was quiet.

Maybe my father tripped or maybe *vertigo* he had a seizure or maybe it was sea legs, but whatever set him in motion, down he went, headfirst. It was a long flight of stairs, made of concrete, and Joyce said, "I suppose we can thank God he didn't break his hip. A broken hip is a death sentence. At our age, it's like glass, the hip." The hip, I was to understand, could shatter *into countless pieces* the way a mirror shatters. "You probably should come down here," Joyce said. "Not that you'll be of any help, but still. He is your father."

The JetBlue flight to Fort Lauderdale was a story unto itself.

At the hospital, I was directed to the ninth floor. Neurology. The nurse on desk duty had a girlish figure but was of indeterminate age because the Florida sun had turned her skin iguana-like. Dry as sand and patchy, and I had to wonder how someone in the medical profession didn't know to wear sunscreen, but the world is riddled with mysteries.

"I'm here to see my father," I said. "Arnie Landsman."

"Oh." The nurse elongated the word *Oh*, as if I were there to see someone important. "Dr. Reynolds wants to speak with you before you go in. Your mother's there now. With your father."

"Not likely. My mother is dead," I explained.

"Sorry. Your stepmom. His wife. She's with him. Don't worry. He's very cheerful," she said, and this she said in such a way that I knew she considered cheerful to be a really good thing to be, like normal. Which was why I didn't say anything about how Joyce was not my father's wife lest I seem not cheerful, and I took a seat on a yellow vinyl chair.

What Happened on JetBlue: I was boxed in next to a frizzy-haired woman, frizzy hair going gray that grew in thickets, like shrubbery in need of pruning, and she was wearing yoga pants, which is the same as going out in your pajamas. On her lap, in lieu of a purse, was a National Public Radio tote bag.

"Business or pleasure?" she asked me.

"Pleasure." I opened my book.

"Me, too. Mostly. My mother's there. In a retirement community."

On a plane we are defenseless against the desperately friendly, the annoying, the needy, and the vaguely creepy-possessive, which is why I should've had the foresight to request an aisle seat. Escape by way of frequent trips to the bathroom. Instead, I had the window seat, and I looked out as the plane taxied the runway, while she went on and on about some shoe store in West Palm Beach. She wasn't an old woman, but she was someone not terrified of becoming an old woman.

"The last time I was there," she was still with the shoe store, "I got these." She lifted her leg, no simple matter in coach, to show me her shoes, which I fully expected to be health-food shoes, mushroom colored and made of tree bark, but they were a snappy apple-green velvet with a kitten heel, and quite something. Because she was going to talk on no matter what, and because I might have liked a pair of apple-green velvet shoes for myself, I went ahead and asked for the name of the shop, which I wrote down on the inside flap of my book, and busy with that, I didn't catch the transition from shoes to swap meets, but there we were. "Most every weekend," she said. "Swap meets. Flea markets." Saturdays and Sundays she spent rummaging through other people's garbage, fishing through flotsam, picking over the remains of the dead in search of photographs of basset hounds. Photographs of basset hounds. "It's like panning for gold," she told me. "I rarely find one, but while looking, you would not believe some of the things I've turned up." She opened a Ziploc bag and offered me some trail mix.

"No, thank you." I turned back to my book.

"Last summer, at the flea market in Chagrin Falls, that's in Ohio, near Cleveland, and twice a year," she went on, because why stop when you've got yourself a captive audience, "they have a big weekend-long flea market—not as big as the one in Brimfield, in Massachusetts, but this one in Chagrin Falls is pretty big." She was from Fort Lee, in New Jersey, not Ohio, but to find what you are looking for often means leaving home. At the Chagrin Falls flea market, going through a bin of ephemera—postcards, recipe cards, road maps, brochures—she came across a packet of letters tied together with yarn. "Not a ribbon. Red yarn," she said. "Like for knitting. The paper was a pale lavender, the same stationery I had back when I was in college. Funny how you just remember those things."

It wasn't only the color of the stationery that was familiar. The handwriting, she'd have known it anywhere because it was her own, and these letters were letters she'd written to another college girl, one she'd met during the summer at a Leadership Retreat with the Campfire Girls. These were not any old letters, and the girl to whom she had written them was not just any girl.

The girl saved them, these letters written to her on pale lavender stationery. She did not read each one as it came only to throw it away. They'd meant enough for her to keep them until they accumulated, until there was a packet of them, but then why not keep them for always?

Maybe ambivalence leaned left before tipping to the right? A retreat with the Campfire Girls wasn't exactly Bloomsbury or Jell-O Shot Night at the Cubby Hole, and perhaps she went on to get married and have children, and these letters, maybe keeping them made her uncomfortable. Or maybe being a wife and a mother, maybe that was what made her uncomfortable, like a skirt too tight at the waist. Unlike the discomfort of keeping the letters, which was more like being queasy, tingly but not only in the stomach. Because it felt nice, that kind of tingle, she kept those letters although she never answered them, and eventually they stopped coming. She kept them, and every now and again, while her husband was at work and the children were at school, *a longing that comes upon you* she would stop whatever it was she was doing—ironing shirts or defrosting the freezer—and she would go to her closet. On the topmost shelf, under some old sweaters she never wore, was the cookie tin where she kept the letters hidden away. Sitting on the edge of her bed, she'd untie the knot in the red yarn, and she would reread the letters, all of them. Then a day came when she took down the cookie tin but did not read the letters inside. Instead, she put the whole kit and caboodle in the trash can out in front of the house, and pickup was the next day. But there are people who go through garbage cans *one man's trash is another man's treasure* and someone might've taken the cookie tin to sell at a swap meet, tossing the letters into a box of ephemera because you never know what people will buy, and maybe there was some value to these letters because why else had they been saved? And in that nice cookie tin, to boot.

Or maybe she died, this girl. Cancer or an accident, and the things that outlive you, who knows what happens to your things then, after you are gone?

All these things we treasure, where do they go? The things handed down to me, the things I keep so I won't forget, those things might very well wind up at a swap meet. It could happen that someday a woman wearing khaki shorts and pom-pom socks will haggle over the cowrie shell that had been my grandmother's, and maybe a gay couple, knowing a good piece when they see one, will snap up the cranberry glass vase, and all the threads connecting these things to me will be cut. Snip, snip *Let go* and there will be no way to remember me at all.

"So I bought them," the woman on the plane told me. "The letters. For fifty cents."

What I was unable to determine was this: Did she think fifty cents was too much to pay for a bunch of old letters? Or was it a steal? Two quarters to buy back a piece of your past? Nor did I ask, although I wanted to, if she reads them now and again. Does she, from time to time, untie the yarn, and if and when she reads them, does the love come rushing back in a gust of wind that knocks her off her feet? Or is it more like a dizzy spell?

Dr. Reynolds looked like a man who chews on his cigar instead of smoking it; someone you might see ringside at the fights. Short and round, and there was something scrappy to his walk. He took the chair next to mine, an orange chair. This hospital had the color scheme of a Tequila Sunrise. "It's not all bad news," he said. "There was significant damage done to sizable sectors of his frontal and right temporal lobes, but his motor skills are unaffected. He can walk, talk, feed himself, go to the bathroom, but his declarative memory, the past, his personal past has been eradicated. He remembers nothing from before the accident."

"Nothing? Nothing at all?"

"Nothing of his own life, but there is some recall of the historical past. And some things that have occurred post the accident. Not everything, but a lot, and that's encouraging."

"Is this temporary?" I asked. "Will his past come back?" Which was a ridiculous question. The laws of physics are firm; the past is past *if only* and it stays that way, which is how we wind up being sorry.

"The truth is, in cases like this, we really don't know," Dr. Reynolds said.

"Can we do anything to help?"

"Try telling him stories," Dr. Reynolds suggested. "Stories about himself, about his life. He'll follow what you are saying, the same as if you were telling him a story about someone else, but sometimes a detail from a narrative can ignite a spark." The narrative form, according to this neurologist and people in other professions, too, engages us in ways that a recitation of names and dates and places does not. "Don't get your hopes up, but it's worth a shot." Dr. Reynolds placed a hand on my shoulder, gave it a light squeeze as if to wish me *bonne chance, mon ami* luck on a mission.

I liked him, this Dr. Reynolds, this man of science who had faith in the power of the story.

My father's room was at the far end of the corridor, and I

was almost there when Joyce stepped into the hallway. Maybe for a respite or maybe she was keeping a lookout for me, but whichever, there she was, resplendent in a pale blue track suit that she wore with a white silk blouse, as if a track suit were a regular suit. "It's not so horrible as we thought," she said. "He's not brain-dead, and he's not at all retarded, but he won't recognize you. Be prepared. He's a little weird."

When wearing nothing but a hospital gown, even the strong seem frail. Maybe it's the vulnerability of the open back, and there was a patch of gray stubble on my father's chin, evidence of a half-assed shave. A gauze bandage was wrapped around his head.

I parked my suitcase in a corner, and Joyce went and sat on the edge of the bed, just as my father had when my mother was dying, which was a seat both protective and proprietary. She gestured toward me, and she asked my father, "Do you know who this is?"

"A pretty girl," he said, and he seemed pleased enough with that, but Joyce said, "No. No, she's not a pretty girl." Which was kind of funny once you got yourself a sense of humor about Joyce. "This is your daughter. Remember? Remember, I told you before. You have a daughter. Sylvia."

"It's good to meet you, Sylvia," my father said, as if I were a total stranger. Which as far as he was concerned, as far as he now knew, I was; and try as you might, you can't muster up love for someone when you have no recollection of who that person is or of the time you spent together. I found myself wishing I'd brought a basket of fruit or a plant, something to hide behind.

I took a seat in the chair near him, but not near enough to touch—a precaution against the urge to rap him on the head with my knuckles, my ear cocked for the hollow thud. Which wasn't a real urge, but I pretended it was, the pretense easier than the truth: distance between us spared me from any awkward demonstration of affection. We were too far apart for either of us to attempt a hug.

A person without a past might be expected to suffer from identity crisis, be disturbed or depressed or in a highly agitated state, but my father wore a smile serene and sweet, as if to remember nothing is its own enlightenment. The sunny disposition made sense, too. When there's no baggage weighing you down, you can float light and happy.

I smiled back at him and we did that—smiled at each other the way people do when they don't speak the same language—because what do you say, what kind of conversation do you have with a person who is now more like Pinocchio or Frosty the Snowman "who came to life one day," than the man you knew as your father?

"So," I said. *You begin* "So, you were born in the Bronx. You had two older sisters and one brother. He moved to New Zealand." I sounded as if I were reading to a child from a picture book, the way people do in those Miss Jane voices, as if children are morons. "Your father owned a fruit and vegetable store."

"Yes," my father broke in, impatient. "Joyce already told me."

Reflexively, I turned to Joyce, who said to me, "You forget? . I've known him forever."

The Scenic Route
239

Joyce *I cannot stomach* was of his earliest memories back when, and here she is central to the new memories forming. Joyce then. Joyce now.

"Fast-forward," I said. "Back from Germany, where you were stationed during the Korean War, you went to a party and there you met the most beautiful girl you'd ever seen. Do you remember her?"

"Why was I in Germany during the Korean War?" my father asked, and Joyce announced that she was hungry. "I'm going to get something to eat," she said. "Does anyone want something from the cafeteria?"

My father laughed and said, "I don't suppose you can get a good pastrami sandwich there?"

All indication was that he had no recollection of his wife of thirty-five years, but pastrami, that he remembered.

"You were stationed in Germany as part of the occupying forces," I told him; I told him the same story that he had once, long ago, told me. "You were a supply sergeant, which gave you free access to chocolate bars and nylon stockings and lots of girlfriends. Does that ring a bell?"

"No," he said.

"This beautiful girl, from the party, my mother, you walked her home, and at her doorstep, you kissed her good night, but instead of asking for her phone number or if she was free next Saturday, you asked her to marry you."

"Really? I did that? That sounds like something from a movie."

I made a mental note, for later, to tell the doctor: pastrami and movies; that it seemed as if he remembered having had experience with both, that had to be indicative of something.

"Yes, it was like from a movie. You loved her very much," I said. "And she loved you very much. You two were really crazy about each other. Always."

My parents did love each other with an ardor and passion you don't expect to find in a house in Westchester County where there also dwelled two children and, for a time, a dog, but they did. All those years, they shared pleasures and disappointments and secrets, and they were affectionate in public and amorous at home. There was never a cross word between them.

My parents never so much as argued.

Except.

Except once. I woke to voices harsh and loud. The padding on the soles of my footie pajamas were like a cat's paws on the thick carpet, and I made no sound as I walked to the landing, where I sat on the top step, like it was a balcony seat to the living room. Footie pajamas. Dr. Denton's footie pajamas. Yellow, and maybe they came in blue, too, and I slept in them until I neared puberty, although I have no explanation as to why I was such a fan of what amounted to swaddling. My parents were wearing the same clothes they'd had on when I went to sleep, so it probably wasn't all that late. My father was no longer shouting, but it was worse than shouting, the way it seemed he was trying to contain the anger. My mother stood there shaking her head as if she had water in her ear, like I sometimes got after swimming, but then she shouted, "It's over. It's over," and she sat down in the blue armchair. She covered her face with her hands, and I watched the way she rocked herself to and fro, the same way she rocked me when I needed comfort. I don't know for how long I sat there watching all this, but well into it, my father saw me. "Sylvia," he said. Not to me. He wasn't talking to me. He was telling my mother that I was there. She looked up and she said, "Sylvia, go back to sleep. Your father and I had a disagreement. It's nothing. It's over. Go to bed."

And it was over. Forgotten, that fight they had. I forgot about it and it seemed they forgot about it, too, because the next day they were happily married again and in love, as always.

Soon after I got married to Vincent, my mother and I met for lunch, and she had some advice to give me. One married woman to another, she said, "Even the best marriages have their ups and downs. Even the best marriages can feel tired, but be patient. It passes," and only then did I remember that night when they shouted hurtful words at each other, and how my mother had shouted, "It's over," and then I understood. My mother, she'd been having an affair. It was the affair that was over. Not the marriage. Not the fight. The affair. Or maybe I'd always known about it, the way we know all family secrets—who pops pills like they are M&M's, who cheats on their taxes, which of them gave birth five months after the wedding—we know these things without explicitly being told; we know, and so I knew that there was a time when something came over my mother and it settled like fog, but heavier and bleaker than fog, and she wanted, needed, a way out from under it. And then whatever it was—boredom, despondency, desperation—it passed, and it was over.

This was not one of the stories I told my father on that afternoon when I told him story after story, not to save my own life but in an effort to resurrect, to breathe life into, what had been his.

When Vincent called to ask me about making our divorce official because he wanted to marry someone else, I said, "Sure. Of course. No problem," and I probably said something about being happy for him, because I was happy for him, although to be happy for someone else doesn't mean that you are happy for yourself.

"It's just a matter of signing the papers," he said.

"Yeah. I know. That's good. That's fine."

"How's Friday for you? I can come by after work."

"This Friday? You mean this Friday coming?"

"Yes. This Friday. Is that okay?" he asked, and I hesitated for no reason other than it was soon; this Friday was only three days away, although I could not say what difference that made.

"Sure. Friday is good. Around six?"

As I knew he would be, Vincent was punctual because he was that way, a reliable person. We kissed hello, a peck on the mouth, quick and dry like chickens pecking at the dirt.

"You look well." Vincent put a manila folder on the coffee table, what was once *our* coffee table; a manila folder that I assumed held the papers I would sign to make it official, the end of the marriage.

"You, too," I said. "You look good," and I opened up a bottle of wine, and we sat on the couch that was once *our* couch, al-

The Scenic Route

243

though I'd had it reupholstered in a bottle-green and teal-blue tapestry, so he might not have recognized it as ours. We drank some and we talked some and the sun was going down and the light had shifted so that we were mostly in shadow now.

Vincent looked at his watch and said, "I probably should be going."

I got a pen and I signed the papers, and I handed them to Vincent and he got up to leave, and when he got to the door, I said, "Vincent."

"What is it?" he asked, and after a skipped beat, I said, "I'm happy for you."

Those stories I told my father, I tried to make them not boring, but there wasn't much to work with, and that fact—that the highlights of our lives, when recounted, were a big snooze—was perhaps hideous and worthy of examination, but like a stand-up comic falling flat, I forged ahead: a raindrop in the school play, I forgot my one line; a donkey bit Joel at the Catskill Game Farm. "A petting zoo," I explained, because my father's expression was quizzical, and my father asked, "Who is Joel?" There was a question loaded with temptation, but I resisted. "Your son," I said, and then I dredged up a story that centered on the only Thanksgiving when my mother put effort and attention into the meal. Sweet potatoes with brown sugar, asparagus with hollandaise sauce, and she baked a cranberry bread, all of which, for my mother, was the culinary equivalent of successfully demonstrating cold fusion. We marveled as we passed around the plates, and then Joel said, "Where's the turkey?"

"She forgot the turkey," I told my father. "The turkey was in the freezer."

Maybe he didn't remember about turkey and Thanksgiving, how they go together, and I didn't go into it because it was like explaining a joke, and explaining a joke winds up making everyone feel foolish. Instead, I went on to tell him about the time I got my arm stuck in a drainage pipe, which in retrospect was a funny story—time can do that, bring levity or new perspective, which is another way of forgetting what was what—when my father yawned.

"You're tired," I said.

"No," he assured me. "I'm not tired."

Trivial stories about people he could not remember, places he could not recollect, must have had the entertainment value of a slide show of a neighbor's vacation to Aruba. "You're not really interested in any of this, are you?" I asked.

"No, guess I'm not." The note of apology was as clear as a C-sharp. "I need to get on with things," he said, "and I can't be in two places at once." Remembered or not, either way those days were gone, and making new memories was plenty to occupy him. "Do you want to watch some television?" he asked. "Judge Judy is on now. She's a riot."

At that opportune moment, Dr. Reynolds came in, much like a mother duck, the way he was followed by a gaggle of interns, residents, consultants, and curiosity seekers. My father was the Chang and Eng of the Delray Medical Center, and who doesn't want to get a peek at the freak show?

Henry told me that when he was a boy, he saw a cow that had wings like a chicken. "At the Salem County Fair," he said. "They had Hitler's car there, too. Maybe it wasn't really Hitler's car, but they said it was. A black Mercedes sedan, and if you gave the man a dollar, he let you sit in the driver's seat."

"And did you?" I asked. And Henry said, "Yes, I believe that I did."

I took Dr. Reynolds aside. "He remembers pastrami and Judge Judy. Not only does he remember who Judge Judy is, he remembers what time her show comes on. How is it he can remember Judge Judy?"

"Because he watched the show yesterday. This is good. The slate was wiped clean, but apparently it didn't break. The pastrami, though," Dr. Reynolds pondered. "That's interesting. I'll be back to check on him later," and, the way ships pass, Dr. Reynolds and his entourage filed out as Joyce poked her head into the room. "Surprise, surprise," Joyce said, as if she had a gift for my father hidden behind her back, but, there was no gift. It was Joel.

My father looked at Joel and then to me, and he asked, "Is he your brother?" My father was giving us a chance, Joel and me, to start over, to quit our hating each other for no real reason or for reasons long forgotten and likely petty, although visceral loathing is not to be discounted. Still, considering the circumstances here, you'd think bygones could be bygones, but Joel looked up at the television, at Judge Judy, and I brought up the handle on my suitcase. "I have to go now," I said to my father. "But I'll be back in the morning."

Walking with me to the elevator, Joyce said, "You know, it's not so bad. I was worried for a while there, that he was going to be a vegetable. Or totally weird. But really, he's very much himself."

"Very much himself?"

"His personality, it's the same," she said, and then she asked me, "Where are you staying?"

"I don't know yet. I'll find a hotel."

"You can stay at our place," Joyce offered. Which was nice of her because when I stayed there that one time before, Joyce made exasperated noises when I left a dirty glass in the sink. "It's handy," she said. "There's room enough for you."

I thought about it. I thought about how you can't leave a dirty juice glass in the sink, and I don't know what I did wrong with the bath towel I'd used, but it was something that annoyed Joyce a lot, and I thought about that, too, but mostly I thought about the montage of photographs, of my father and Joyce then and my father and Joyce now, as if there had never been anyone but them, and how now that had come to be true, and I said, "I'll be fine. Thanks, anyway."

The next morning, I found my father sitting up in his hospital bed, sharing a laugh with Joyce, a laugh that he would remember.

Henry was tearing up the road that hugged the Dalmatian coast, but at Rijeka we hit a traffic jam, which could have been the result of a jackknifed truck or a six-car pileup or a parade, but it turned out to be the line for the ferry we were taking to the island of Lozenj.

There was no shade around anywhere, and the sun—sun that reflected off the sea—beat down on the car where for hours we waited for a ferry that, as best as we could determine, might *You're sure it was this evening?* or might not come. Henry shifted his weight, fidgety, and was drumming his fingers on the steering wheel, and you'd have thought that at an area where you had people waiting and waiting for an indeterminate amount of time, people roasting like meat on a stick, because it was that kind of hot, you'd have thought that someone, one former Communist, would've found sufficient entrepreneurial spirit to set up a snack bar in the vicinity—a gold mine. A snack bar or, at the very least, mustered up the spunk to strap on a cooler and sell bottled water the way frankfurters are sold at the ball park, but capitalism doesn't take all cultures by storm, which is not always a bad thing. There is money to be made in the land of opportunity, but a free market economy also has endless shelf space for fucking up.

'You're telling me? Like I don't know?'

A dollar bill sent out in a chain letter, Mary Kay cosmetics, the snapping up of houses for no money down to flip them like cards in a stacked deck, the books and the videotapes on how to make millions as a motivational speaker or thousands stuffing envelopes at home, money sent to the televangelist that God would return to her fivefold, these crackpot ventures never did bring in more for Ruby than a day's worth of wishful thinking, at best. More often than not, her designs to get rich quick yielded problems or disasters, which was why I was sure she was mistaken when one Sunday afternoon, not all that long ago in terms of real time but lifetimes ago in terms of how things turned out, Ruby put down her coffee cup and leaned in, as if we were about to cook up a scheme. "Remember that good idea you had," she said, "the one about how to make some money?"

"Me? I had an idea about making money? I don't think so." Even if I had come up with a good idea to make money, which seemed unlikely, I knew better than to wave the red cape of a bull market at Ruby.

"It was a while back. When your father sold his house. You told me about Laura and Joel taking the oak furniture, and how they made a pile of money from selling it."

A snipe I took at my brother and his wife, tossed off without forethought, and I never gave it a second thought, either, because who remembers a snide quip made years before in regard to a pair of people about whom you regularly made snide quips, but Ruby, she took it, tucked it away in the back of her mind, where it rested the way a bullet lodges in fatty tissue, harmless unless it breaks free and travels to a vital organ. "I don't know that they really sold off the furniture," I said. "It just seemed like the kind of thing they'd do."

"That's right. They would, because they'd know how to turn a profit. I'm going to do that, sell off antiques and make some money."

"And where are you going to get these antiques?"

"Yard sales. At yard sales you can always get good items on the cheap. And you know what those high-dollar antique stores charge for junk. Or like your brother did, I'll go to the auction houses."

"Ruby," I repeated, "I made that up, about my brother. It's not a fact."

"So what? It's still a good idea. I figure over some five or six weekends, I can clear fifteen thousand dollars. That's all I need. Fifteen thousand dollars would fix everything."

Buy low and sell high. This much I knew from my grandfather, my father's father, and even though in his case the transaction involved nothing more complicated than a bunch of radishes, I understood that this is, in theory, how business works. But the theoretical is not the corporeal, and in the world of dollars and cents, there are more losers than winners. My own deficit in the arena of get-up-and-go spares me from that particular failure, but just because I'm not motivated does not mean that I am ignorant, and if someone else, pretty much anyone else, had said to me, "There's money to be made in buying low and selling high," I would have said, "Yes, that's how it works." That's what I would've said to someone else, pretty much anyone else other than Ruby. To Ruby, I said, "You might make some money, but there's money to lose."

She wouldn't hear that part of the equation. "It's easy money,

Sylvia," she said, and that—easy—was where it went wrong before it even got started.

Because nothing is ever that easy.

Buy low, sell high; to make money, you have to spend money. To haul away the treasures to be bought for a song at yard sales, Ruby needed something like an SUV or maybe a minivan. Most new businesses operate in the red for months if not years before a profit is turned, and so be it: she traded in her black Saab at a sizable loss and drove off in a blue Ford pickup truck. Dark blue pearl, that's what the color was called. "It was either this dark blue pearl or orange," Ruby said. "Those were my choices. Orange. I don't know what that's about. Who'd want an orange truck?"

And yes, that truck came in handy when at the first yard sale she hit, in Darien in Connecticut, because rich people have higher-quality garbage, she scored a three-piece Art Deco bedroom set, cherrywood, complete with the blue mirrors, and how would she have gotten *that* home in a Saab?

Home? Not to a high-dollar antique store or to an auction house. She took the Art Deco bedroom set home. "I got such a good deal on it," she said, "I couldn't see a reason not to keep it."

Here was a reason not to keep it: Two weeks before, she'd bought herself another bedroom set, a new one, from a furniture store on the Upper East Side, for no money down, which still, no matter how you slice it, is not free. "But that one is about nothing special," she said. "This Art Deco set, it's particular."

Two days went by and Ruby bought herself a boat because

she always, always wanted a boat, which was news to me, that she'd always wanted a boat, and now that we were into June, won't that be nice to have a boat to take out on a summer day? "It's nothing fancy," she said. "Just your average motorboat." She had it docked in a slip in a marina in Bayonne, in New Jersey. "The marinas here were full up," she said. "It's just as well. That Seventy-ninth Street Boat Basin, that's a pricey place. And I couldn't really afford the one on Twenty-third Street, either."

I could've said, "So what? It's not like you can afford the boat. In for a penny, in for a pound," but that wasn't a helpful thing to say to Ruby.

"What I really, really wanted," she said, "was a cigarette boat. Those babies can fly, but for a cigarette boat, they wanted a down payment, and you know I couldn't come up with cash money."

Cigarette boats are not eco-friendly, but Ruby wasn't much of an eco-friendly person; she had other things on her mind, things that didn't reach into the future, and if you expect more from people than they have to give, *each according to his means* you're setting yourself up for disappointment.

The ferry to the island of Lozenj was painted a dingy gray, and the floors were sticky. When we looked out the window, we could not see anything except dirt and grime, and Henry said, "It smells like old puke in here."

"Could be," I said. "Or something dead. A rat in the wall."

Out on the deck there was no place to sit, which might

have been why, despite the stink inside, no one else was there but the two of us, gripping the handrail for balance, standing close together, shoulders brushing gently like soft kisses. The air was of the sea and the spray from the Adriatic wet our faces, and this was a moment I wish I could have captured like a firefly in a jar on a summer night, a moment to keep like a souvenir.

The road from the port to the town was like a length of twine tangled around the cliffs above the shore, but we did not get killed in a crash along the way, despite how likely it seemed that we would. Town was one hotel, one restaurant, two cafés, and a small shop that sold bottled water and vodka and Russian plonk along with crackers, cigarettes, air freshener, postcards, and nail polish.

"There doesn't seem to be a whole lot to recommend here," Henry said. "Do we want to stay?"

"I don't know that we have a choice." In that way, islands are like boats and planes; you can't just up and walk off whenever you damn well please.

The hotel was built by the Communists and had all the charm of a municipal building, circa 1971. Although our room was spacious, huge even, it might have been better had it been smaller because the royal blue indoor/outdoor carpeting went wall to wall, and that was a whole lot of ugly carpet to confront. The nautical motif bedspread and the art on the wall, two prints of seagulls in flight framed in black plastic, were homely, but the plumbing worked well, and I didn't demand much more than that from a hotel room. Henry, though, he stood there as if the blue carpeting were the sea and he were adrift, adrift and the prospects for rescue were grim. "It's too awful," he said.

"It's clean," I pointed out. "The toilet flushes, the shower's got some muscle to it, and the sheets are fresh. It's just for one night."

Henry tried. He did, he tried. "I know. One night. What's one night?" He tried, but still he was genuinely pained by the ugly room, as if he'd found himself in the most wretched of circumstances and not just for one night, but for always.

"Think of it as an adventure," I told him. "A story you'll tell. A horror story. An atrocity story about the one night you spent in an ugly hotel room and how you've never been right since."

"I know, and I am appropriately ashamed of myself," he said.

And I said, "As well you should be." And because I didn't want to think about how sad he was made by it or what that might say about him, what it meant to be undone by the tribulation of one night in a not-so-swank hotel room, I said, "Now let's go to one of those nice cafés and have a drink," and that made things better. For the both of us.

Ruby was sitting on my couch, but her feet were tapping out a routine—forward, 1-2-3, back, 1-2-3—on the floor. "I had two lessons this afternoon," she said. "One salsa and one East Coast swing. You can't be anything but happy when you're dancing."

One hour of salsa and one hour of East Coast swing at Arthur Murray's Dance Studio.

Arthur Murray's Dance Studio? Wasn't that from the time of martini shakers, Dean Martin, the Stork Club, and roadhouses with neon signs that flashed DINING AND DANCING? There was such a roadhouse, a holdover from the 1950s or maybe even from before that, near where I grew up.

Michael's Dining and Dancing, legendary for serving beer to the underage. Friday nights, the parking lot would be symphonic with the sounds of barfing, the way a bird calls and then there is a pause and another bird answers, like a piccolo responding to a cello.

"Ballroom dancing?" I asked. "People still do that?"

"Where have you been?" Ruby said. "It's the newest big thing."

It didn't surprise me any to learn that, as a boy, Henry had gone to dance class. "After school," he said, "on Wednesdays, from the time I was nine until I was twelve, I attended Miss Haggarity's Dance School for Young Gentlemen and Girls." It didn't surprise me, but it did reenforce the strangeness of him.

"Did you hate it?" I asked.

And Henry said, "No. I rather enjoyed it, although I didn't like that I had to wear a suit."

The Biggest New Thing: "Just teach 'em with the left foot and don't tell 'em what to do with the right foot until they pay up." Arthur Murray could have said that, except it was William Jennings Bryan who said it. William Jennings Bryan is perhaps best remembered for his role in the Scopes Monkey Trial—he was the one *against* evolution—and he was also a great supporter of Prohibition, so it's a safe bet that, despite the left foot–right foot metaphor, he wasn't riding high on the Dance Craze wave, the wave of ragtime that swept the nation literally off its feet, because there was something unsavory about those dances. Ragtime was whorehouse music, honky-tonk, and the dances had names like the Grizzly Bear and the Bunny Hug, and we all know where *that* leads, but then along came the dance team of Irene and Vernon Castle, a married couple and as wholesome as milk. Pretty much, they were the Pat Boone of their day, and they cleaned up the Kangaroo Kant, made the Chicken Scratch respectable, and they traveled from city to city, where night after night they demonstrated their watered-down versions of the Animal Dances and their de-eroticized tango to packed houses of young men and women eager to watch, and to learn, to dance.

In New York, Irene and Vernon opened a dance club, along with a dance school, which was where a young man named Moses Teichman took lessons. Moses, who was known to his friends as Murray, was an excellent dancer. Good enough to win the blue ribbon at the Grand Central Palace Dance Contest, which was the Westminster of the dance circuit. Between his jobs as a draftsman at the Brooklyn Navy Yard and as a newspaper reporter, Murray taught dance at Castle House and later at other places, too.

Everyone was dancing, but then the war came, World War I, and the Dance Craze wound down, like a clock.

World War I. The Great War. Think about that, about referring to a war as Great, the superior of Good. Or maybe "Great" refers to the magnitude, as in, the Great Big Fucking Horror Show of a War that was without any purpose other than to introduce the world to shell fire and mustard gas. That war. In 1916, before the United States threw its hat into the ring, Vernon Castle, who was a British citizen, did what countless other honorable but foolish young men did. He enlisted, and with the British Royal Flying Corps, he flew more than one hundred daring combat missions over the Western Front.

The following year, having heroically completed his tour of duty in Europe, Vernon Castle returned to America to teach our young aviators to fly combat missions, too, which was a far cry from teaching them the Maxixe and the Squirrel and the Bullfrog Hop.

Due to the American distaste for all things German at that time, 1917, Murray (né Moses) Teichman changed his name to the entirely un-Germanic-sounding Arthur Murray.

When the war ended, Arthur Murray went to Atlanta, where he studied business administration, and a few years later, in what was a truly brilliant conflation of all his talents—draftsmanship, dance, and sales—he started up a business selling footprints. Cut-out footprints to be placed on the floor in the pattern of the dance you wanted to learn. Follow the shadow feet and 1-2-3-4, you were doing the Foxtrot or the Hesitation Waltz. A big success, this business was, but Arthur Murray wasn't one to stop there. Making a deal with the Statler Hotel chain for use of their ballrooms, he then trained a small army of dance instructors, and he sent them off to give lessons the Arthur Murray way.

A franchise was born.

And the franchise grew, and when Cuba became America's playground and Latin dancing became all the rage, Arthur Murray got his own television show, which had a ten-year run despite his speech impediment. Arthur (né Moses) stammered when he spoke just as did the biblical Moses, who, we could say, led a conga line across the Red Sea.

During a training flight, Vernon Castle's plane crashed and he was killed.

From a one-time worldwide high of some three thousand six hundred, the number of Arthur Murray Dance Studios shrunk considerably, but by no means have they gone the way of the Automats or the Biltmore Hotel or that pink place for ice cream.

"All I want to do now," Ruby said, "is dance."

"There's a plan."

"You have no idea how happy I am." Ruby moved her shoulders in time with her feet, and she was right: I had no idea how happy she was. "Wait until you see the outfits." From the glossy shopping bag that she'd set alongside the couch, she took out what I supposed was a dress. Green spandex and covered with sequins, which I could imagine wearing only if for some reason I wanted to dress up as a mermaid. The other dress in the bag was red. A rhinestone starburst was at the center of it. The neckline and cuffs were rhinestone-studded, too. "You need them to be flashy," Ruby explained, "to show up better on television. Otherwise you look washed out."

"Television?"

Ruby explained how all the big competitions are televised. "They start out small. Local competitions, the way beauty pageants do, how you've got to be Little Miss Debbie Cakes before you can go on to be Miss Teen Alabama. It's the same with the dance competitions. You win the local ones first, and then you move on to the big time. There's a movement afoot to make ballroom dancing an Olympic sport. Like figure skating. Check out the shoes," she said; shoes that were silver T-straps with a three-inch Marie Antoinette–type heel.

The suit Henry wore to the dance lessons he took as a boy was navy blue. "Every year I got a new navy blue suit just for dance class. And a yellow bow tie." He seemed pleased by that, the yellow bow tie. "The girls wore puffy dresses with crinolines. And white ankle socks."

'Crinolines?'

Ruby put the shoes back in the bag, "You would not believe what these things cost," she said. The dresses stayed draped across her lap, as if they provided warmth or comfort, like a blanket. "But it will even itself out because I took the package deal. One hundred and one private lessons," Ruby said. "Private lessons are an hour. That's one hundred and one hours of private lessons. *Plus* unlimited group lessons. Unlimited. Whenever I want. *And* I get free admission to all the dance parties, *and* entrance fees for the competitions get waived. All that for just under ten. Tell me that's not good value. Long term."

"Just under ten what?"

"Thousand."

"Ten thousand dollars? You gave Arthur Murray's Dance Studio ten thousand dollars?"

"I didn't *give* them ten thousand dollars, Sylvia. I paid for lessons in advance. Well, you know. I didn't exactly pay. I put it on my card. Pieced out over a few cards." Pieced out over a few cards because no one card gave Ruby that kind of credit, her risk factor being on the high side.

Trying to talk sense to Ruby when she got like this was futile. Instead, I said something like, "Well, as long as you are enjoying yourself. That's what matters."

Henry allowed that truer words were never spoken. "Pleasure is the finest of pursuits."

"Define *pleasure*," I said.

And Henry said, "Right this very minute," but because of that way he had, of not always emphasizing one syllable over another, I didn't know if he meant "right this very minute" *was* his definition of *pleasure*, or was he asking did I *want* his definition of *pleasure* "right this very minute," as if maybe I'd put him on the spot. like when someone asks who is your favorite author, and you go blank; or asked if you want to turn off grandpa's life support, and you need some time to think that through.

Pleasure might very well be the finest of pursuits, assuming you really are enjoying yourself, but already Ruby had rushed headlong, way past pleasure for its own sake. "When you win the big competitions, those are cash prizes they give away. You get a trophy *and* cash. There's money to be made in dance," she said, and yes there was, because clearly, the Arthur Murray people, they were raking it in, which you can do when you don't have a conscience.

Gathering dust in the marina in Bayonne, Ruby's motorboat was depreciating in value the way sand runs through an hourglass. The car payment on her dark blue pearl Ford pickup truck was overdue, and she still hadn't gotten around to replacing the taillight that got crushed while she was backing up and forgot to look. Lucky thing it was a tree she hit and not another car, because her insurance rates were already sky-high, but the hell with the taillight. She wouldn't be driving the truck any time soon regardless. The parking garage was keeping it for collateral until Ruby paid what she owed them, and who knew how much that was and who cared?

Ruby danced.

Like Zelda Fitzgerald, who first got inspired to dance at the age of twenty-seven, the age when most dancers retire their toe shoes. Zelda studied ballet under Lubov Egorova, a one-time prima ballerina from the Russian Imperial Ballet, and those Russian ballerinas, they weren't playing. Eight hours a day, eight grueling hours a day, Zelda danced and she danced and she danced until one pirouette too many sent her whirling into the nuthouse. Like that, Ruby danced. Every night after work and all day on Saturday and all day on Sunday and on all those days when she called in sick, Ruby was learning the steps to the Foxtrot, the tango, the Viennese waltz, salsa, and East Coast swing. On Friday nights, at the parties hosted by the Arthur Murray Studios, she danced until midnight, when the parties were over and everyone had to go home, and even then she jitterbugged her way to the bus stop.

While dancing, it is impossible to worry or to give a shit about anything except the music and moving with it.

The boat got repossessed.

Ruby danced.

Ruby danced for seven weeks, and for her first competition, she wore the red dress with the rhinestones. She competed in salsa and tango and East Coast swing, for which she won herself a plastic trophy, bronze-colored, with a placard affixed: East Coast Swing. And beneath that: Third Place.

"The gold trophy should've been mine," Ruby said. "I deserved to win the gold."

She deserved the gold trophy and she could've lived with the silver one, but that bronze piece of crap? No. This competition was fixed. "And you know how I can get when things aren't fair."

I knew how she could get.

Ruby pitched her bronze trophy at the judge who, she said, was probably fucking that two-left-footed bitch who won, and even though the trophy was light-weight plastic and would not have done damage had it connected with the judge's head, it was better for everyone that she missed. The plastic trophy hit the wall, and Ruby was escorted out. "I'm banished from the studio. I never loved anything so much as this, Sylvia, and now they won't let me back."

"Apologize," I suggested. "Show remorse. Promise you'll never do it again. Remind them that everyone deserves a second chance."

"You think that might work?" Ruby asked.

"You've got nothing to lose," I said, and indeed the Arthur Murray Dance Studios found itself in a position to forgive, and Ruby resumed her dance lessons and she returned to the Friday-night dance parties, and for the next competition she entered, she bought yet another grotesquely ugly gown. Turquoise with purple spangles and glitter *glitter!* glued to the fabric, and she borrowed money from her mother to pay her phone bill and she borrowed money from me to cover the minimum balance on two of her credit cards and she borrowed money from her mother again, and at this next competition, she again got a bronze trophy. For salsa, not for swing, and she did not hurl it, the plastic trophy, at the judge or anyone else. She took the trophy home, and she put it somewhere, maybe in a drawer.

Everyone does *do over* deserve a second chance, although we don't often get one, and even when we do get a second chance, we're likely to make the same mistake again. The things we learn later rather than sooner tend to result from harsh lessons, but mostly we learn nothing at all.

Ruby's Ford pickup truck, it got repossessed.

The next morning Henry made damn well sure that we were on that first ferry out of Lozenj, and when we hit the dry land of the continent, he drove as if putting distance between us and there had purpose. I leaned in to rub his shoulders, and he took one hand from the steering wheel to unbutton his polo shirt the way a man in a suit will loosen his tie to unwind after a long, hard day.

We stopped for a late lunch in Verona, and after lunch Henry bought me perfume called Eau de Juliette that came in a white box covered with red hearts. From there, we moved on to Pavia, where there used to be a leaning tower like the Leaning Tower of Pisa, except the one in Pavia leaned more and then it fell. We saw some cathedrals, but we didn't go in any of them, and we stayed in a hotel that was originally a monastery, but now it was furbished with all the amenities, and very nice amenities, at that.

Breakfast was unhurried. The coffee was particularly good, and Henry was reading last week's *Wall Street Journal,* folded in that way, into thirds and then in half, so that it doesn't flap around, the way I kept the road map when trying to follow our route. But now I had the road map spread out alongside my coffee cup, everywhere east of the Adriatic hanging over the edge of the table, like a runner for the tablecloth. "Not that I know much about such things," I said, "but given the way the stock market fluctuates, aren't you pretty much watching a rerun of a horse race? Wouldn't it be more helpful to read the *Journal* when it's current?"

"Probably," Henry said, "but I don't do any investing myself."

Much the way a child pins the tail on the donkey, spun around and heading ass-backward, my finger circled the map and landed on Calais. "Calais. Sounds like calla lily, doesn't it?"

'Calla lily. There's that great line from Stage Door *about calla lilies. When Katharine Hepburn says, The calla lilies are in bloom. On second thought, maybe it's not really a great line, but it's the one that stays.'*

We finished our coffee and we got back in the car, and we drove in that direction, the direction of Calais, via Switzerland.

"Switzerland," Henry said, "should never be a destination but only a means for getting from one country to another. Like a bridge, and you've just got to get across it, is all."

Which was the same thing Ruby used to say, more or less, about the men who came between the husbands, and also she said something similar about the episodes that she referred to as her spells. She'd know when one was coming, a spell, the way a bum knee forecasts rain, as do swallows flying close to the ground, and she'd say, "I just have to go through it," which made it sound more like a tunnel than a bridge, but the idea was the same: a means of getting from here to there. She would do her best to prepare for it, call in sick to work or give notice, and then she'd curl up at the far corner of her couch, curl like the pattern of a snail's shell, as if to curl inward, headfirst, was to be tucked in tight and would keep her from spiraling downward.

Henry and I, we didn't write them down, the names of places we liked best, the places we'd like to live, to live together, but it was a list we said aloud, as if it were another word game we were playing as we drove through Switzerland. Like the way we played Z my name is Zachary and I come from Zurich, where I sell xylophones.

"Xylophones?" I said. "No. Xylophones begins with an *x*."

"Yes." Henry conceded that it did. "But it sounds like a *z*."

"Sounds like. But isn't."

"Well, it should be a *z*," Henry said.

Lots of things should be, but aren't.

Prague, Bohemia, Slovenia, Vienna, and pretty much all of Italy except Venice, but only because Venice was no place to drive a car, and and despite that, we'd never been there together, we agreed on living in Spain, too, and although not spoken, it was understood that the other side of the Atlantic was not to be considered. We talked about which would better suit us: A house in a small village? Or farm country? Or mountains? Or an apartment in a big city? And if we do wind up in an apartment, should we look for one with a garden or would we prefer a balcony?

I could not say how much of this talk was for real and how much was just talk, the way, as if constructing a platypus, some couples will conjure up a baby—my eyes, your nose, and what will we do if it's a girl and she gets your legs—despite no intention whatever of having a baby, and definitely not having a baby together.

But talk we did, of cities and towns, and do we favor dark colors for drapes and upholstery? Or might we go light and airy? Would we get a dog for a pet? As to how we would live, where we would get the means to live, that was a spoiler, and Henry said, "It's a bridge to cross when you get there," and then we were no longer in Switzerland.

Sailing, swimming, windsurfing, bicycling, sand-castle construction, and there was an aquarium, a museum dedicated to the zeppelin, and the sky over Lake Constance was poolside blue. Holding hands, sweethearts, Henry and I, we walked along the promenade. "Such pep," Henry said. "Everyone so diligently energetic. Looking out on all this physical exertion in leisure is draining on me. Let's get us a cocktail."

'Trifling. Didn't I tell you? Trifling like nobody's business.'

And so we did just that; we went for a drink, and then we went to our room, and from there we went to the restaurant adjacent to our hotel, where for dinner I had a grilled vegetable plate and Henry ate quab, which was a fish. The local wine was fruity, and at the end of the meal, Henry asked me, "Are you feeling lucky?"

"Very," I said. "I'm feeling very lucky."

"Then wait here. I'll be right back," and when Henry returned to the table, he was wearing a white button-down shirt and a blue sports jacket.

"Where'd that come from?" I asked.

"My suitcase," he said, and then he said, "Shall we?" and off we went to a casino, where we played roulette, *roulette!* betting high and low but always on red. In the end we came out fourteen euros ahead of the game, and Henry suggested that we spend our winnings on a nightcap.

The next day we were back on the road, driving for hours, and maybe we were still in Germany, but we might have crossed into France, but whichever—France or Germany—we were going through a long stretch of farm country.

All through the winter and all through April, Ruby danced, but *with April showers* come May, she stopped. She stopped dancing as surely and as completely as the little ballerina in the music box stops twirling when you close the lid.

She stopped dancing, she quit her job, she quit going out, and she quit answering her phone, which was why I went over and let myself in, which I could do because I had keys to her apartment, just as she had keys to mine. The shades were drawn as if it were photosensitivity from which she suffered, and the television was on, but it was on Channel 8, which was all static and interference. There was no evidence that she'd been eating: no dirty dishes in the sink, no bag of Pepperidge Farm cookies on the coffee table, no empty to-go containers, and her ribs showed through her T-shirt.

She didn't quite sit up, but she shifted in my direction, and she was good and ripe, too, because it's not like she was taking showers or brushing her teeth. "You reek," I told her. I could tell her that she smelled bad because we were friends that way, friends who could tell each other the truth even when it was not a compliment. "You've got to take a shower."

"Go home." Ruby made as if she were looking at something out the window, but she wasn't looking at anything.

"I will. In a minute. I just want to be sure you're okay."

"I'm as okay as you are," she said.

"Yeah," I said. "Except I'm going to work and I'm not stinking up the room."

"How nice for you to be so fragrent." When she got like this, Ruby wasn't delightful or even likable or tolerable, and I wasn't about to respond and she wasn't about to say anything more, and we sat there listening to the steady buzz of the static from the TV, as if it were music, until the phone rang and I jumped the way you do at a birthday party when a balloon pops. The balloon is there in plain sight, and you know it's just a matter of time before it pops, but when it does, it's as if you'd never expected *that* to happen. Ruby, though, she seemed not to hear the phone.

"Do you want me to get that?" I asked. "It could be important."

"It's not important," Ruby said, as if nothing could be important. "It's Ms. Wilson. From the collection agency."

The answering machine picked up, and sure enough Ms. Wilson, or someone who identified herself as Ms. Wilson, was offering to work out a payment plan, and if that wasn't agreeable, Ruby could expect to find herself in court.

"Sylvia," Ruby said, "go home. Leave me alone."

"Not until you eat something." I was firm about that, because then, if she ate something, I could feel satisfied about myself, the way we feel good about ourselves when we give money to a worthy cause, in that slightly smug way, so pleased with our own goodness, as if we'd actually done something brave or noble.

"I'm not hungry," Ruby said. "Go away."

"I'm not leaving until you eat," I told her, as if a bite of bread or a banana would soothe more than my conscience.

"If I eat something, will you go home?"

I said yes, and that was the deal we struck.

The refrigerator was empty except for condiments, and the handle to the kitchen cabinet was sticky like a half-eaten lollipop, but I did find three cans of Campell's Chicken Noodle Soup and a box of Saltine crackers. While the soup was warming on the stove, I folded a napkin and put a spoon alongside a bowl set on a dinner plate. I tried to make it look nice. Like when you are served dinner at the hospital and, next to the covered dish, there is a little bud vase on the tray, to lift your spirits or to fool you into thinking that this might be nice food.

Standing over her, I watched Ruby eat, and when she finished half of the chicken noodle soup and all of a Saltine cracker, she placed the plate, bowl, and spoon on the floor beside the couch. Satisfied with that much, I let myself out, locking the door behind me, and over the next two days, I called every few hours. Not that I expected her to answer the phone, but I left messages, content that she'd hear them, to let her know I was thinking of her, as if in such a state she gave a shit who was thinking about her or not. Mostly, I suppose, I was just trying to do the decent thing. Do the decent thing, and you can rest easy.

Germany or France, whichever, we were cutting between fields of sunflowers and fields where brown cows grazed when, at a fork in the road, Henry veered left and then stopped behind an old toolshed set between a house and a barn.

On the chimney top of the farmhouse was a nest made of sticks. Not twigs but sticks woven into a basket that could have been a laundry basket for a big family. One leafy branch was placed just so, at the edge, like a welcome mat, and in the nest were three fledgling storks. *Storks!*

It's something remarkable how every year the storks migrate from the south of Africa, from Zimbabwe and Tanzania, to middle Europe, where they build their nests, lay eggs, eat frogs, hatch their young, and teach them to fly, to fly home to Africa before winter sets in. And every spring, they come back again.

Across the way, on the roof of the barn, was the mother stork. She was white with black wing feathers and her long legs were the same shade of red as her beak, as if her shoes and purse matched. Suddenly, majestically, she spread her wings out wide and flapped them once, twice, three, four times, and from the nest the three little storks flapped their wings, as if they were waving to their mother. I grabbed hold of Henry's arm, and we watched the mother stork lift off the way a helicopter does, straight up, albeit a little cockeyed, and then, in a seemingly effortless glide, she flew once around the barn before landing, but the fledglings, for all their frantic wing flapping, did not rise up from their nest.

Again the mother showed them how it was done—flap, rise, and glide—and back around she came, and again she flapped her wings, and in the same way we struggle for recollection, as if they'd closed their eyes tight and squeezed, the fledglings struggled to take flight, and again they failed to fly.

Henry and I would not be there to see it happen, but they would fly, those baby storks. Maybe that day or maybe the day after they would get the hang of it, of this I was sure. They would fly home.

What Happened Next: Ruby got up from the couch to wash down twenty-four capsules of Sleep-Eze with vodka. She took another slug from the bottle, the bottle of vodka she'd pinched from a party the previous December. "Smirnoff," she'd said. "How chintzy is that? Serving Smirnoff at the office Christmas party?"

Now the bottle of vodka was tucked under her arm as if it were a baguette she were carrying home from the bakery, as if that's why she needed the bread knife, to slice French bread. A bread knife with a wooden handle and a serrated blade that was eight inches long and last used for scraping gum off the bottom of her shoe.

Sleep-Eze. Vodka. Bread knife.

The vodka and the bread knife she took with her into the bathroom, where she undressed. Leaving her clothes—a rank T-shirt and black panties—where she dropped them, she ran the bathwater. Warm. A warm bath, and how return-to-the-womb is that? To return to the time before you were born shares common ground with ceasing to be. Either way, the world exists but you do not.

Sleep-Eze. Vodka. Bread knife.

Here was the plan: to recline in the tub and, while nipping at the vodka, let the warm water wash over her until it was deep enough for her to fully submerge. Then, turn off the faucets, cut open her wrists, and fall into a dreamless *Hey Mr. Sandman* sleep in the warm bath and she wouldn't have to wake up, not ever, and so it would be like she never was.

Tomorrow would come, but Ruby, she wouldn't have to be there for it.

According to Chinese legend, the stork carries worthy men to a blissful eternity.

.　　　　.　　　　.

These things happen all the time in New York. Other cities, too, no doubt. When you live in an apartment building, there's always a chance that the upstairs neighbor will run the bath and then get distracted by a phone call or something on television or a commotion on the street, and the tub will fill, fill to the brim, and then the damn thing overflows and water is dripping from your ceiling. You go upstairs, cursing a blue streak, and you bang on the door, just as the woman did, the woman who lived in the apartment directly below Ruby's, to tell Ruby that her tub was overflowing. The woman knocked and knocked, and next she pounded, and then she no doubt muttered something about what kind of fucking idiot runs the tub and then goes out without turning it off? Meanwhile, this woman's ceiling had buckled and water was coming down her walls like heavy rain against a windowpane, and she went to find the building superintendent because he had keys to all the apartments, and although that, having keys to all the apartments, might or might not be legal, no one ever complained because of situations such as this one. Also it's not uncommon to lock yourself out, and who wants to have to call a locksmith?

The building superintendent was from the former Soviet Union and had a mustache similar to the one Stalin wore, but, unlike Stalin, he was a good man. He knocked on Ruby's door, and then he knocked again, and when he again got no answer, he closed one eye and looked into the peephole, which is only for looking out, so it's not like he could see anything, but it satisfied him that no one was at home, and therefore it was necessary to let himself in to turn off the faucets.

The way nature abhors a vacuum, sometimes when telling a story, to get it to make sense, to make sense of it, you need to fill in the blanks, add details, create dialogue, or remember things you couldn't possibly have known.

The bathwater was pink.

The building superintendent slapped Ruby's face, not hard, but with enough force to wake her up, except she didn't wake up. He knew she wasn't dead because he'd seen plenty of dead people in his life. Before he came to America, when he lived in the Soviet Union and it was not yet the *former* Soviet Union, people died like flies, and often an empty vodka bottle was at the scene there, too.

In ancient Egypt, the *ba*, a stork with a human head, was the physical manifestation of the soul as it migrates to reunite with the body in the afterlife.

To fall asleep, and either drown or lose enough blood to die by exsanguination, whichever came first, was a good plan, insofar as a plan to kill yourself can ever be a good plan, but as does sometimes happen even with the best of plans, it didn't work out that way. In the time it took for the tub to fill, Ruby grew so very tired, and she wasn't thinking clearly, either, which was why she forgot to turn off the faucets before slitting her wrists, and she was so very, very tired that she didn't have the strength required to cut deep enough and the blade wasn't razor-sharp, and she got only to one wrist before her eyes closed. Her eyes closed, her energy drained away, but her blood did not, and because she fell asleep with her neck supported by the lip of the tub, as if it were a pillow, and her head resting against the wall, she didn't drown, either.

Ruby's stomach was pumped and, as next of kin, her mother was called, and she drove, without stopping for so much as a bathroom break, from Virginia to New York University Hospital, where she sat by Ruby's bed, watching over her daughter.

Another Thing About Storks: In Hebrew, the word for *stork* translates to "good mother."

Watching over her daughter with the same kind of equanimity as if she were watching over a plant. She didn't do any of that silly hand-wringing or blaming herself or blaming anyone else, and there was a glint of something metallic, like steel, in her eye. Something strong and stoic or maybe it was triumph.

Three days of psychiatric observation is required by law for all attempted suicides, and at the end of those three days, it was determined that Ruby was no longer a danger to herself or to anyone else, and she was released from the hospital. There was a Band-Aid on her wrist.

Ruby and her mother went from the hospital to Ruby's apartment, where they stayed long enough to pack up three suitcases and four boxes: clothes, books, CDs, laptop, and an accordion file of necessary papers from the bank and the IRS. In her wallet that nestled in her purse, Ruby's mother had the name of a fine psychiatrist written down on a piece of paper and tucked away. A fine psychiatrist in Richmond who had been recommended by that nice doctor at New York University Hospital. That nice Russian man, the one who was the building superintendent, helped them load up the car. "Now, you take whatever you want," Ruby's mother told him. "The furniture and dishes and whatnot. Whatever is left, you can throw out or give away or sell. That bedroom set is worth some money. It's Art Deco, you know."

From the West Side Highway, they took the George Washington Bridge and from there picked up the New Jersey Turnpike and onto Interstate 95, I-95 South, and at a rest stop where they went for lunch, Ruby called to tell me that *what every Southern mother really wants* they were in Delaware already. Because I was at work, she left the message on my answering machine: "I'll call you from Virginia."

When I finished telling Henry this story, he said to me, "None of it was your fault. How could you blame yourself? For what? You didn't do anything."

"Exactly," I said.

The Last I'll Say About Storks: Aesop was a man with many fables, and all of them featured anthropomorphized animals, and also they all concluded with a moral of one sort or another. Aesop had two fables in which a stork was a main character: "The Fox and the Stork," and the moral to that one was, "One bad turn deserves another," and then there was "The Farmer and the Stork," which opens with a farmer setting a net to trap cranes because cranes ate his seeds. Along with the cranes, a stork got trapped in the net, too. The stork pleaded with the farmer to spare its life on the grounds that a stork is not a crane; a stork does not eat seeds. Which is true. Storks eat lizards and frogs. "I am a stork," the stork said, to which the farmer said, "It may be as you say, but I know only that I have taken you with these robbers, the cranes, and you must die in their company," and the moral of the story is this: "Birds of a feather flock together."

20

We stopped at Contrexéville to buy bottled water, a loaf of bread, and a wedge of cheese, a pungent *fromage du pays*. Also chocolate and fruit and a bottle of wine. It was out of the ordinary for us, and as far as Henry was concerned, it was throwing all caution to the wind to forgo a proper lunch someplace nice, but who says you can't go wild every now and again?

While Henry drove, I took an orange from the grocery sack, a blood orange. The rind was mostly orange-colored, as we've come to expect an orange to be, but with a blood orange, here and there—the way women apply blush to their cheeks—were brushstrokes of scarlet. Once it was peeled, all vestiges of the color orange were gone. The fruit was deep red, the same red as wine and garnets, and *garnet earrings from Karlovy Vary* I fed a slice of the blood orange into Henry's mouth and one into my own mouth, and it was perfectly sweet *I won't forget* and juicy. I like to think I've got a talent for picking out a good piece of fruit, a talent passed on to me from my father's side of the family, and then I fed Henry another slice of orange while, at a speed that was a hairsbreadth under reckless, we zoomed through Bar-le-Duc, and from what I could make out, it was a cute place. A river ran through the valley and on both sides were hills abundant with grapevines. Off in the distance, I could see the clock tower. It must be that every town and city in Europe has a clock tower, and the clock tower is most often erected alongside a church, as if working in concert to remind you that the hour looms. I didn't care to be reminded of that, and I asked Henry, "Do you want me to peel another orange?"

It was late morning when we got to a lonely stretch of road that cut through the forest at Saint-Mihiel, a forest that was dense and dark with fir trees. Henry pulled over and put the car in park. From the backseat, which was the repository for, among other things, discarded city maps, empty water bottles, and a towel, he got his camera and the small blue blanket and the bread and wine and cheese. "Grab the fruit, would you?" he asked.

Patches of sunlight broke through the thick trees the way summer sunlight is recalled in retrospect and seen in dreams, too, and it was quiet. The kind of quiet that is not an absence of sound but something in its own right. Quiet broken only by the occasional *tseekut,* a songbird calling to its mate, *tseekut, tseekut,* and we walked *tseekut* until we came upon a small clearing. Henry shook out the blanket and we sat, and he opened the bottle of wine and I tore off hunks of bread for makeshift sandwiches, which we ate. We passed the bottle of wine back and forth between us, and I was happy, a kind of happy that, if manifested into tangibility, would've taken the shape of a daisy.

When the bottle was empty, I stood up to slip out of my dress, and crumbs from the bread fell away. I took off my underwear, too, and my shoes, and Henry, fiddling with his camera, looked at me through the lens. "You do have a most aesthetically pleasing form, the way you are both petite and curvy." Then he pointed just to the left of our picnic area and said, "How about there? At the base of that tree."

Again looking at me through the lens of the camera, and not quite satisfied, Henry came and posed me as if I were a dancer, my feet in fourth position, one foot crossed to the middle of the other. He took some six or seven pictures of me that way and then he paused. "Put your hands over your eyes, but don't cover your face. Just the eyes." And I did. I put my hands over my eyes like a child expecting a surprise, and he said, "Oh, so lovely." The stream of sunlight warmed me and *tseekut, tseekut,* the songbird called, and when he finished taking pictures, I took my hands away, and there was Henry. Which was a surprise, the way it overwhelmed me with love to see him again, and here's the thing about filling up with love, filling up with desire: it's the opposite of filling up. It's about becoming empty, as if the contents of yourself poured out as fast and entirely as water from a bucket and you need, urgently you need more, and that need to be filled overtook me. I put my arms around Henry's neck, and on the blanket spread out over a bed of dirt and pine needles, like Adam and Eve prior to the incident with the apple, we went at it like a pair of bunnies, and it was that kind of wonderful and I expressed myself accordingly, and would have again expressed myself had we not heard something like a commotion. Voices calling out, and five or six men and women, Norwegians, came rushing toward us until they were close enough to know that my cry was not a cry for help and thus their Heroic Intent was reduced to Embarrassing Moment. They went like bumper cars banging up against one another looking for a way out, and we were not especially delighted to see them, either, but we did have to admit how very decent it was of them, the Norwegians, that somewhere in a dark and dense forest they heard a woman cry out and they didn't stand around debating whether or not to mind their own business. This Good Samaritanism, it had much to do with our deduction that they were Norwegian, because Norwegians, we believed, were good like that. Virtuous people. The Danes, too, but we called this group Norwegian because of their sartorial splat: short pants, thick socks, sandals, and fanny packs. They held walking sticks, and their camping gear was packed into canvas rucksacks they carried on their backs.

At the car, Henry rewound the roll of film and put it in one of those small black canisters with a gray snap-on lid. In the glove compartment were more of those film canisters, and whenever he took a sharp turn, they rolled around in there like marbles.

We did not stop again until we got to Verdun.

'All Quiet on the Western Front. *They made that into a movie, but we haven't seen it. My mother prefers movies that are uplifting.'*

The quiet of the battlefields at Verdun, what had once been the battlefields at Verdun, now reforested with oak trees and evergreen trees, that was yet another kind of quiet. Not like a church mouse or the hush of a snowfall or like the quiet of the forest at Saint-Mihiel. This was quiet as sorrow is quiet, and as we walked among the trees, Henry and I fell silent in kind; to speak would be to disrupt the uneasy peace. The ground, too, was uneasy, not quite natural land formation because of where the trenches had been.

Later, we learned that to walk through the old battlefields was a bad choice to make because mines are buried there still, and even after almost ninety years, it was possible that a mine could detonate. Also buried in that ground were things like bayonets and spoons and human legs never found and bodies without legs that were never collected and canteens and horses' heads and arms and hands and mess kits and gas masks because that's what war does: it tears people apart, separates people from their things and from their limbs, and buries it all in the ground.

.   .   .

World War I, and my maternal grandfather did what so many boys did; he lied about his age so that he could enlist, which, you could say, is one of the better justifications for telling the truth because look where his lie landed him: on a battlefield in Verdun.

Boys go to war because they are boys, because they are young, and the young are foolish, impetuous, naive. Get 'em when they are green, when they think war is some sort of sporting event and the very worst thing that could happen is they could lose. Lose not life or limb or mind but a game, like football or Parcheesi, because young boys believe that they will live forever and that nothing bad will happen along the way.

Such a boy was my grandfather when he enlisted. A boy no older than fifteen. A gentle boy who painted pictures of wildflowers and weeping willow trees. A boy soldier who was more of a mascot than a warrior, but that didn't stop them, in 1917, from shipping him off to France along with the other soldiers, to Verdun, where it was raining.

Historians of war will tell you that by the end of 1916 the Battle of Verdun was over, and technically speaking that is true. Officially that particular battle had come to a close. The town was destroyed, the buildings reduced to rubble, the inhabitants reduced to ghosts. Officially it was over. In theory it was over, but in actuality the half a million dead on that front wasn't enough to call it quits. The fighting at the battle lines of Verdun went on just the same as it had before it was officially over, and that's what it was, a battlefield, when my grandfather got there.

The rain never let up. Every day it rained, and at night, too, and they, the soldiers, were wet, always wet, soaking wet. Their clothes were wet and their boots were wet and many of the soldiers got fungal infections between their toes because their boots never dried. The wet ground turned to mud, and soldiers were deep in mud, and mud got in their boots and under their fingernails and in their mouths and in their noses and in their food. They ate mud and they drank mud and they breathed mud. And still it rained, but it could not rain enough to clean the air of the stench of gunpowder and mustard gas and of the dead and the decay and the whiff of fear that comes with shell fire and sniper fire. Sniper fire. Ours? Theirs? Who knew? Who cared? And when the shells exploded, there was pandemonium. Horses bolted and men were shouting and men were screaming, screaming to move it, screaming to take cover, and screaming for God to save me, and for God to forgive me and *They dropped like Flakes* crying, crying for their mothers, and in this chaos of scrambling and shooting and crying and screaming and begging and running, he, my grandfather, fell to the ground. He fell, facedown, but he had not been hit by a bullet or a piece of shrapnel. Running, he slipped in the mud and he fell. That was all. He slipped, like Charlie Chaplin on a banana peel. Silly, really. He slipped in the mud and his ankle twisted and snapped into two or three pieces. A broken ankle. Trivial, piffle, when on all sides of him men were losing their arms and their legs, when their intestines were spilling out, when their lives were gone—snap—just like that. A broken ankle was reason almost to be grateful. Be grateful and get on with it because he could go on, because he wasn't among the dead or dying. He was hurt, but not wounded.

With his elbows bent at his sides, his palms flat to the ground, he pushed against the ground for leverage, to get up, to hop to wherever, anywhere was preferable to being face-down in the mud while all around him shells were explod-ing and horses were screaming and men were screaming. He pushed, pushed himself up, but his hands slipped in the mud; he pushed again, and again his hands slipped. The mud was too deep, too thick, too wet to support his weight, and my grandfather called out for help. He did not call out for a medic; the medics were busy holding back the flow of blood that was mixing with the rain and turning the mud to the color of a brick. He called out for someone, anyone, to help him up, that's all, help him to stand up, to literally give him a hand to pull him up, but no one would stop for him and the rain would not stop and my grandfather reached out and caught hold of a boot. The soldier whose boot he'd grabbed, a soldier he knew, Murphy, Mumphrey, something like that, looked down at him, and my grandfather said, "Help me up, would you? Help me to stand up," but Murphy, Mumphrey, shook him loose, as if shaking off a dog who got hold of the cuff of your pants, shook him loose and left him there.

When it was all over, *Who won? Who cares?* it was night and my grandfather was too cold and too tired and too wet to try again to stand up. He lay there in the night, in the dark. A puddle of rainwater had formed around him. Although it was too dark to see that the puddle was pink, pink from the blood of the dead and the dying, he could smell it, the blood, and also he was a boy who'd painted with watercolors, flowers and trees and sunsets with watercolors, and he knew exactly what happens when red pigment is diluted, the shades of pink that come. He lay there, this boy, in the mud, trying not to hear the weeping and the *wasted and wounded, it ain't what the moon did* pleading of those who were not yet dead, but who soon would be. You can try not to hear that kind of crying, but try all you might, you are going to hear it. You are going to hear it for the rest of your life.

Time passed. How much time had passed? He did not know. Maybe it was early the next day or maybe later the next day when a cease-fire was called. One of those gentlemanly cease-fires; cease fire so we can collect our dead and dying and you can collect yours, as if there were still such a thing as basic human decency. Soldiers and medics returned to the field to gather *ye rosebuds* up their dead and their almost dead, and there they found the boy soldier who was my grandfather who was neither dead nor dying unless you count the withering of the heart to be a kind of death. Otherwise, he suffered only from a broken ankle. A broken ankle. An ankle that twisted and broke and never quite righted itself, and he never quite righted himself, either. He was twisted with disgust, with loathing and contempt for humanity, from whom he came to expect nothing. Never again was he the least bit sweet, and all because of a broken ankle on the battlefield at Verdun.

.   .   .

It's as if they were destined, my mother's side of the family, not for tragedies but for mishaps; and it was those small misfortunes and those missed opportunities that left them lonely or sad or peculiar or broken.

Or maybe that's how it is for everyone.

"Tragedy bestows dignity," Henry said. "The little adversities are more likely to render you awkward."

Henry and I, we were not tragic figures, either. Our misfortunes were nothing more than off-chances not taken, or taking the easy way out. Our lives were charmed.

We walked farther along weathered paths, weaving around trees. We walked for an hour or maybe more, and because the afternoon was dry and very hot, it was not entirely ridiculous to think we were seeing a mirage or that we had come upon Xanadu, because suddenly, out of nowhere, there we were in the shade *midway on the waves* cast from a dome that turned out not to be a stately pleasure dome but the dome of the Ossuaire de Douaumont. The ossuary. Where the bones were kept. The bones of some one hundred thirty thousand soldiers, French and German, both, and some Americans and Australians, too. Or at least it is assumed that it's a mixed bag of bones; no one could identify them because all that remained of these men, some one hundred thirty thousand men and boys, was that: bones. The bones, and there was no name to attach to a rib cage or serial number to a skull. What to do with all those bones? Here in the ossuary they were interred, heaped into a pile like junked cars or green turtles in a tank at Woolworth's, and there were no lines of demarcation to tell so much as where one man began and another man ended.

There, at the jumble of human remains, the remains of the unknown soldiers, the unidentified young men, the boys never heard from again, the once loved but now gone and forgotten, Henry and I shared no words, because what can you say in the face of such a thing? After a while, we quit looking, and only then did Henry say, "Sobering, if you stop to think about it."

"Yes, when you stop to think about it."

If you stop to think about it, Henry said.

If implies a choice: You can think about it, *Thinking on things, that's where you trip up* or you can choose not to think about it.

'Or you can think about it tomorrow. I can't count how many times we've seen that movie now. My mother will never get her fill of Gone with the Wind. *Because of Scarlett's attachment to the home place.'*

When you stop to think about it gives you a choice, too, but only in the timing. Only in the timing, but sometimes timing is everything, and sometimes better-late-than-never is not better. Sometimes *late* and *never* amount to the same thing. Sometimes, it has to be *now* or never.

Flanking the ossuary on all sides were meadows of white crosses planted in rows like corn, and each cross was identical to the next, as if to drive home the point: a dead man is a dead man is a dead man, and it doesn't get any more wasteful than that, than being one of too many dead to count laid out in a way that speaks only of numbers but says nothing of who you were. Row upon row of white crosses. Like at Arlington National Cemetery in Washington, D.C., where I went with my parents and Joel for three days, where we also saw the White House, the Capitol, the Washington Monument, and the Lincoln Memorial. At the Smithsonian, I got two souvenirs: a dollhouse-size porcelain tea set and a book about Betsy Ross. If there was a gift shop at Arlington, I got no souvenir from there, but when we got home, I remembered it well enough to turn my sandbox into a cemetery. I buried dead bugs, broken toys, a baby bird that did not survive its fall from the nest onto our patio. It did not yet have feathers, that baby bird. I marked the graves with crosses made from twigs and twine, but someone—my mother or father or both—uprooted the crosses, exhumed the bodies, and put the lot of it in the trash. "That was no way to play," my mother said.

When something predatory, maybe a fox or a weasel, got at my pet white rabbit, which we kept in a pen in the yard, my mother told me that the rabbit ran away, as if the rabbit's leaving me by choice were less distressing than its death, even if that death was on the ugly side, which I suspect it was, because out the window I saw my father picking up white fluff from the lawn, fluff I'd first thought was dandelions after they go from yellow to the puff of white seed.

A year after my mother died, my father, my brother, and I went to the cemetery for the unveiling of her gravestone, which was to be without fanfare or ceremony. The stone had been erected, and we would go and have a look at it; that was all.

A slab of white marble, traditional in its shape, as my mother would have wanted it to be. Simple and cherub free. A proper memorial tablet, and her name—Elise Landsman—was engraved in block letters, but below her name, in the space traditionally reserved for date of birth and date of death or testimony such as Beloved Wife, or Devoted Mother, was this: Refreshingly Different. As if she were a soft drink.

Like Dr Pepper or Sprite.

I don't know how it happened that my mother's gravestone came to read like an advertisement for soda, and we didn't do anything about it except shuffle our feet and act weird, until my brother got into his car and I got into my father's car with him, and we called it a day, and my mother, who prided herself on being anything but different, would now be remembered for all eternity as refreshingly so. Except, of course, she won't be remembered for all of eternity, and as far as I know, no one has ever again been to the place where she is buried.

21

Two or three times a week, Ruby called me to talk on the phone. Other times, I called her. I talked to her about the things I'd pretty much always talked to her about: the men I dated, the books I read, the friends I saw for lunch, how everything was fine, how this perfectly pleasant life was my life, and why would a perfectly pleasant life make a person want to scream? The things Ruby talked about now, on the phone, were not the things she'd always talked to me about.

On this night, it was Ruby who called me, early, before dinner. "Hey, Sylvia," she said, "do you remember that song? 'Blame It on the Bossa Nova'? Blame it on the bossa nova. Now, isn't that the truth? Blame it on the bossa nova, is right."

"That song was well before our time," I noted.

"Yeah," Ruby said, "but it did me in, just the same. Those dance lessons. It was those dance lessons that sent me over the edge."

I asked Ruby to hold on while I poured myself a glass of wine, and when I came back to the phone, she was singing, ". . . on the bossa nova with its magic spell."

And I broke in and said, "You sound good. Not the singing. I mean you. *You* sound good." Which was true. She did sound good. Not *too* good, which was also good, that she sounded not *too* good, because for Ruby *too* good was not good either. But she did sound good, and don't forget she was living with her mother, which is never easy for anyone. "Do you feel good?" I asked.

"Well, I couldn't feel any worse than I did, so yeah, I suppose that means I feel better," and I didn't say anything and I don't even know what exactly, if anything, I was thinking, but I'd drifted off for a moment, and because *not* talking on the telephone is disconcerting to the person on the other end, Ruby said, "Sylvia? Are you there?"

"Was it awful?" I asked her. I meant, Was it awful being you?

"Sometimes," she said. "Sometimes it was awful. But you want to know the truth, Sylvia?"

That question—Do you want to know the truth?—is a rhetorical one, and I was not expected to answer it, but I wanted to answer it. I wanted to say, "Maybe not. Maybe I don't want to know the truth. Maybe I'm better off not knowing." Some information you get, it's like a hot potato or a live grenade, and what are you supposed to do with that except wait for it to blow up in your face?

And as is also the way with rhetorical questions—Do you want to know the truth?—the one who asked the question is the one who answers it, and Ruby said, "The truth is, Sylvia, there were times when I couldn't imagine anything more wonderful than being me; those times, it was like my name was up in lights, like I was the Music Man with my own big parade. We just watched that one, *The Music Man*, the night before last. Did you know that Shirley Jones, who played Marian the Librarian, was the mother in *The Partridge Family*?"

I think I did know that. A better question is why I knew that.

"Ma-ri-an," Ruby sang, "the li-brar-i-an," and then like it was a medley, she segued into "With a hundred and ten coronets close at hand."

"So," I said, "there were times then when you were happy?"

"No. Not that. I was never happy. Ecstatic. But not happy."

"And now?"

"Now? No. Not happy now, either," she said. "But I'm okay. I'm pathetic, mind you. I'm fat. My hair is falling out. I'm a substitute teacher at the local high school, and I spend every night watching movies from Netflix with my mother. But I'm okay." Then she said, "I've got to get my mother off the musicals though. Tonight she has a Judy Garland–Mickey Rooney double feature planned."

"It's time you came back," I said. "Don't you think?"

"How can I come back? I'm fat, and my hair is falling out."

"You can wear a wig. My mother wore a wig after the chemotherapy, and really, it looked just like her own hair. You couldn't tell the difference."

"I can't come back," Ruby said. "I don't have the means to come back."

"My treat," I said.

"Not that kind of means. There's more to it than the money."

"Like what?" I asked.

"Guilt," Ruby told me. "I swear, Sylvia. I never saw my mother so pleased with me as this. It'd break her heart if I left."

"But what about you?"

"Me? I bathe regularly and that's something."

I laughed at that because I knew she wanted me to laugh at that and not because I thought it was funny.

"I'm clean," she said, "and I'm calm. Mostly that's the drugs, but also it was a load off me, a relief to learn that it was something."

"What was something? I'm not following you."

"It's like, remember back when everyone was dead tired? How being exhausted was going around like it was something fashionable?"

"Yeah. I remember. But what's that got to do with you?"

"All those people carrying on about how they were tired all the time, and all the other people thinking, So what, you're tired, big deal, everybody's tired, and then it got called chronic fatigue syndrome, and all the tired people felt better because they weren't just tired. They had chronic fatigue syndrome."

"Yeah. I remember that."

"That's the same way I felt better. When I learned that I had something real. With a name to it. Like a thing."

"What was real?" I asked. *No ideas but in* "What thing?"

"A real sickness. Documented. After I got diagnosed, when I could attach a name to it, that made it real, that I'm able to say I have bipolar disorder makes me feel better. Not that I go around announcing it, but for myself it makes a difference."

Bipolar disorder is the same as manic-depressive disorder, but in my opinion, bipolar, as a descriptive, pales in comparison. Bipolar. That could just as well be about climate change or an Arctic expedition, but that's just how the words go.

"Why does calling it bipolar make you feel better than calling it manic-depressive?"

"Bipolar. Manic-depressive. Makes no nevermind," Ruby said. "It's not which word. It's that there *is* a word."

"But you knew what was wrong."

"No, I didn't. I didn't know there was something *wrong* with me. I knew there was plenty wrong with my life. But not with me. *You* knew what was wrong? How did you know?"

How did I know?

DIAGNOSTIC QUESTIONNAIRE (STEP 1)

Instructions: Please check all that apply:

Has there ever been a period in your life when you were not your usual self and you . . .

had an inappropriate sense of euphoria? □
were so irritable that you started fights? □

had loss of appetite or were overeating?	☐
telephoned friends in the middle of the night?	☐
did things other people thought risky, excessive?	☐
spent money that got you into trouble or debt?	☐
had thoughts of death or suicide?	☐

Return completed form to your mental health care professional.

"How could you have *not* known?" I asked. "What did you think was going on?"

"I thought I was a profoundly unhappy person. Except when I thought I was walking on air. I thought I had poor judgment skills. I thought I was not likable. I thought I had lousy luck and bad taste. But you knew? You knew what it was? You knew I had something that could be diagnosed? And treated? You knew I had something that could be made better with a pill? And you didn't say anything? All these years, you knew? Why didn't you tell me?"

"I assumed you were aware of it," I said.

"You assumed I was aware of it? You assumed that I knew? You assumed that I knew, and what? That I liked it that way? That this was good for me?"

"Well, no. Of course not, but I, I just assumed you knew. That's all."

"You knew there were drugs to help?"

"Yes, but . . . I assumed you knew," I said.

"Well, I didn't know, but even if I did know, why didn't you encourage me to do something about it? To get help?"

"I didn't think it was my place to say anything," I said, which, I admit, sounded lame, and Ruby thought so, too. "Not your place? All these years you let me be a crazy person because it wasn't your place to say something? You let me go on like that, marrying losers, losing friends, losing jobs, getting into debt that I'll never get out of? You were my friend. My best friend. My best friend in the world, and you stood there and let me go on being miserable because it wasn't your place to say something? I tried to kill myself, but you never said anything, you never did anything, because it wasn't your place? Fuck you, Sylvia. Fuck you and your place."

I waited to see if Ruby was going to hang up on me or not, and then she did.

The ultimatum: I would come to Thanksgiving dinner only if Hannah and Nathan were not invited. "Them or me," I'd said, and my mother relented. "Okay, okay"

Unless you subscribe to the school that there's no such thing as accidents, it was no big deal that I got to Grand Central Station moments after my train had pulled out, off on its merry way. Trains to Pound Ridge ran every hour. I needed only to call, to say I would be late.

There once was a time when lined up all along one wall of Grand Central Station were telephone booths *It's a bird, it's a plane* with glass doors you could close for privacy, and a phone call cost a dime or maybe a penny. I vaguely recollected those phone booths from childhood, or maybe I'd seen them in an old movie, but regardless, they were long gone, and in their stead were pay phones out in the open. Five or six of them circled around a pole, like a maypole or a late-twentieth-century hitching post.

The phone rang. Twice, and Aunt Hannah picked it up and said hello. Aunt Hannah? I said hello back and I asked to speak to my mother, who said, "Sylvia? Where are you?"

"You promised," I reminded her. Like maybe she forgot.

"Oh, Sylvia. Don't." My mother affected that voice, the one she used whenever I was being unreasonable and ridiculous. "She's an old woman with no family but me. It's Thanksgiving."

"But you promised."

"Fine. I promised," she said, as if the promise itself was the failing, as opposed to the breaking of it. "So I should send her away? Is that what you want?"

"You promised."

And around and around this conversation went, me feeding coins into the pay phone, and my mother telling me it's Thanks-giving and why can't I be generous, and me repeating, "You promised," and around and around it went until it went berserk, my mother snapped, "What is your problem?"

And all those people milling about the phone bank, people carrying pumpkin pies in white boxes tied with string and bas-kets of fruit and bottles of cider to bring to the feast, all those people waiting for the trains to take them home for the holiday, all those nice people got to hear me shout, "His hand in my un-derpants. Is that enough of a problem for you?"

Because I had a stubborn streak, which is rarely an attractive quality, I would wait it out, wait for my mother to call me, and some two weeks later, she did just that. She called me, and in the true spirit of the ostrich, she made it sound as if we'd had ourselves a delightful conversation just days before, and no one apologized for any reason.

Mostly we go about our lives as if those things that happened, didn't happen.

Ruby hung up on me, and when I called her again the next day, she again hung up on me. Five or six times more I called her to say I was sorry, and each time I called, she hung up on me, and she was right about it all. I always told her the truth about everything, about everything else; I told her the truth about everything except the one thing that might have made a difference. That was the one thing I didn't tell her. "And don't ask me why," I said to Henry. "Because I don't have an answer. Or at least not one that I can face."

"If you had told her," Henry asked, "would it have changed anything? Would she have gotten herself some help?"

"I don't know. Probably not. But that doesn't matter. What mattered was that I didn't tell her."

Giving my words back to me, as if he were returning a book that spoke to him as it spoke to me, Henry said, "We're all guilty of something, Sylvia."

"Yeah, we sure are."

22

As much as Henry and I ever had a fixed plan the same way we had notions of destination and indefinite roadways for eventually getting us there, the plan was to follow the Route du Champagne. At some point or other along the way, we'd take a left toward Calais, which was pretty much what we did except for that detour at Valmy that wound up taking us nowhere except back to Valmy, and so it was there that we stopped for the night at the Château Picard, which, in its day, was a château for real. Built on a hilltop in 1880 or some year like that, it looked like a palace, and there was even a winding staircase leading to the doorway. The roof was made of glazed tiles. The floors were glazed tiles, too, white and sky-blue tiles laid out in a harlequin pattern, and there were stained-glass windows and fireplaces and a swimming pool and a spa and a wine cellar with a tasting room. Because we liked this hotel, we liked it a lot, Henry booked a room for three nights. A room with a balcony from which we could see trees and vineyards and more vineyards until we could see no farther. The balcony floors were tiled in that same harlequin pattern, white and sky-blue.

Hungry and thirsty as we were, we did not bother to dress for dinner, taking time only to wash our hands and our faces. In the pair of sinks, sinks side by side, in a bathroom that was head-to-toe pink marble and had a tub big enough for swimming laps, we washed off the dust and the grime of the summer heat.

When on the Route du Champagne, dinner is mostly Ruinart, although Henry did eat some snails and I had a salad, and Henry raised his glass to me, as if he were making a toast. "Madame de Pompadour was a frivolous woman," he said, "but an observant one."

"And this has to do with what?" I asked.

"It was her observation that drinking champagne renders a woman all the more beautiful."

"Sure it does," I said. "Especially when the man she's with has drunk enough of it."

"*Au contraire*," Henry said. "*In vino veritas,* and that is why you so often find men crying into their beer."

"Crying into their beer, but going home with whomever says yes because whoever says yes is all the more beautiful."

"You are not easily flattered," Henry remarked.

"No, I'm not."

"That's because you're a cynic," Henry said. "But you do know that cynics, all of them, deep down, are romantics at heart."

"What, then, are romantics? Deep down."

"Liars, " Henry said.

Two bottles of champagne rendered Henry and me nothing if not tipsy, and as we wound our way back to the château *le château!* we held on to each other, as if we believed that two loopy people were steadier than one would be. As opposed to twice as loopy.

Together we fell onto the bed, and after what might be delicately described as a fumbling and drunken interlude, but nonetheless a mutually satisfying one, we were closer to sober now. "I am going to soak in that scrumptious bathtub," I said. "Care to join me there?"

"I do," Henry said, "but first I'm going to make myself a drink. Will you have one too?"

'A drunk for a son and a cripple for a daughter.'

"No, thanks." I got up from the bed, leaving Henry tangled in the sheets.

On one of the glass shelves in the bathroom was an assortment of gels and salts and soaps *pour le bain*, all in an array of the colors of a peach: muted yellow and pink coral. I turned on the bathwater and added a pinch of this and a little of that, and frothy white bubbles *bubbles!* effervesced. I eased myself into the tub, and the water might well have been the waters of the river Lethe, as if ache and memory are braided and only if you have forgotten everything there is to know can you feel that kind of relaxed. Relaxation that slipped into serenity offering a new perspective, an appreciation for my father's lack of enthusiasm for bringing it all back. With not one thing on my mind, I stayed there, in bliss in that bubble bath, until the bubbles fizzled out and my fingers had pruned up on me.

I reached for a towel.

A towel that was more velvet than terry cloth. Soft and thick, and I wrapped it around myself, tucking in the end as if it were a sarong, and I ran my hands along my waist and over my hips just to touch the towel more.

I expected to find Henry on the bed. Nursing his drink or maybe he fell asleep, but he wasn't there. Two empty mini-bottles of cognac on the night table faced each other like queens on a chessboard, and the door to the balcony was open. Light from the chandelier over the bed slanted out, casting a glow around Henry, who stood at the balcony's railing, his back to me, as if he were enjoying the view of the vineyards, which were not visible at night. He was wearing his blue jeans but no shirt, and he was barefoot. As if sensing my presence, he turned in my direction. He had a highball glass in one hand and he raised the glass along with that index finger to his lips. International sign language for No Talking. With his other hand, he held his cell phone to his ear.

Things out of context can result in a synapse gap, when your neurons simply can't make the leap to make sense of something that makes no sense. Such as a non sequitur, and there is that same kind of disconnect at something too weird, like that time when I was at Brighton Beach and I ran into Marty Zorn, who was a colleague from work, and he was wearing a Speedo, and I got confused. In that way, Henry talking on a cell phone was a concept I could not grasp, which I admit is ridiculous because who in the Western world doesn't have a cell phone? And pretty much everyone in the rest of the world has one, too. Everyone has a cell phone, yet Henry's cell phone baffled me. It baffled me for no reason, I suppose, except that I'd not seen it before. Other than to waiters and hotel clerks and shopkeepers and each other, we spoke to no one else, and we never spoke to anyone on the phone.

That which appears unexpectedly can be a nice surprise, although it can just as easily be a blow, like a brick falling on your head, but mostly, as is also the way with tumors, the unexpected is benign. A tumor, as we know, is an abnormal mass of tissue, a lump that forms somewhere. Such as the breast, the liver, the brain, the ovaries, the throat.

I went back to the bathroom, where I sat on the edge of the tub, dipping my fingers in the water, which was cool now. All that remained of the bubbles were bits of foam fixed to the porcelain like moss or mold growing. It was the middle of August, the exact date I wasn't sure of—maybe the sixteenth or even as late as the twentieth—but it was August.

I unplugged the drain, and I waited.

I waited.

To know that, generally speaking, the unexpected is likely to be neither remarkably good nor frightfully bad did nothing to quell the uneasiness that settled over me, that funny feeling that was, in fact, not at all funny unless you subscribe to the idea that all comedy, ultimately, eventually, when played out to its conclusion, will reveal the misfortune it masks.

I waited.

Time passed this way, with me just sitting there on the edge of the bathtub, until Henry knocked lightly on the door, a formality, the rap on the door before opening it. "Sylvia," he said, and I waited, and then Henry said, "She tired of the guru."

On the Saturday morning cartoons, Bugs Bunny, or maybe it was the Road Runner, but one or the other of them, would be racing along and step beyond the edge of the cliff, and there was that moment when *Let go* we knew before Bugs Bunny knew that there was no ground beneath his feet. Ignorance of the fact that there was no ground beneath his feet kept him suspended in air because what you don't know can't hurt you. But invariably he would look down and understand his predicament. He'd pump his legs, pump madly, as if the energy generated would keep him from falling or move him along, but of course it can't and it didn't, and he'd plummet into the abyss. The difference between the cartoons and the corporeality of the physical world was this: after falling off a cliff, Bugs Bunny had only to get up, dust himself off, and he was back in business.

I knew that the summer would come to an end the same way we know that someday we are going to die, but *someday* is not today. Not now, not yet, not here. I wasn't ready. I had not begun to prepare. I needed more time. I'd been promised more time, as if more time, in the end, would have changed something.

Henry took me by the hand and led me to the bed, and we lay there, side by side, holding hands like dolls cut from folded paper, as if there could have been a string of us. We dared not look at each other, and we dared not speak because we knew what would come out would not be words that made any sense—no words could make sense of this—but rather something like the sound of glass breaking. We stared up at the ceiling, as if the ceiling were the sky and we were expecting snow to fall. After a while of staring up at the ceiling like that, I said, "So, does this mean we're not going to Calais?" and we both laughed and we kept laughing for a good while, but that did not make anything better.

Breakfast on the terrace, and *in my end is my beginning* we had fresh croissants with black cherry preserves. When we were finished eating but were not yet done with our coffee, not yet done, *not yet done* I fished through my pocketbook for my wallet. From one of those compartments never used, I took out an old cocktail napkin, folded into fourths and worn by age to a velveteen texture. Although I couldn't say for how many years exactly I'd carried this napkin in my wallet, it was for a long, long time, and whenever I got a new wallet, I transferred the cocktail napkin to it along with my credit cards, driver's license, library card. Unfolding it, taking care not to stain it with black cherry preserves, I showed Henry the note which read: "Sylvia, When talk turned to smiles, I wanted to whisper in your ear how sexy I think your mouth is." It was signed: "R."

"Who is R.?" Henry asked, and I told him, "I have no idea. I do not remember who R. is, who R. could be. I do not remember who wrote these words to me or the circumstances of them. It's just one of those things I kept, one of those things I could not bring myself to throw away."

"But why keep it if you don't know who wrote it?"

"I suppose for that very reason. To remind me how we can forget, how we do forget. How I forgot someone who wrote me a sweet note, such a wonderful thing, a sweet note on a cocktail napkin, but still, I don't remember him. It's a terrible thing to forget what was good and those we loved," and then Henry asked, "Do you want me to ruin my life for you?"

Douceur de vivre: cashmere sweaters, fine wine, sterling flatware, hotels that were once châteaus, an active social life *our kind* in Paris, towels like velvet.

"Do you want me to ruin my life for you?" Henry asked, and what could I say to that?

Charles de Gaulle Airport. With a
first-class ticket in hand because Henry
had insisted on it, he insisted on buying me
a first-class ticket home, I went through the
metal detectors. Waiting for my carry-on
bags and my shoes to be X-rayed, I turned
to the Plexiglas partition, to look at Henry
once more, but Henry, he was already
gone.

There are no happy endings.

The end of all things—a book, a life, a
summer, a marriage, the last bite of cake,
the last of innocence lost, a love affair—is
always sad, at least a little bit sad, because it
is the end, the end of that.

That is the end of that, but because the

future dangles promise like a bell on a stick, because possibilities *a Cinzano ashtray* remain, we go on.

Except.

Except, how do we go on when what was best is behind us? When the longing is not for someone you have not yet met but for someone you knew and lost?

I never did finish telling Henry the story about my mother's aunt Semille, in whose memory I am named. Semille, who loved glass beads, opera, and a boy she did not marry, but many years later fate brought them together again. That story, Semille's story, was yet another story with a good beginning, yet another story that I wish had had a different end. But there are no happy endings unless we cut the story short, and as far as I know, there are no rules of etiquette to a miracle, either. Nowhere is it written that you are obliged to use the miracle you got, or to be glad of it even, but my mother, a sap for a love story and raised on Metro-Goldwyn-Mayer irrepressibility, could not imagine that Semille would be anything less than rhapsodic at reuniting with her old flame, at finding him, in New York, a miracle, at Temple Emanu-El some forty or even fifty years after breaking his heart. Breaking his heart and turning her own heart into something small and cold and hard. Like a marble.

"What did you say to him?" my mother asked Semille, as if love lost were the same as other things lost, like when my mother was a girl and she misplaced her gold locket. For days she cried about that, but when the locket turned up in her school bag, it was the same as if it had never been lost in the first place.

"Say to him? What could I possibly say to him?" Semille

wiped at her eyes. "I said nothing to him. I ran out of there before he had the chance to see me."

"Why? Why didn't you talk to him?"

"I was a beautiful young woman when he saw me last," Semille said. "When he loved me. Better that he remember me as I was then."

"But he's old now, too," my mother reasoned, and hers was not an unreasonable conclusion, as if reason had anything to do with this.

"I deserve to be alone," Semille said, and she said no more than that, because it was the truth.

Hers was not love lost; it was love denied. And this is all that I know about Semille. Maybe it's all that I need to know. Maybe it's enough. Maybe it's more than enough to know that she had an affection for glass beads and that she wept not for what she lost but for what she let go. "I deserve to be alone," she said, because she knew it was her own damn fault. Semille wept not because she did something stupid; she wept because she *didn't* do something stupid. Sometimes, to do something stupid—to disobey your parents, to rush into battle, to speak out of turn, to ruin your life—is a far better thing to do than to do nothing at all.

The moral of the story is this: sometimes, to do nothing, to do nothing at all, is the sorriest thing ever.

Yes. We should've said something, we should have done something, even something stupid, something that chanced ruining our lives, because to do something stupid, something reckless, something honest, is to be brave, but Henry and I, if we were nothing else, we were cowards, and that was the end of that.

Insights,
Interviews
& More . . .

An Interview with Binnie Kirshenbaum on *The Scenic Route*

Marion Ettlinger

All the characters in The Scenic Route *are flawed people, many of whom engage in behavior that is somewhat immoral. Why not write about admirable people?*

Each and every one of us is a flawed being; admirable people occasionally engage in less than admirable behavior. It would be dishonest to write characters who are all good, all the time. It would also be boring. Our imperfections make us human. Without human error, we would be machines. Sylvia is passive, Henry is weak, Ruby is broken, but they are not evil or horrid. They need not be admired (although they do have admirable moments) or even liked (although I like them very much); I care only that they be human, and by extension, they are flawed, imperfect beings.

Is Sylvia having a mid-life crisis? Do women experience mid-life crisis the same way men do?

Mid-life crisis? I'm more inclined to call it a mid-life reckoning. Sylvia is taking stock of her life, and instead of having a future of possibilities to look forward to, she sees a future of only memories and regrets.

Manifestations of mid-life crisis might be different for men and women. There's the stereotype of the man buying himself a red sports car and taking up with a woman half his age, but the impetus for that behavior isn't, I don't think, gender-specific. We all come to a time when we realize our own mortality, when we begin to question who we are, what we have achieved, are we happy? When lives are pretty much settled, the routine can seem unbearable and sad. We might long for all that we did not do and most likely will never do. Sylvia is trying to understand how she got to this state, as if understanding will afford her purpose, and somehow ease her sorrow.

Some of the stories, incidents, and times that Sylvia recounts repeat themselves in variation. How intentional was this?

The scope of human experience, boiled down to its essence, is limited. What makes any experience unique is the individuality of character. Much of this book addresses the need to remember and be remembered. The periodic return to the years of World War I ▶

An Interview with Binnie Kirshenbaum on *The Scenic Route (continued)*

was deliberate for the reason that Sylvia states—the astronomical death toll—and yet it's a war that, these days, tends to be forgotten, thereby compounding the tragedy of it.

The title* The Scenic Route *resonates on several levels: travel, storytelling, and life itself. Why do Sylvia and Henry take the scenic route as opposed to the direct path?

They travel scenic routes because destination is irrelevant. They don't care *where* they are going so much as that they *are* going. It's an obvious observation about life, often an inspirational observation, that the journey is what counts, but it is also an anti-inspirational observation. No matter how hard you might try, no matter how many twists and turns and back roads you take, fate is not to be escaped. Despite having taken the scenic route, Sylvia, Henry, and Ruby all end up where they began.

And what about the scenic route of storytelling?

That's a question I'll answer with a story: My husband is a scientist; his study of life has a clearly defined thesis. One day I was telling him a story and, to paint a fuller picture, I was giving him a background story which led to an anecdote. There he stopped me and said, "Get to the point," to which I said, "Point? There is no point. It's a story."

Story is how we explain ourselves, understand ourselves, how we are remembered, how we remember others. We're not but one story; we are a sum total of stories. Stories upon stories that lead to other stories, looping back to more stories. That circuitous way of telling stories allows Sylvia to get at the truth about herself.

And what of those incidents or people best forgotten?

Nothing and no one are really best forgotten. We might want to forget because it makes life easier, more pleasant to forget that which causes hurt. But easier and more pleasant isn't complete; it's not true. We need not dwell on the hurt, but to lose memory is to lose a part of yourself.

To whom is Sylvia telling her stories, and why now?

Sylvia tells her stories to Henry, except for that overriding one, "The story of Henry and me," which is told as she imagines telling it to Ruby. The need to tell Ruby that story is Sylvia's roundabout way of apologizing to her friend and owning up to her own failings. She wants to forgive herself, and she wants to forgive Henry, too.

Flawed and ultimately sad, your characters are left with little hope for happiness, yet there are some very funny moments in this novel. This is true of your other books, as well. Would you talk about that dual nature to your fiction? ▶

**An Interview with Binnie Kirshenbaum
on** *The Scenic Route (continued)*

In reviewing one of my novels, the poet
and critic Richard Howard referred to me
as a "stand-up tragic," which delighted me.
I find what is sorrowful and dark in life is
richer to write about, but I also believe that
humor is a mechanism for survival. When
confronted with that which is too sad, too
uncomfortable, too painful, we make a joke.
If we can laugh, we can go on. ∾

6

Three Stops Along the Way to *The Scenic Route*

By Binnie Kirshenbaum

1) I was eleven years old when my mother and I were invited to lunch at the Rothmans' house. The Rothmans had been friends of my grandparents, and they—the Rothmans, not my grandparents—had once been rich. Very rich. Money that had afforded them maids, a chauffeur, gardeners, an art collection, but, hit hard by the Great Depression, they never recovered. The servants had been let go, the Bentley sold, the art auctioned off, and some forty years later, when I met them for the first and only time, all that remained of their once luxurious life was the house. The land, the guest cottage, and the stable belonged to other people now. "Every year," my mother told me, "they scrape together the money to pay the taxes on that house. It makes no sense. Two old people living all alone in a crumbling mansion like that."

It was October; leaves on the trees were gold and orange, and as my mother drove along the private road to the Rothmans' house, I nearly cried out, so sharp was the pang of longed-for autumns past, as if in that moment I realized the close of childhood, that I was soon to outgrow Halloween, and that what is gone is gone for good.

The Rothmans' house, a Greek Revival mansion, was indeed falling apart; the inside of the house, in an equally shabby state, was even more wondrous: frayed silk seat cushions, threadbare carpets, chipped ▶

vases, and chandeliers crisscrossed with cobwebs worthy of Miss
Havisham. To be in that house was to be in a book; a house of stories
populated with characters who traveled on ocean liners and suffered
the kinds of misfortunes specific to literature.

Lunch was Welsh rarebit—a grilled cheese sandwich eaten with a
knife and fork—served on cracked Royal Albert plates all the more
beautiful for the evidence of their fragility. Although I itched to explore,
sure that there was treasure in every room, I sat like the well-behaved
child I was and imagined what it might be like to be Mr. and Mrs.
Rothman, those many years alone in a big house that was splendor gone
to seed. What I remembered and imagined of that day stayed with me,
tucked away, to surface while writing *The Scenic Route,* as my inspiration
for Aunt Thea and Uncle John wasting away in a crumbling mansion,
for Beatrice's dignity despite greatly reduced circumstances, and for how
Henry's identity and his sorrow were inexorably bound to the trappings
of wealth.

And the ache for what is gone, I remembered that too.

2) On a Sunday afternoon, sitting on the couch, my thoughts were
drifting when I fixed on a Victorian-era photograph that hangs on
the wall along with some other old photographs.

Generally speaking, I consider old things—furniture, jewelry, dishes,
lamps, hats—to be more pleasing to the eye. There is also the fact of
superior craftsmanship, but mostly I prefer old things to new things
because old things have history, stories to tell. Although I rarely know
what the story is, knowing that there *is* a story creates texture and sparks
the imagination. For example, engraved on the inside of my wedding
ring, bought in an antique shop on Bleecker Street, is "Emma and Frank
1892." How could I not be curious about Emma and Frank, who they
were, where they lived, and whether their marriage was a happy one?
Or not?

The story (within the story) in *The Scenic Route* about the woman
Sylvia meets on the plane was rooted in a packet of letters I'd bought
some years before, for a dollar, at a flea market in Connecticut. Written
over the course of five months in 1944 and tied neatly together with
twine, the letters were to an infantryman named Edward Stilton from his
hometown sweetheart, Catherine. Home was in Ohio. Chatty letters, they
offered a glimpse of American life at a time when most all the young men

were overseas. Gasoline was rationed, and Catherine's sister worked in a munitions factory. On November 4, 1944, Catherine wrote her last letter to Edward: "Dear Edward, There is no easy way to tell you this news. Yesterday I got married to someone else." Was his heart broken to bits? Did he come home from the war? Or did he die on the beaches of Normandy? Maybe he came home missing an arm or a leg. Did he and Catherine, in their small Ohio hometown, pass each other daily on Main Street? Were they still in love? Or did hate fester between them like gangrene?

The photograph that gave me pause that Sunday afternoon was of my great-grandmother, and although it's been hanging there for years, this was the first time that it occurred to me: I knew next to nothing about her life, who she was. I did not even know her name, and there was no one left to ask. I had no stories about her to tell. That is what a life is, a series of stories recounted (which accounts for all the stories in this novel). But no stories about my great-grandmother were passed down from generation to generation the way her gold locket was and her photograph. If not for the things of hers that remained, she would've been forgotten entirely, as if she'd never lived. The value of our possessions, our things, is not monetary; it is derived from their substantiation of memory and time. Proof that we were here, and that stories are contained in their matter.

Other than that they married in 1892, I know nothing about Emma and Frank, yet because I wear Emma's wedding ring, I think of them and I wonder about them, and something else I wonder about is this: How did Emma's wedding ring, one hundred years later, wind up in an antique shop on Bleecker Street?

And what will become of my things after I am gone? If my trinkets are discarded and the gold melted down for scrap, who will remember us: Emma, Frank, my great-grandmother, and me?

3) Good fortune is not to be taken lightly, and I am well aware that I am indeed fortunate. Pretty much, I got the life I dreamed of back when my life was still ahead of me, when I was wide-eyed, when the list of Things To Do seemed endless, when the future was uncertain, when life was rife with surprises and wonderful things could happen

And wonderful things did happen. Some lousy things happened too, but disappointments, loss, heartbreak—all could be mitigated by that ▶

same promise of possibility. The phone could ring; a door could open; there was tomorrow.

Then one day, for no discernable reason, an overwhelming sadness came over me, like _nebbia,_ except this fog did not lift. And when I was asked, "What do you want that you don't have?" I said, "Nothing," and this was true. I wanted for nothing.

Like daylight in winter, my list of Things To Do grew shorter, eclipsed by another list, Things I Will Never Do, and its subset, Things I Will Never Do Again. However many possibilities remain from the middle years onward, they are outweighed by impossibilities and responsibilities; the disruption from the unexpected brings more irritation than joy. I don't mean that life is without pleasure. There is pleasure. But drugs to stay awake all night because I was out having fun gave way to pills for sleeping; unabashed joy eased into a placid calm, which brought not the serenity expected but grief. I wanted for nothing except that wide-eyed belief that life is rife with possibility, and I too asked, "Where do I go from here?" ᜒ

Excerpt: *An Almost Perfect Moment*

IN BROOKLYN, in a part of Brooklyn
that was the last stop on the LL train and a
million miles away from Manhattan, a part
of Brooklyn—an enclave, almost—composed
of modest homes and two-family houses set
on lawns the size of postage stamps, out front
the occasional plaster-of-paris saint or a
birdbath, a short bus ride away from the new
paradise known as the Kings County Mall, a
part of Brooklyn where the turbulent sixties
never quite touched down, but at this point
in time, on the cusp of the great age of disco,
when this part of Brooklyn would come into
its own, as if during the years before it had
been aestivating like a mudfish, lying in wait
for the blast, for the glitter, the platform
shoes, Gloria Gaynor, for doing the hustle, for
its day in the sun, this part of Brooklyn was
home to Miriam Kessler and her daughter
Valentine, who was fifteen and three-quarter
years old, which is to be neither here nor yet
there as far as life is concerned.

Therefore, on this Tuesday afternoon,
mid-November, it was in a way both
figurative and literal that Valentine stood
at the threshold between the foyer and the
living room, observing Miriam and her three
girlfriends—she, Miriam, called them that,
despite their middling years, *my girlfriends,*
or simply, *The Girls*—who were seated
around the card table, attending closely
to their game.

Four Bam against Six Crack, the mah-
jongg tiles clacking into one another sounded
like typewriter keys or fingernails tapping ▶

11

on a tabletop, something like anticipation, as if like Morse code, a message would be revealed, the inside track to the next step on the ladder to womanhood, such as the achievement of the big O or the use of feminine hygiene products, things Valentine had heard tell of but had yet to experience, things for *later, when you're older.*

For Miriam and The Girls, mah-jongg was not recreation, but passion. Nonetheless, and in their Brooklyn parlance, a nasal articulation, they were able to play while carrying on a conversation, which was not so much like juggling two oranges, because, for them, talking was as natural as breathing.

"Am I telling the truth?" Judy Weinstein said. "I'm telling the truth. Could she be a decorator or what?"

"She's right, Miriam. You could be a decorator. Two Dragon. It's a showplace here."

"When I'm right, I'm right. She could be a decorator."

Even if her taste wasn't to your liking, there was no doubt Miriam had an eye for placement and color. The living room, recently redecorated, was stunning, in an Oriental motif. Red plush carpeting picked up the red of the wallpaper that was flocked with velveteen flowers. A pair of cloisonné lamps capped with silk bell-shaped shades sat on black enamel end tables flanking the gold brocade couch. A series of three Chinese watercolors—lily pads and orange carp—framed in ersatz bamboo hung on the far wall. A bonsai tree, the cutest little thing that grew itty-bitty oranges which were supposedly edible, was the coffee-table centerpiece.

"This room takes my breath away. I ask you, does she have the eye for decorating or what?"

"They make good money, those interior decorators."

Waving off foolish talk, Miriam asked, "Are we playing or are we gabbing?" To fix up her own home was one thing. To go out in the world as a professional, *who needs the headache?*

Miriam took one tile—Seven Dot—which was of no help at all, from Sunny Shapiro, while Sunny Shapiro with a face that, in Miriam's words, could stop a clock, applied, on a mouth that was starting to wizen like a raisin, a fresh coat of coral-colored lipstick, the exact shade of coral as the beaded sweater she wore.

Studying her tiles, a losing hand if ever there was one, Miriam Kessler fed a slice of Entenmann's walnut ring into her mouth. Like she was performing a magic trick, Miriam could make a slice of cake, indeed an entire cake, vanish before your very eyes. Miriam swallowed the cake, her pleasure, and then there was no pleasure left until the next piece of cake.

Her grief cloaked in layers of fat, Miriam Kessler was pushing 239 pounds when she last stepped on the bathroom scale back in September or maybe it was August. Mostly she wore dresses of the muumuu variety, but nonetheless, Miriam Kessler was beautifully groomed. Every Thursday, she was at the beauty parlor for her wash and set, forty-five minutes under the dryer, hair teased and sprayed into the bouffant of her youth; the same hairdo she'd had since she was seventeen, only the color had changed from a God-given warm brown to a Lady Clairol deep auburn.

Despite that Miriam never skimped on the heat, rather she kept the thermostat at a steady seventy-two degrees, Edith Zuckerman snuggled with her white mink stole, and so what if it was as old as Methuselah, and from a generation ago, hardly with-it. The white mink stole was the first truly beautiful thing Edith had ever owned and she wore it as if the beauty of it were a talisman. As if nothing bad could ever happen to a woman wearing a white mink stole, never mind that she had the one son with the learning problems and her husband's business having had its share of ups and downs.

Oh-such-glamorous dames, adorned in style which peaked and froze at their high-school proms, The Girls were as dolled up as if on their way to romance or to the last nights of the Copacabana nightclub, as if they refused to let go of the splendor.

But it was Judy Weinstein who seemed to command the lion's share of Valentine's attention. Judy Judy Judy was a vision in a gold lamé jumpsuit. Not the gold lamé as precursor to the Mylar of Studio 54, but lamé, lahr-may, they called it, of the fashion flash of the fabulous fifties. And her hair, Judy's hair was bleached to a platinum blond and woven as intricately and high on her head as a queen's crown. Her fingernails, dragon-lady long, were lacquered a frosted white.

Some seven or eight years back, on a Friday morning, it must have been during the summer or some school holiday because Valentine was at home, Miriam had said to her daughter, "Go and ask Judy if she's got a stick of butter I can borrow." Miriam was baking an apricot strudel, the recipe calling for two sticks of butter when Miriam discovered she had but one. Valentine knocked on the Weinsteins' door, and Judy called ▶

out, "Come in." It was that way still, this part of Brooklyn, like a small town where there was no need for police locks and Medeco locks and home alarm systems.

Although Judy did sometimes go for the silver lamé and also had in her closet a breathtaking copper lamé sweater set, the gold lamé was her trademark, and when Valentine went through the Weinsteins' living room into the kitchen, behold! There was Judy in a gold lamé hostess gown, her feet shod in gold shoes, pointy with three-inch spiked heels, her face was fully made up, eyeliner whipped into cattails, fuchsia-pink lipstick, enough mascara to trap flies. Diamond earrings dangled from her lobes, which shimmered as if made of pearls instead of mere flesh, while her hands were confidently braiding dough for the Sabbath challah bread. Valentine must've been so overwhelmed by the glory that was Judy Weinstein that she seemed to forget entirely why she was there, what it was her mother had wanted. True, Valentine had set eyes on Mrs. Weinstein pretty much every day, but this might have been the first time she saw light like sunbeams reflecting off the gold and platinum, light radiating like that of the pictures in her book of Bible stories. All Valentine managed to do was gape until Judy phoned Miriam and said, "Valentine is standing in my kitchen with her mouth hanging open. Butter? Sure. I've got butter."

Now Miriam licked the residue of the sugar icing off her fingers and exchanged two of the tiles on her rack for two from the center of the table. So absorbed were they with their game and their talk, not one of these four women had heard Valentine come in the door or noticed that she'd come near to them.

Not until Edith Zuckerman called Five Dot did any of them look up, and only then did they see Valentine. See Valentine and gush. With words detouring through the sinuses and in voices husky from years of smoking Newport mentholated cigarettes, Juicy Fruit gum snapping, they carried on, "Will you look at her? Every day she gets more beautiful."

"What a face. I ask you. Is that a face?"

"She's right. That's some face. Gorgeous. Ab-so-lute-ly gorgeous."

"Honest to Gawd, Miriam, you should put her in the movies with that face. Quint. I've got a cousin who knows somebody big with the studios. I'll give him a call for you because, really, the kid could be a star with that face. I ask you, am I right?"

"She's right. When she's right, she's right."

"I'm telling you, I'm right. She even looks like that actress, Olivia Whatshername."

"Olivia Newton-John? She looks nothing like Olivia Newton-John."

"No. No. Not that Olivia. The other one. From *Romeo and Juliet*. The one who was Juliet in the movie. Olivia Whatshername."

"I don't know who you mean."

"Girls. Girls. Are we gabbing or are we playing?" ·

"All I'm saying is that the kid is gorgeous. Is she gorgeous or what?"

"The kid is gorgeous."

"Mah-jongg."

All tiles were dumped to the center and flipped facedown to be washed, which is the mah-jongg equivalent to shuffling a deck of cards. Sunny Shapiro was East, the one to go first this round, and when the women looked up again, Valentine was gone. Even though Miriam knew that the plush carpeting, wall-to-wall, muffled the sound of footfalls, it sometimes threw her for a loop the way Valentine moved silently, as if the kid walked on air, the way she appeared and disappeared without warning, as if she were something you imagined instead of a person.

Although Edith Zuckerman would never say so, not even under torture, because she loved Miriam like a sister, Valentine gave Edith the creeps, the way the kid looked as if she knew everything, as if she had imbibed the wisdom of the ages, as if she knew all your secrets, including the ones you didn't dare admit even to yourself. Yet, at the very same time, she managed to look like a moron, as if the most ordinary things— a Dixie cup, the television set, a doorknob—took her by complete surprise, as if she'd never seen such remarkable things, as if she were a plastic doll with wide eyes painted on and a hollow head. ↶

Have You Read?
More by Binnie Kirshenbaum

AN ALMOST PERFECT MOMENT

In Brooklyn, in the Age of Disco, Valentine Kessler—a sweet Jewish girl who bears a remarkable resemblance to the Virgin Mary of Lourdes—has an unerring gift for shattering the dreams and hopes of those who love her. Miriam, her long-suffering mother, betrayed and anguished by the husband she adores, seeks solace in daily games of mah-jongg with The Girls, a cross between a Greek Chorus and Brooklyn's rendition of the Three Wise Men, who dispense advice, predictions, and care in the form of poppy-seed cake and apple strudels. When her greatest fear for Valentine is realized, Miriam takes comfort in the thought that it couldn't get any worse. And then it does.

Sagacious, sorrowful, and hilarious, *An Almost Perfect Moment* is a novel about mothers and daughters, star-crossed lovers, doctrines of the divine, and the colorful Jewish community that once defined Brooklyn.

"[A] terrific writer . . . both funny and compassionate."
— Frances Taliaferro, *Washington Post*

"Engrossing. . . . Cinematic, effortlessly beautiful descriptions will spark the reader's imagination, and myriad plot twists and turns will keep you guessing."
— *Chicago Tribune*

Brazen and given to transgressions, the narrator of this mordantly witty novel is an aloof, tough-talking, married Manhattan woman who carries on three affairs simultaneously, blithely breaking seven of the Ten Commandments in her search for a safe place to land. Rootless, bouncing from bed to bed, she knows she is pure of heart. If only she could find where her heart got lost. Irreverent and achingly honest, she points to the small but infinitely deep cracks in our masks, drawing the reader into her world of misadventure—erotic, comic, and deeply unsettling. Juggling four men—her husband, "the hit man," "the multimedia artist," and "the love of her life"—she can't decide whether she is out to prove or disprove the Talmudic wisdom: If you don't know where you're going, any road will take you there.

"Not many young female novelists can deal with sex, the appetite for it, and the loss of such appetite with as much candor, lack of self-protection, and humor as Binnie Kirshenbaum."

—Norman Mailer

"[A] a dark and powerful look at a troubled spirit."

—*Publishers Weekly*

HISTORY ON A PERSONAL NOTE

From New York City to the former East Germany, from rural Virginia to affluent suburbia, the characters in these short stories grapple with love, loss, greed, perversion, and other awful truths as they try to transcend their limitations with occasional humor and dignity. In "History on a Personal Note," Lorraine, a Southerner, wonders if her German paramour will find the inspiration to leave his wife amid the destruction of the Berlin Wall. In "Viewing Stacy from Above," a pregnant woman descends into a pit of despair as she contemplates the constraints of motherhood. In "Money Honey," a young adulteress who ditches her husband is reprimanded by an extended family of elders whose morals are even more dubious than her own.

Contemplative, allegorical, and witty, *History on a Personal Note* takes us into a world laced with black humor and makes us laugh—until it hurts.

"Kirshenbaum has a strong moral aptitude and a ballistic sense of humor, launching anti-assumption rockets with cool precision. . . . Her candor about the female psyche is not unlike Margaret Atwood's, but her feisty voice, gutsy humor, mischievous dispassion, and gift for setting scenes and conjuring moments of realization are all her own."

—Booklist

Don't miss the next book by your favorite author. Sign up now for AuthorTracker by visiting www.AuthorTracker.com.